Kate pulled alongside the prison bus and glanced inside the vehicle.

Nearly a dozen men sat in the uncomfortable seats behind the wire mesh screen that protected the driver and the armed guard in the front.

One of the prisoners sat at the window. Sunlight glinted from his unruly shoulder-length blond hair, picking up the streaks and highlights that summer had burned into it. His face was chiseled, but a few days' dark beard growth covered his cheeks and jaw. Wide-spaced hazel eyes peered out from under dark brows that arched with sardonic amusement. Despite the shaggy look, the dimple in his chin plainly showed.

He glanced at his watch, then back at Kate. The amusement left his features and concern filled them.

Then the double explosion ripped through the Jeep's interior.

Dear Reader,

When I look back on life, as I'm sure we all do, wondering how we got to where we are whether for good or bad, I think about the storms I've weathered. Personal storms. Broken hearts. Tragedies. Another choice I could have made.

Sometimes it seems as if everything I am today is defined by storms I've passed through. But all those things have made me stronger or made me see a little more clearly. Sometimes they made me focus on the little things. And sometimes they broadened my horizons.

More than that, though, I'm an avid storm watcher. I love spring and the wonderful electrical storms that the season brings. There's something simply exhilarating about lightning streaking across the dark sky. It touches something elemental within me and makes me feel so alive! Those of you who feel the same way know what I'm talking about. And those of you who don't probably think I need counseling.

Kate Garrett has been weathering her own personal storms for years. But now she's about to step into the eye of a particularly nasty tropical storm, in the midst of escaped convicts and a sexy man who presents a danger that Kate has steered clear of for years.

I hope you enjoy this one!

Meredith Fletcher

www.bombshellromance.blogspot.com

MEREDITH FLETCHER

STORM FORCE

Published by Silhouette Books

America's Publisher of Contemporary Romance

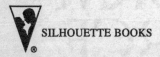 SILHOUETTE BOOKS

ISBN-13: 978-0-373-51434-2
ISBN-10:   0-373-51434-4

STORM FORCE

www.SilhouetteBombshell.com

Printed in U.S.A.

Books by Meredith Fletcher

Silhouette Bombshell

Double-Cross #14
Look-Alike #90
Storm Force #120

Silhouette Single Title

Femme Fatale
  "The Get-Away Girl"

MEREDITH FLETCHER

doesn't really call any place home. She blames her wanderlust on her navy father, who moved the family several times around the United States and other countries. The one constant she had was her books. The battered trunk of favorite novels followed her around the world when she was growing up and shared dorm space with her in college. These days, the trunk is stored, but sometimes comes with Meredith to visit A-frame houses high in the Colorado mountains, cottages in Maine, where she likes to visit lighthouses and work with fishing crews, and rental flats where she takes moments of "early retirement" for months at a stretch. Interested readers can reach her at MFletcher1216@aol.com.

This book is dedicated to Mary Beth Bulmer,
who lived in Florida for years and makes one of
the best Key lime pies in the world!

And to Tara Parsons and Tashya Wilson,
who make it all possible AND presentable!

Chapter 1

Bright morning sunlight slashed across the bug-smeared windshield of Kate Garrett's five-year-old Jeep Cherokee as she sped along the two-lane highway. Staring into the glare through the map of scattered insect anatomy crusted with road dust, she felt the stress of the day already getting to her. Discomfort knotted up across her shoulders and at the base of her skull. If the frustration kept up, she knew her jaws were going to ache, and that would be the first step toward a killer migraine. She *so* didn't need that.

"Are you listenin' to me?"

Kate tucked the cell phone more firmly under her chin. "Yeah, Dad, I heard you. Tyler called you and told you one of my clients is shooting the local wildlife."

Tyler Jordan was the eighteen-year-old she'd hired to help with the Mathis contract. He was a local youth and good with the Everglades areas all along the Tamiami Trail, but he didn't much care for the fact that he worked for a woman. Tyler's father had worked for her father. As a result of their fathers' influence, they'd gotten stuck working together.

"That guy's out there shootin' up everythin' that moves," her dad said.

"I got that," Kate went on. "I told you I was on my way out there." She cursed silently. When she'd first seen Darrel Mathis she'd known the man and his buddies were going to be trouble.

"Stupid cell phones," Conrad Garrett fumed in his coarse gravelly voice. "Oughta be a law, I tell you. You were breakin' up."

Despite the fact that one of her high-paying clients was off in the bush chasing after wild boar through the Florida Everglades, Kate had to grin at her dad. He claimed to hate new technology, but he was always the first to upgrade to a new cell phone or computer. And he was the one who had bought her kids the new PlayStation 3, then promptly sat down to beat them at every game they wanted to play. Steven and Hannah, her eight-year-old son and five-year-old daughter, didn't always seem comfortable with her, but they loved Grampa Conrad.

"If I didn't have a cell phone we wouldn't even be having this conversation," Kate pointed out.

"Yeah, well I'm tellin' you that if they were gonna put in new digital networks to replace the old analog ones they should have at least put in ones that worked."

Kate loved her dad. He'd held it together for her and her two sisters and brother after their mother had died of ovarian cancer. Kate had only been four years old. She barely remembered her mother.

But she remembered how her dad had taught her to swim and camp and track and hunt. She'd learned how to fish and run trotlines a couple years before she'd gone to school. She was the baby of the family and the only one who hadn't promptly moved away from Everglades City when the first chance presented itself. Her sisters and brother couldn't wait to be somewhere else and seldom visited. Janice and Carol were married and lived in Atlanta, Georgia, and Doug was in the navy. Kate and her dad only had each other these days.

During Kate's younger years, her dad had worked as a hunting and fishing guide through the Everglades, managing big-game expeditions as well as deepwater fishing. Kate had gone everywhere with him.

Her dad had gotten to where he couldn't stomach the tourist clientele coming in from northern Florida and out of state wanting to fish and hunt in the Everglades wilderness. These days, he worked as a marine consultant, specializing in shallow-water recovery and occasionally dabbling in treasure hunting. Her dad was always and forever finding some new trade or learning a new skill. He'd passed part of that restlessness on to all of his children, and he blamed himself because they'd all left.

"You gotta get out of the guide business, baby girl," her dad said.

Kate smiled and shook her head. She was twenty-eight years old, divorced for three years, and running her own business shepherding hunters, fishermen, tourists and the occasional university professor through the Everglades. She hadn't been anybody's "baby girl" in a long time.

"Not all of us can get certified to do marine salvage," Kate responded. She checked the road up ahead and saw a big white bus. The rear of the vehicle had Everglades Correctional Institution stencilled across it in blocky black letters. Department of Corrections was written below in smaller letters. She could barely distinguish the passengers but she imagined the hard-eyed men in shackles and orange jumpsuits inside the bus. Everglades Correctional Institution was over in Miami proper and she wondered what the bus was doing traveling the back roads.

"I could get you certified for divin' and recovery," her dad offered. "Be no problem at all."

"Dad, I don't want to be certified. You like diving. I don't. Being underwater makes me feel like I'm drowning."

"Marine salvage is doin' good business," her dad said. "And now that we're in hurricane season again, I'm bettin' there's gonna be a lot more business. There's a storm movin' in. Should be here by tonight."

Kate looked up at the eastern skyline. Darkness already roiled on the skyline. By this afternoon the Miami coastline would start feeling the fury of Hurricane Genevieve.

"Why, if I had a little bit of paint and knew you were interested," her dad continued, "wouldn't be no trouble at all to add *and Daughter* after *Garrett Marine Salvage*."

Just like you added and Daughter *to everything else you were doing when I was growing up.* In addition to the guide business, Kate had also spent time overhauling boat engines, replacing decks and coaming, and piloting airboats. Her childhood hadn't lacked for something to do.

When she'd been growing up, though, she hadn't felt the need to stand on her own two feet. Now, with the divorce behind her and only visitation with her kids granted instead of custody, she wanted to be her own person. More than that, she *needed* to be independent.

"All I'm sayin'," her dad went on, "is that you should think about it. There's more money in salvage work than in the guide business."

"I'm doing all right for myself." Kate bristled slightly. Her ex had pointed out her inability to care for their children in the manner to which they'd become accustomed—expensive summer camps, nannies and international vacations—every time she'd scraped together enough money to hire a lawyer to make an attempt to adjust the visitation. But she'd returned to what she had known, to what she had loved. There was nothing like being out in the wilds of the Everglades away from civilization. She just hadn't been able to convince her kids of that.

"You got some almighty prideful ways," her dad said.

"I wonder where I got that," Kate replied.

"And did anyone ever tell you that stubbornness was unattractive in a young woman?"

"I prefer to think of it as determination."

Kate slowed as she caught up with the D.O.C. bus. Her dad meant well. She'd never had a person stand by her like her dad did. Through thick and thin.

"Maybe you could just do marine salvage part-time," her dad suggested.

"We've been over this," Kate said. "You travel too much. How could I maintain a home for Steven and Hannah if we lived and worked off a boat together?"

"We'd find a way, baby girl," her dad said in his rough, prideful way. "You and me, we've always found a way."

A lump formed at the back of Kate's throat. "I know, Dad." She paused, looking around at the thick forests and the sweeping plains of sawgrass that hid the cypress swamps. Mangroves grew in salt water and cypress grew in fresh water. Big Cypress Swamp was all fresh water until the sea invaded it during the occasional tropical storm.

"And that boy of yours," her dad said, "why he'd love a chance to play at being a pirate lookin' for lost treasure."

Maybe with you, Dad, Kate thought. Steven remained distant from her despite her best attempts to get closer to him. Every time he looked at her, Kate got the feeling that she just didn't measure up, that he faulted her for leaving.

Looking back on her marriage and divorce, Kate had to admit that he was right. She'd never belonged in Bryce Colbert's world. He was computers and international deals, long business trips spent in Europe and interviews in *Forbes* and *Money*.

She'd always been her father's daughter. At home in the small towns in southern Florida with the bush and mosquitoes. Tall and athletic, she didn't look like the tiny fashion dolls Bryce seemed to prefer. She was five feet ten inches tall, had curves that turned the heads of most men, and a thick mane of auburn hair she wore past her shoulders that had humbled the hairdressers in several New York salons. Freckles scattered over the bridge of her pug nose couldn't be hidden by cosmetics. Her eyes were such a dark green they sometimes looked black.

This morning, since she was going to be in the brush, she wore heavy khaki pants, a black T-shirt under a tan Banana Republic vest and hiking boots. Wraparound amber-tinted sunglasses protected her eyes and she wore her hair tied back. Back when she'd met her future ex-husband, she'd been dressed much the same. She was definitely *not* Bryce Colbert's kind of woman.

But Bryce had blown into her world like a hurricane and swept her off her feet. He'd been ten years older, with one marriage already in flames and a string of jilted lovers behind him. Kate hadn't known that then.

Nine years ago, Bryce had hired Conrad Garrett to lead him and a small party through the Everglades on a hunting expedition. Bryce had brought a woman with him, but she didn't take to the rough living conditions and the fact that he was paying more attention to Kate than to her. The woman left in a hurry.

At that time, Kate had felt a glow of pride that she was able to turn the head of a man like Bryce Colbert. He was so confident and so sure of what he wanted. Kate hadn't responded to Bryce's advances at first, which had only seemed to increase his desire for her. In the end, though, she'd been thoroughly captivated by Bryce's charm and he'd been driven to win her. That kind of infatuation, and she knew now that's what it had been, was nothing but trouble.

Shortly after the marriage, Kate had gotten pregnant with Steven. The marriage started falling apart almost immediately, but Kate busied herself with raising her child. There was nothing in the world that she loved like her son and daughter. For the first time she'd known what had prompted her father to set his life aside for her till she was grown.

During the six years of her marriage she'd lived in New York and tried to fit in. She'd worn the dresses Bryce had bought for her, gone to the salons he'd pointed her to, and taken classes to learn how to entertain in his home. Only later did she realize how hard she'd worked to become a trophy wife. She'd been competing in an arena that she didn't even care about, but Bryce had somehow brought out the desire in her to be the perfect Stepford wife. In the end, she knew she hadn't been much different than the fish, deer and wild boar trophies she sent home with her clients.

Even before the divorce, Bryce had resumed dating. He hadn't even tried to hide it. Or maybe his infidelity had gone on longer than Kate had known. Now, she didn't want to know. Whatever had drawn him to her in the beginning was gone. Bryce had gone back to the same kind of woman he'd always pursued.

Five years old and impressionable, Hannah always talked about the women her daddy dated. She didn't see the pain it caused Kate, and Kate wouldn't have let her daughter see it for anything. Hannah was fascinated by the clothing and jewelry the women wore, how her daddy was always dating "princesses."

Kate wasn't jealous. For the most part. During the marriage, and especially during the divorce when his attorneys had painted her as a gold digger in court and in the three years since, when he'd fought off every attempt she made to see more of her kids, she'd learned that marrying Bryce Colbert was the biggest mistake she'd ever made.

Of course, she'd made some good ones later too. Agreeing to guide and care for Darrel Mathis's group was one of those.

"Maybe we could talk about this later," Kate suggested. "You're breaking up at this end."

"Sure, Kate, sure," her dad agreed. "Didn't mean to step on any toes."

"You didn't." Kate hated to make her dad feel like he'd said or done anything wrong. "I've just got my hands full today."

"When Tyler called me this morning—"

Kate fully intended to address the "Tyler issue" as soon as possible. Tyler had called her dad no doubt thinking that calming down a drunken hunter was more a man's work. Wisely, though, her dad had called her.

"—I thought about goin' out there myself," her dad said. "Takin' care of it for you."

"That would have been a mistake, Dad." Kate heard the icy anger in her voice.

"I knew it," her dad told her. "That's why I called you. But I also knew you had to pick up the kids from the airport in Miami today."

Kate glanced at her watch. It was 6:14 a.m. She made herself take a deep breath. "I've got plenty of time to do that."

"Yeah. Figured you did."

Hearing the hesitation in her dad's voice, Kate relented a little. "I appreciate the thought."

"Sure. No problem. Did you ever find out why the Toad's sendin' the kids down?" Her dad never used Bryce's name, as if by not acknowledging it he could strip away her ex's dignity. Toad was short for "scum-suckin' toad."

"No." Outside of the four weeks she got to see Steven and Hannah in July every year, Kate rarely got to have her children. She spent Christmases—either before or after, according to Bryce's plans—in New York. Surrounded by the snow and the hustle and bustle of the city, she always felt like an alien.

"Did you ask?"

"No."

"You should've."

"I'm getting to see my children," Kate said in a tight voice. A lump formed in the back of her throat as she thought about all the times she couldn't see them. Her vision blurred and tears threatened to leak down her cheeks. She steeled herself. "I'm not going to question that."

"Yeah, I guess so," her dad agreed. "I should be clear here in a day or so. Okay if I come by?"

"Of course. They would love that."

"What about you? Or have I worn out my welcome this mornin' bein' a busybody?"

Kate grinned, knowing that despite her dad's gruff demeanor he really was feeling awkward now that he'd said everything he had. "I'm willing to tolerate it," she told him.

"That's good," her dad said, sounding a little relieved. Most people, except for the ones that really knew him, wouldn't have noticed the change. "Mighty good. I'll call you before I come over."

"Just come, Dad."

"I will. An' if you need anythin', let me know."

Kate said she would, told him she loved him, and pushed the end button. She tapped the brake to slow down and slide behind the D.O.C. bus as it rounded a sweeping curve between towering cypress trees. Her thoughts ran to her kids again.

Her dad was right: she should have asked Bryce why he was sending Steven and Hannah. During the past three years, he'd never let her see them any more than the court order had declared. For Bryce, custody was all about power and controlling his financial vulnerability. From all accounts, Bryce didn't spend that much time with Steven and Hannah, but paid others to. She kept having visions of her kids growing up in a vast, empty apartment among strangers.

Put that away, Kate told herself. There's nothing you can do about it right now. You're working to change that. Stay with it.

The two-lane highway straightened out again. Kate knew for a fact that the Florida Highway Patrol and the Collier County Sheriff's Department didn't monitor the highway. In fact, she was surprised that the D.O.C. bus was using the route. The road was well off the beaten path.

Her cell phone rang.

Kate scooped it up and answered automatically. "Garrett Guides. Kate Garrett speaking."

"Kate, where the hell are you?" Tyler Jordan sounded scared and pissed and out of breath all at the same time.

"On my way," Kate said.

"Well, you need to hurry. That damned idiot is out there shootin' up half the Everglades. He gets around some of the regulars through here, they're gonna shoot the ass offa him."

"I'm getting there as quick as I can," Kate said. "Faster than my dad would have. He was over in Miami when you called him. If you'd called me first, I'd have been a few minutes closer by now."

"This didn't seem like something a—" Tyler caught himself just in time and closed his mouth. "Like something *you'd* want to deal with," he finished lamely.

A gunshot cracked over the cell phone connection.

"That was Mathis?" Kate asked.

Three other gunshots followed in quick succession.

"Yeah," Tyler said. He swore vehemently. "He's a crazy son of a bitch, Kate. If it's movin' out there in the brush, he's shootin' at it. Damn wonder he ain't shot nobody. He's an anesthesiologist, right?"

"Yeah."

"Something tells me that man's been raidin' his own goodie box."

"Give me fifteen more minutes," Kate said. She put her foot down harder on the accelerator, getting ready to pass the D.O.C. bus. "I'll be there."

Another gunshot echoed over the phone connection.

"Sure," Tyler said sourly.

Kate pulled alongside the D.O.C. bus. She couldn't help glancing inside the vehicle.

Nearly a dozen men sat in rigid-looking seats behind a wire mesh screen that protected the driver and the armed guard in the front.

One of the prisoners sat at the window. Sunlight glinted from his unruly shoulder-length blond hair, picking up the streaks that summer had burned into it. His face was chiseled with a few days' dark beard growth lightly covering his cheeks and jaw. Wide-spaced hazel eyes peered out from under dark brows that arched with sardonic amusement. Despite the shaggy look, the dimple in his chin showed plainly. He wore the familiar orange inmate jumpsuit.

He glanced at his watch, then back at Kate. The amusement left his features and concern filled them.

"Just do what you can," Kate said into the phone. She tried to shake the prisoner's gaze but found it hard to look away. The man was handsome and she couldn't help wondering what he had done to get locked up. "I'll be there as soon as—"

The double explosion ripped through the Jeep's interior. At the same time that she realized the sound had come from beside her and not from the cell phone, Kate saw the bus's front tire shred and come apart. Chunks of rubber flew through the air and slapped against the Jeep, knocking bug debris from the windshield.

Throwing the cell phone down, Kate put both hands on the wheel and tried to speed up as the bus crossed the dotted lines. Before she was able to get clear, the bus slammed against the Cherokee's right rear quarter panel.

Although the collision barely caught the Jeep, the vehicle wobbled and the tires tore free of the highway pavement. Kate tried to shove the transmission into four-wheel-drive with the shift-on-the-fly selector but by then it was too late.

The Jeep swapped ends, spinning out of control. Metal screeched as the bus slammed into the smaller vehicle again, driving it like a battering ram, striking again and again. The passenger window shattered and fell away. The side mirror crumpled inward and fell off.

Kate struggled to recover, jerking the steering wheel and alternately hitting the brakes and the accelerator. Evidently the bus driver was trying to do the same thing because the bigger vehicle tore free. As she tried to regain control of the Jeep, Kate watched in horror as the D.O.C. bus fell over on its side.

Careening wildly across the two lanes, the bus left a trail of sparks. The sound of tortured metal shrilled over the area, startling dozens of birds from the trees and filling the sky with feathery clouds for a moment.

Then Kate lost sight of the bus as the Jeep left the road and skidded into the swampy treeline. She held on grimly as the vehicle crashed through the brush. The seat belt felt as if it was cutting her in two as it restrained her. She came to an abrupt stop against a cluster of knobby-kneed cypress trees in black water.

Even though he'd been prepared for the explosion and the eventual wreck, Shane still jumped at the sound. Seated in the stiff seat, he grabbed hold of the chains secured to the D-ring in the floor between his feet. He lifted a foot and jammed it against the seat in front of him.

Some plan, he told himself. You're going to be lucky if you don't get somebody killed.

That wasn't the plan. The plan was all about escape. For himself and for the men he'd fallen in with while in prison. The man who had rigged the explosion worked in Hollywood doing elaborate movie stunts for guys like Richard Donner and John Woo. All stuff with big explosions and flying cars.

It's a hell of a lot easier watching a stunt like that than being involved in it, Shane thought as the bus started to flip.

All around him, the prisoners cried out, scared and surprised.

Except for Raymond Jolly. The big man sat braced in his seat, broad face implacable. He glanced at Shane with those dead eyes. "You ready?" he asked.

Shane leaned forward to reach Jolly's hands and took the

lock pick he'd fashioned from a piece of wire he'd snared while the prisoners had been at the hospital. They'd been tested for an outbreak of the latest flu everyone was talking about in the media. Shane's nose still hurt from the deep swab.

Working quickly, he picked the lock. The cuffs fell open. By the time the bus was sliding along on its side, finally slowing with a deep grinding noise, he had his legs free.

He pushed himself up and checked the driver and the guard. The guard's attention was locked on the wounded driver. Shane walked across the seats, duckwalking from seat to seat as he used his hands on the seats above him.

Reaching the wire-mesh door, he used the lock pick again. The guard heard the noise a beat too late. Shane opened the door as the guard started to raise his shotgun. Grabbing the weapon's barrel, Shane shoved forward, closed his hand into a big fist, then hit the man in the face.

The guard stumbled backward, releasing the shotgun.

Grabbing the shotgun, Shane rammed the butt into the side of the guard's jaw. Go down! Shane thought.

The man's eyes rolled up inside his head and he sank into a boneless heap.

Shane breathed a sigh of relief. He wasn't going to kill anyone.

"Shane!" Jolly yelled.

Reaching down, Shane took the guard's keys and tossed them back to Jolly.

Jolly caught the keys and quickly uncuffed himself. He handed the keys to the prisoners next to him, then he made his way forward and joined Shane.

"Gonna have to climb out the window." Jolly plucked the sidearm from the fallen guard. He grinned crookedly at Shane. "Woulda been better if the bus had fallen the other way."

"Would have been worse if my buddy hadn't been able to rig the bus," Shane pointed out.

"Yeah." Jolly looked at the two fallen guards.

Shane knew the man was thinking of killing them. Raymond Jolly was a merciless man and had killed before. "If you kill one of them," Shane said in a calm, non-threatening voice, "I guarantee you're going to amp up the pursuit. Escaping prisoners is one thing. Escaping prisoners who capped guards while they were helpless is another."

Jolly hesitated for just a moment, then nodded. "Let's hit it." He shifted his attention to the driver's-side window and surged up.

Shane's stomach unknotted. He followed Jolly, climbing from the bus. He'd heard the sound of the Jeep colliding against the bus. Now he wondered what had happened to the woman.

He slithered free of the bus, surprised at all the smoke. Then he realized the bus was on fire.

Dazed, Kate fumbled for the cell phone in the floorboard. The Jeep's engine sputtered and died before she could get the clutch pushed in. She punched in 911 and looked at the spiral of black smoke wafting up from where she had last seen the D.O.C. bus.

When the phone didn't connect, Kate looked at it. No signal.

She switched the ignition on and heard the engine catch. Then she pressed the accelerator and tried to back out of the swamp. The tires spun, even in four-wheel-drive, and refused to find purchase.

Thinking that the men might be trapped in the burning bus, Kate forced her door open and got out. The swamp water was almost up to her knees. Working her way around the vehicle, she opened the rear deck and took out the fire extinguisher from the other gear she kept on hand. Then she turned and slogged up the muddy hillside to the road.

The bus lay on its side, sprawled two-thirds of the way across the road at an angle. Bilious black smoke poured from the engine compartment.

Surely somebody is going to see that, Kate thought. There were enough hunters and fishermen in the area that someone would call in a fire.

She sprinted across the street. The fire extinguisher banged against her thigh at every step. Although the extinguisher wasn't much, it was all she could think to do. Her mind whirled. The driver and guard would be free, but the prisoners were shackled in the back. She couldn't bear the thought of watching anyone burn to death.

She attacked the flames in the back immediately, hosing down the smoke and flames with the extinguisher. The white clouds warred with the black smoke. Her eyes burned and watered.

Movement to her right drew Kate's attention. She turned and spotted a man in an orange jumpsuit coming through the smoke. He carried a fire extinguisher too and helped her spray the flames. In seconds the cold white powder crusted the engine compartment and the flames disappeared.

As she staggered back, almost overcome by the smoke, Kate saw that the prisoner was the blond man she'd spotted through the window. Blood wept from a cut over one of those hazel eyes.

"Guess you came along at a good time," he said in a deep, resonant voice. Then he shrugged. "Of course, I guess you could say it was a bad time too. Another few minutes earlier or later, you'd have missed this altogether."

Another prisoner joined the blond one. The new arrival was broad and chunky. His thick-jowled face looked menacing. A thick scar bisected one eyebrow. His hair was oiled and combed straight back.

"You the girl in the car?" the new prisoner growled.

Kate stepped back. "Where are the guards?"

"Guards didn't make it," the prisoner grunted. Then he smiled. "Where's your car?"

Lifting the fire extinguisher to use as a weapon if she needed to, Kate didn't answer. If the guards were dead and the prisoners were free, she was in a hell of a mess.

The menacing prisoner lifted his arm. He held a pistol pointed at her. "Where's your car? I won't ask you again."

"In the swamp," Kate said. "It spun out of control across the road."

The prisoner held out a hand. "Gimme the keys."

Before the man or Kate could move, the blond man stepped forward and grabbed Kate. He stood behind her and wrapped a hand around her upper body, holding her trapped for a moment, and fished the Jeep's keys from Kate's vest.

He held the keys up, dangling them from his thumb. "Got 'em, Jolly."

The prisoner with the gun smiled. "Good job, Shane."

Moving quickly, Kate stamped her heel against Shane's shin, scraping skin with her hiking boot. He yelped in pain, but that was quickly muffled when she slammed the back of her head against his nose. She made a desperate grab for the Jeep's keys, but Shane closed his fist over them.

Jolly aimed the pistol at Kate.

Moving quickly, Kate threw herself around the end of the bus out of Jolly's line of fire. *Guards didn't make it.* The cold, flat declaration ricocheted through her mind. She was out here alone with escaped prisoners.

On the other side of the bus, Kate ran. Guide work was

physically demanding. She exercised and ran every day even though finding the time was almost impossible, keeping herself in peak condition. Her life and the lives of the people who hired her depended on her ability to take care not only of herself but of them as well.

Footsteps slapped the pavement behind her. Curses rang out.

Kate ducked and slid down the muddy hill on the other side of the road from where the Jeep had gone off. A gunshot cracked behind her and leaves fluttered down from the cypress trees in front of her. She didn't quit running, leaping and dodging through the cypress forest with the sure-footed grace of a deer.

Fifty yards into the swampy tangle, hidden deeply in the brush, Kate stopped behind a tree and glanced back at the bus. Shane and Jolly hadn't pursued her.

As she watched through the residual smoke coming from the bus's engine compartment, Shane, Jolly and four other prisoners in orange jumpsuits disappeared over the other side of the road.

Knowing they were going for her Jeep, Kate edged through the cypress forest, working her way forward. Jolly had a pistol, but there might be more weapons on the bus. Once they found out the Jeep was mired in the swamp, they might come for her. After all, she knew the area. If she had a chance to get to the bus and get a weapon—a pistol or a shotgun—she was going to. But if she had to flee farther back into the swamp, she was prepared to do that too.

She halted at the edge of the treeline and listened to the Jeep's engine catch. The transmission whined, then she heard the wheels grab hold. Evidently with six bodies aboard, the Jeep had found enough traction to extricate itself.

A moment later, the Jeep roared back on to the road with

Shane at the wheel. The tires slung mud off, found traction again, then dug in.

Kate watched in disbelief as her Jeep accelerated and disappeared down the road. The adrenaline hit her then, strong and savage, and took away nearly all her strength. She leaned against a tree and shuddered, hoping that someone had seen the smoke and was coming to investigate.

She couldn't stay here. She had a client with buck fever and she had to pick up Steven and Hannah from Miami International Airport in a few hours. Taking a breath, she steadied herself and started for the overturned bus.

Chapter 2

Kate paused beside the bus, breathing hard. Slow down, she told herself. The men inside this bus have been convicted of armed robbery, drugs, murder and rape. You can't just charge in there. But what about the guards? She sighed. She couldn't let anyone burn to death.

During her guide experience—with her dad and on her own—she'd had several close calls. Snake bites and other injuries to clients as well as herself topped the list. And she'd ended up being the medic for her dad and her siblings when they'd gotten hurt. Taking care of people was just second nature to her.

She studied the bus, wondering how best to handle the situation. No matter what she did, there was some risk. At least it didn't look as if it was going to catch on fire and burn again.

"Is the bus gonna explode?" someone yelled from inside.

"Man, why didn't those guys cut us loose while they were at it?" someone else griped.

"Can anyone reach the driver? He's got a set of keys on him."

"Dude," someone else said, "I think that guy Jolly or one of his *cabrones* took the key ring."

Kate jumped up and caught hold of the edge of the bus, then hauled herself up. The men inside the bus saw her through the windows and started screaming for help, wanting to know if the bus was on fire. They beat on the windows with their free hands, the other hands manacled to the D-rings in the floor. Several of the prisoners yelled at her, urging her to get inside and set them free. Some of the comments bordered on suggestive. Kate ignored it all, hoping she wasn't going to find the guards dead.

The driver's window was open. Kate looked inside and saw the uniformed guard lying spread-eagled across the bus doors that were now flat to the street and unable to be opened. The guy was in his fifties, heavy-set and balding. She couldn't help thinking he was somebody's husband, somebody's father, maybe even somebody's grandfather. But she had no idea how she was going to get him out of the bus if it caught on fire again.

Holding on to the edges of the window, Kate let herself down into the bus. She knelt beside the fallen guard. Blood covered his face, still leaking from a deep laceration on his forehead. Bleeding's good, she told herself. Bleeding means the heart's beating. He's alive. But he had to stop bleeding to stay that way.

The wound wasn't going to stop bleeding on its own. It was too wide, too deep. Judging from the look on his head, he'd have a concussion at least, but something short of a skull fracture, she hoped.

"Hey!" one of the orange-jumpsuited prisoners called out. "Hey, *chica!* Get his keys! Get us out of here before we burn up!"

Several other prisoners echoed the demand/plea. A few of them were crying or praying.

"You're not going to burn up," Kate stated. She reached under the dash and freed the large first-aid kit secured there. Sorting through the supplies, she found a gauze pad and a roll of adhesive tape. She pulled on a pair of surgical gloves and cradled the guard's head in her lap. Working quickly and from experience, she wrapped the wound, fashioning a turban that would compress the laceration and help aid the clotting to stop the bleeding.

"Damn you, woman!" someone swore. "You can't just leave us in here to die!"

Kate didn't take the verbal abuse personally. Being a single woman in what was essentially a man's profession drew a lot of ire and harsh speculation as to why she did what she did. A lot of men felt threatened. None of them seemed to understand or accept that she just loved being part of the world her father had introduced her to. There was a real freedom in being a guide, in staying out in the wilderness where she wasn't under someone's constant scrutiny.

"You're not going to die," Kate said, not looking at them. They were captives, chained to the D-rings mounted in the floor. Most of them had to stand now, or sit on the opposite seats because they were at the end of their chains.

"This frickin' bus is on fire, lady," someone snarled. "Look at all the smoke."

"*Was* on fire," Kate said calmly. "I put it out before your buddies stole my vehicle."

"Jolly ain't no buddy of mine," someone said. "That bastard had this whole thing wired, this escape an' all. Blew up the bus. An' he didn't invite nobody else in on it."

Kate let that pass without comment. The prison pecking

order wasn't her concern. Finished with the wounded guard, satisfied that she'd done all she could do under the circumstances, she turned her attention to the second guard.

He was younger, probably twenty-four or twenty-five. He was slim and good-looking. Or at least he would have been if it hadn't been for the massive swelling on the side of his face. Somebody had hit him really hard.

Reaching into the first-aid kit, ignoring the continued caterwauling of the prisoners, Kate took out an ammonia capsule and snapped it under the younger guard's nose. The acrid stink caused Kate to choke and cough, but it woke the guard.

He came around fast, jerking his head to get away from the ammonia. He cursed and reached for his pistol but found only an empty holster. His eyes were wide and frightened as he looked up at her.

Kate looked at his prison ID, noting the picture and the name. If something had been planted on the bus to cause the tire to blow it, it could have been an inside job. Just because the guy was wearing a prison guard uniform didn't mean he was a good guy.

"Bill," Kate said in a neutral voice. "Bill Maddox. Can you hear me?"

"Huh?" Maddox blinked at her. Awareness gradually seeped into his eyes. He touched the side of his face. "Damn but that guy can hit."

Kate held up two fingers. "How many fingers am I holding up?"

Maddox looked and blinked. "Two."

She smiled at him, feeling some of the control returning to the situation. "Good. You've been in an accident, but you're going to be fine. Do you know what happened?"

"Yeah. Something on the side of the bus blew up. Pete lost

control and we flipped. By the time I recovered, Shane Warren was out of his seat, off the chain and through that security door. He hit me before I could pull my weapon." Bill shook his head slowly. "I've never seen somebody move that fast in my life."

"Can you sit up?"

He managed it with help and Kate left him propped against the top of the bus.

"I've got to try to get help," Kate said. "Your friend needs someone to look after him."

"Where's Pete?"

Kate pointed at the older guard crumpled against the doors.

Maddox started to get up, then his legs turned rubbery and he sat back down hard again. The prisoners jeered at him, making fun of his inability to stand.

"Easy," Kate said, looking him in the eye. That was important to a shock victim, she knew. The victim had to feel that he could take care of himself. "You're probably a little light-headed right now. After everything you've been through, that's to be expected. Just go slow and you're going to be fine."

Leaning back, Maddox started taking deep breaths.

"Breathe slowly," Kate made herself say calmly. She knew she sounded much more calm than she felt. She'd practiced sounding that way during stressful situations. She demonstrated till he started breathing that way too. "You breathe fast like that you're going to get your blood too oxygenated, you'll hyperventilate and you could pass out. That won't help Pete." Give him someone else to take care of, she thought. That way he'll stop worrying about himself so much.

"Okay," he said. "Thanks. Are you a nurse?"

Kate checked an immediate impulse to ask him why he thought she couldn't be a doctor. She made herself smile reassuringly. "No. But I've done a lot of first aid."

"How did you get here?"

"I saw the accident happen. Thought I'd stop by and lend a hand. Unfortunately, some of the prisoners managed to escape and stole my Jeep."

Maddox looked into the back of the bus. "Who?"

"Somebody named Jolly. Another guy named Shane."

Maddox cursed.

"There were four other guys," Kate said, "but I didn't get their names."

Looking back through the prisoners, Maddox said, "Phil Lewis, Monte Carter, Deke Hannibal and Ernie Franks. They were the ones that helped Raymond Jolly pull the Desiree Martini kidnapping."

That rang bells. Desiree Martini had been the twentysomething heiress of Gabriel Martini, the international shipping magnate who operated out of Miami-Dade. The kidnapping had taken place a few months ago. The last Kate had heard, law-enforcement officials had "feared the worst" and the ransom money hadn't yet been recovered. Jolly had stashed it someplace before the FBI had apprehended him.

"We need to call 911," Kate said. "Let them know we're out here."

"Sure." Maddox pulled his cell phone from the holster on his belt. He checked it, shook his head and immediately regretted that. "No signal."

"It happens down here in the low areas," Kate said. "Let me borrow it and I'll hike up on one of the hills. See if I can get a signal there."

"I can do it." Maddox tried to get up again but couldn't manage it. Ruefully, he handed Kate the phone. "I'll just stay here and take care of Pete."

"You do that," Kate said.

"What should I look out for?"

Kate stood and shoved the phone into her pocket. "Keep his head elevated. That'll relieve some of the pressure and naturally help slow the bleeding. If he throws up, don't let him breathe it in. Turn his head and get it out." She gave him a reassuring smile. "Should be cake."

"Cake," Maddox echoed doubtfully.

"I'll be right back as soon as I get through to someone." Kate climbed up and caught hold of the window. She heaved herself out and dropped over the side of the bus. She forced herself to jog, not run, not allowing herself to give in to the panic that throbbed inside her.

She had to run a quarter-mile to reach a rise. Even then she only had one signal bar showing. But when she punched 911, she got right through. As she explained the situation—giving her location and knowing the phone GPS coordinates would back her up—she looked back at the overturned bus. A thin trickle of black smoke continued to pour from the engine compartment. The quiet of the Everglades made everything she saw feel surreal.

She couldn't help wondering where Raymond Jolly and his cohorts had gotten off to in her truck.

"Hell of a mess you got yourself involved in, Kate."

Standing to one side of the accident site, Kate watched Sheriff Harvey Bannock walking over to her. "Didn't exactly have this on my schedule either, Sheriff."

Bannock smiled and wiped the back of his wattled neck with a handkerchief. "Damn, but it's humid." He looked to the south where the ocean lay only a few miles away. "Supposed to be blowing up a storm out there that'll be on us soon. They're calling it Genevieve."

"That's what Dad said."

"How come the bad ones always get those sexy names?"

Kate shook her head and watched as the prisoners were led from the overturned bus into another one under the close supervision of shotgun-toting prison guards. Several of the prisoners had complained of medical problems, insisting they needed to be taken to a hospital and not back to the prison. Besides the prison bus, there were several sheriff's deputies, paramedics and a few of the local reporters. Miami had even sent a news helicopter.

Bannock was a thickset man who'd been sheriff in the county for twenty-five years. His florid face came from too much drinking, but he ran a tight ship. His iron-gray hair was neatly clipped and he wore a jacket over a Colt .45 he'd carried as an officer during his tours through Vietnam. He looked like somebody's grandfather with his jeans and cowboy boots, but the mirror sunglasses and no-nonsense attitude were all cop.

He was also a good friend to her and her dad. He threw a lot of out-of-town business her way with recommendations and business connections he had. Sometimes Kate thought it was because he felt sorry for her, but Bannock always insisted it was because he could trust her to treat people right and not over-charge them or allow them to poach or indiscriminately kill.

That reminded her of the Mathis party Tyler Jordan had called about.

"You okay?" Bannock asked.

"I'm fine," Kate said.

"You look a little jacked."

"Maybe a little," Kate admitted.

"Prison guard Bill Maddox said you took care of every-thing inside the bus."

"Is the other guard going to be okay?"

"The EMTs had him talking. They tell me he's going to be fine. Part of that's because you bandaged him up. A few stitches, a stay at the hospital tonight for observation, he'll be home this time tomorrow."

Kate glanced at her watch. So far she'd been at the site for almost two hours. She still had Mathis to deal with, and guessed that Tyler Jordan was probably beside himself right now. He might even be prompted to quit. She sighed. All she needed was to be left shorthanded with Steven and Hannah coming so unexpectedly.

"Problems?" Bannock asked.

"I have a client who's turned the site I put him on into his own private shooting gallery. Tyler called me this morning. I was on my way out there when this happened."

"I'll send a deputy around when I can. Where's the site?"

Kate told him.

"Don't know how soon I can get a man there," Bannock said. "We're battening down the city, getting ready for this thing. But I'll have him there as soon as I can."

"I appreciate it." Kate was antsy, feeling the need to go burning through her.

Bannock wiped his sweating face. "I'm gonna cut you loose, Kate. Ain't no reason for you to hang around here. If I have any more questions, I'll give you a call or come by."

"Thanks, but since they took my Jeep, leaving's not exactly an option."

"There might be a way," Bannock said. "Clyde Burris wants an exclusive interview with you."

Clyde Burris worked for one of the weekly newspapers out of Everglades City. Kate bought advertising space from him and sometimes allowed him to do interviews with out-of-state clients who wanted a little extra publicity before they returned home.

"I really don't like the idea of talking to the news," Kate said.

"That's the good part," Bannock said. "It ain't the news. It's Clyde. And when other media agencies call you, and I guarantee they will because the story's a good one—'Local Woman Hero,' Raymond Jolly, and the unsolved nature of the Desiree Martini kidnapping—you'll be able to tell them that you've granted an exclusive to Clyde." He paused. "That's guaranteed to get him picked up on every stringing service across the nation."

Kate didn't doubt that. As she recalled, the Desiree Martini kidnapping had been huge news a few months ago.

"How's that going to help me get to my site?" Kate asked.

Bannock sighed. "I have to do the math for you too? And here I was believing your daddy when he said he raised a bright girl."

Not too bright, Kate thought sourly. I married Bryce Colbert and didn't see him for the louse that he is.

"Just tell Clyde you're willing to do the interview in the car on the way to your site. He's taken all the pictures of a wrecked bus that he can publish. What he needs is a bigger story. Something with a little more homegrown flavor, and a personal look at the 'hero' of this little shindig. And Tyler Jordan's driving one of your trucks, isn't he?"

Kate nodded.

The sheriff spread his hands and smiled. "There you go. You can drop Tyler off at home and keep the truck so you can pick up your kids at the airport. I've even provided you transportation. Problem solved."

Kate had to admit that the arrangement would work out fine. She wasn't even surprised that Bannock knew she was picking up Steven and Hannah. It was a small community, and Bannock kept a close watch on things.

She took a deep breath. "Let me know when you find my Jeep?" It was a point of pride more than anything. She didn't want Jolly and Shane to get away scot-free.

"You bet. I'm going to have to keep it in impound for a few days. It's evidence now."

"Sure." Kate thanked him again, then walked over to Clyde Burris and laid out the deal. The reporter quickly agreed and guided her to his car, changing tapes in his microcassette recorder as they walked.

By the time she reached the site, Kate felt all talked out. Clyde, slim and nervous and a chain-smoker, had kept at her the entire trip, somehow managing to change radio channels and keep up with all the local breaking news at the same time.

There was a lot of speculation about what had caused the bus to wreck, from an organized prison breakout all the way to a terrorist attack.

Clyde had kept returning to that too, but Kate hadn't been able to tell him any more than she already had. She'd been curious about the blond man with Jolly, though. According to Clyde's sources, Shane Warren was pulling a thirty-year shot on a drug charge and second-degree-murder rap. Supposedly the Atlanta district attorney was even looking at him for killing an undercover narcotics agent.

"Not a good guy," Clyde had summed him up. But the reporter had been curious as to why Shane Warren had ended up with Raymond Jolly.

When they arrived at the site, Kate thanked the reporter for the ride and got out looking for Tyler. The young man was sitting sullenly in the guide truck listening to a Toby Keith CD. His auburn hair hung down to his shoulders. Aviator sunglasses covered his eyes. His skin stayed red all the time and was covered with freckles. At eighteen, he was short and skinny like his father, but still in possession of out-of-control hormones and way too much male attitude.

"I'd about given up on you," Tyler said. His stained straw cowboy hat was more crumpled than creased, and had bright-blue peacock feathers jutting from it. His black T-shirt was festooned with marijuana leaves. Not exactly the kind of message Kate wanted to send out to clients. She could imagine the T-shirt showing up in pictures people showed their friends and family back home.

"Where's Mathis?" Kate asked, walking by him. She checked her watch. Damn, but the time was getting away from her. She was going to have to hurry if she was going to pick up Steven and Hannah on time.

"The cabin. Got back about twenty minutes ago and started drinking. Him and his buddies." Tyler uncoiled from the four-wheel-drive pickup and got out.

"Bring the video camera."

Remaining sullen, Tyler asked, "Why?"

"Just do it," Kate commanded.

Tyler cursed. For a moment, she didn't think he was going to do what she said. Then he reached into the truck to get a compact video camera. He reluctantly followed her.

Kate held a stun baton in one hand. So far, Tyler hadn't seen it. The weapon was one Kate had learned to use out in the bush. It was an Asp Electroless Tactical Baton specially made for a humid environment like southern Florida. When closed, it measured only nine and a half inches, but the release button expanded it to twenty-six inches of carbon steel guaranteed to stand up under repeated impacts. The weapon only weighed a pound and a half.

Her father had introduced them to her when she'd been fifteen, and even made her take courses with it at a martial arts dojo till she knew what she was doing. *You're a woman, baby girl,* her dad had said, *and you're workin' in a man's world. Some of them guys you take on are gonna show a mean side ever' now an' again. No matter that you can scuffle an' fight, you're likely gonna be givin' away a hundred pounds or more an' maybe a few inches of reach. It'd be stupid for you to work in them conditions an' not be able to properly take care of yourself.*

Over the years, Kate had worn the weapon out in the bush. She'd used it more on snakes, wild pigs and alligators than men. But she'd used it on men before too. It usually shortened the fight any belligerent drunk might want to provoke to a matter of seconds, with no one getting seriously hurt.

"Did you take video of Mathis shooting the wildlife?" Kate asked. That was why they kept the camera. Sometimes as an added feature to the hunt, and sometimes to shoot evidence of poachers.

"Yep. Lotsa footage." Tyler shook his head. "Dumbass. He wants a copy. Even paid me in advance."

Kate breathed out in an effort to stay calm. Guys like Darrel Mathis just didn't understand that shooting video of what they were doing was for a court case, not a vanity recording they could show their friends later.

"We booked five buddies," Kate said. "How many are still with him?"

"Three."

"What condition?"

"About as drunk as Mathis."

"Any idea what set him off?"

"They've been drinking since last night," Tyler said. "I don't think they've come up for air or been to bed." He was silent for a moment. "What are you going to do?"

"Ask them to leave."

"Great." Tyler snorted. "I'm sure they'll just pack right up and go. Is the sheriff sendin' somebody around?"

"They're tied up with the escaping convicts."

"Goin' up there is stupid. He's just gonna laugh in your face."

"Just make sure you keep the camera on." Kate willed herself to go cold inside. Sometimes a paying customer went willingly, maybe feeling remorseful about what they'd done, and sometimes they were so drunk they were easy to handle. And sometimes Sheriff Bannock had a deputy that could stop by when Kate pressed charges and produced a digital recording.

The camp was a neat, compact affair, one of the permanent sites she maintained under contract with the landowner. Keeping the guests from shooting up the wildlife—and sometimes the landowner's livestock—fell under Kate's purview.

There was a single log cabin with three small bedrooms, a living room, a kitchen and two bathrooms with shower facilities. An outside patio provided a brick grill and oven so any game taken could be cooked and prepared fresh instead of packed away and frozen for transport back home.

All of it sat in a hammock of broad-leafed oak trees that looked alien against the backdrop of the cypress trees that were generally the norm this far south in Florida. Most of the hardwood trees never ventured into the wetter climates near the coastal areas.

Shade covered the gleaming SUVs and luxury cars parked under the carport. Any one of them would have cost more than what Kate made in a calendar year as a guide, but she didn't owe for anything. After her divorce from Bryce, she'd been very careful with her money, saving as much as she could before giving it to attorneys to fight the impossible fight for more time with her children.

Kate didn't resent her moneyed clients the income they had, but it did remind her of Bryce and the fact that she'd never be able to match what Bryce was able to give Steven and Hannah on what she was doing now. But there was something to be said for being free.

She'd built her cabin in the off-season, after securing the lease. She'd felled the timber, cleaned it up and negotiated furnishings, plumbing and kitchen appliances from building contractors she worked with when hunting and fishing was slow. She'd taken pride in her work. And in the fact that her dad had helped her put it together these past few years.

She only had three sites with permanent housing. The rest were campsites. Permanent housing was a plus. The clients didn't have to drive in every day from Everglades City or one of the outlying areas, and they didn't have to rough it in a tent. Being able to get drunk, bring women out or watch satellite television if the hunting trip turned into a lazy vacation made the difference to a lot of clients.

At the door, Kate hooked the Asp to her belt, took a deep breath, then knocked.

"Who is it?" a male voice demanded.

"Kate Garrett, Dr. Mathis," Kate said.

When dealing with clients, her dad had taught her always to refer to them as Mr. or Mrs. or, in this case, doctor.

"We're fine, sweetheart," Mathis said. "Don't need anything. But I appreciate you stopping by."

"We need to talk, sir." The "sir" part sometimes came hard, like it did in this case, when a client turned out to be a trigger-happy fool.

The door opened. Darrel Mathis glared down at her. He was a big man, six feet four inches tall, a lot of it running to fat. His jet-black hair and goatee came out of a bottle, as evidenced by the untreated three-days' growth of ash-gray whiskers on his cheeks. He wore camouflage pants spotted with blood and a black T-shirt.

"That sounded awfully official," Mathis said.

"Yes, sir," Kate agreed. "I'm afraid it was. I'm here to ask you and your friends to leave."

Mathis looked at her for a moment, then he grinned and stepped back into the cabin. Behind him, three men in varying degrees of sobriety sat at a card table. Clothes lay scattered everywhere, as well as rifles and bows. A porno movie played on the wide-screen television to their left. The dramatic groans of the stars filled the silence in the cabin.

No one made a move to switch off the television.

Kate got the feeling that she'd walked into an NRA frat party.

"Our guide," Mathis said drunkenly, gesturing to Kate. "Says she's here to throw us out."

The three men sat there, obviously not knowing what to do.

Then Mathis started laughing, and the other three joined him. Turning back to Kate, Mathis said, "This is Friday, sweet cheeks. I'm paid through till Sunday. Come back and throw me out then." He gestured at the cabin. "I'll probably be ready then. I have to tell you, the atmosphere isn't exactly what I'd thought it would be."

He said that with air-conditioning pouring into Kate's face. She'd worked hard to get air-conditioning to the cabin, had to pull extra shifts at the construction work to afford the units and the gasoline-powered generators to run them.

Mathis tried to close the door.

Kate shoved her foot into it before the door met the jamb.

The hiking boots protected her feet from a lot, including weather and impact. She didn't even feel the door close on it.

"Dr. Mathis," she stated firmly, "you're leaving. *Now.*"

Mathis got red in the face and cursed, not nearly as inventively as Kate thought a medical school graduate should be able to. She stood before him and didn't react, didn't let any of it touch her. The last time she'd let herself be hurt by anything a man said had been in divorce court, when Bryce had accused her of being unfaithful in their marriage and had got several of his friends on the stand to swear to the affairs they'd had with her.

None of it had been true. But the judge had believed it. Or maybe he was paid to believe it.

"Get your foot out of the door," Mathis said.

"No, sir," Kate said.

"And *you,* you little pipsqueak!" Mathis roared, throwing a big finger at Tyler. "What are you doing with that camera?"

"Figured they might have an anesthesiologists' convention sometime in the near future," Tyler said. "Thought maybe I could send them footage of you blowin' up Little Bunny Foofoo with a thirty-ought-six. I'm bettin' they'll find it real entertainin'."

Kate really didn't want Tyler baiting Mathis, but she knew she couldn't divide her attention.

"Shut that camera off!" Mathis yelled. "Or I'm going to come out there and beat you to a pulp!"

"An' that's assault," Tyler added in that smartass tone he had down so cold. "My, my. Your legal difficulties *do* continue to multiply."

"Dr. Mathis," Kate said calmly, "we can do this with the sheriff's office in attendance, or we can do it without them. I'm amenable to doing it without them because they could want to arrest you."

Mathis cursed, then he reached out, obviously intending to grab Kate by the face and shove her back from the door. Kate grabbed Mathis's wrist and yanked, swiveling her hip to put her weight into the effort and pull the man out into the yard. She stuck her foot out in front of him and tripped him.

Caught off-balance, Mathis fell, landing hard on the ground and rolling. "Now you've done it, bitch!" He pushed himself to his feet and doubled his big hands into fists. "I tried to be nice to you, but you wouldn't have it that way. Hell no. You want to be some tightass ice princess? Well, now we'll see who's laughing. I didn't come out here to get made fun of by some backwoods hillbilly."

He came at her swinging. There was no finesse to his effort. He was just brute strength focused on hate and powered by rage.

"Dr. Mathis," Kate said, putting her right hand on the Asp at her hip, "I'm asking you to cease and desist. Before someone gets hurt."

"You're the only one who's going to get hurt."

Kate knew there was no use talking to him. Either Mathis was too drunk or too full of himself to listen. She took two steps back, dodging punches at her head.

"Dr. Mathis," she said, "this is your final warning."

"I'll give you a final warning!" he roared, punching again.

Pulling the Asp from her hip holster, Kate pressed the stud and extended it to the full twenty-six inches. She kept it hidden by her leg. When Mathis reached for her again, still roaring with rage, she whipped the Asp around and hit him in the elbow, not enough to break anything, but enough to numb the limb. She darted to the side and hit him again, this time in the right calf, temporarily crippling him. Still moving, she walked behind him and hit him in his left thigh, numbing that leg as well.

Mathis fell.

Kate wasn't even breathing hard. She left Mathis lying on the ground, cursing and moaning in pain. Inside the house, worried that one of the doctor's buddies would try for a rifle and throw the whole situation ballistic, she looked at the men.

They stood staring at her in open-mouthed astonishment. Even Tyler looked astonished, but he kept the video rolling.

"You can't do that," one of Mathis's buddies said.

"It's done," Kate said. "It's over. Grab your belongings and get out." She walked back out of the cabin on trembling legs. Don't throw up, she told herself.

"You know," Tyler was saying to Mathis, "I take a lot of crap about workin' for a woman. Ever'day, it seems like somebody's got some smartass thing to say about it. In fact, as I recall, *you* seemed to have taken some shots at me over it this mornin', while you were out there shootin' holes in deer an' birds an' anything you spotted. But you know, workin' for a woman just kind of takes on a whole new complexion when you see her kick somebody's ass. I mean, who'd expect it?" He grinned. "I didn't. I *know* you didn't. I can tell by that bug-eyed look of surprise on your pasty face. As you can see, I just kind of developed a whole new appreciation for my boss." He looked over at Kate. "Want me to call the sheriff's office now?"

Kate nodded, afraid to talk because she didn't trust her voice and didn't want to sound confused or mad or scared. Actually, she was all of those things. She glanced at her watch. More than that, she was definitely going to be late picking up Steven and Hannah now.

Chapter 3

Late! Kate hated to be late. She glanced at her watch as she strode through the Miami International Airport to Traveler's Aid. She fought back an unaccustomed sense of panic. Sheriff Bannock had sent a deputy around to collect Dr. Darrel Mathis, but it had taken more time than Kate had counted on.

All around her, people were coming and going, moving like cattle through the increased security measures. They stripped off their shoes and subjected themselves to almost invasive security measures. And a few that got singled out for one infringement or another did get subjected to invasive security measures.

Forty-eight minutes late. If Bryce knows… Kate stopped herself. He can't know.

Feeling panicked, Kate stopped at the car-rental desk and asked directions to Traveler's Aid. The young woman behind the desk pointed at the sign that Kate had missed. She thanked the woman and walked over to the aid center.

Steven and Hannah sat in chairs against the wall. Steven wore a perfectly tailored dark suit and looked like a junior executive even at eight years old. He had his father's dark hair—carefully styled, of course, not a hair out of place. But he had his mom's dark-green eyes, which had irked Bryce because people always mentioned how much he looked like his mother after they saw Steven's eyes.

Hannah had long blond hair, the color a throwback to family on both sides that had added weight to the infidelity charges Bryce's attorneys had trotted out to muddy the waters of the divorce. At five, Hannah was an angel. Sometimes, when Hannah was working with one of the animals Kate sometimes found out in the wild and nursed back to health, Kate would just sit and watch her daughter, wondering how anyone like Hannah could ever come into the world without some kind of special fanfare. She wore a beautiful dress that would have bankrupted Kate's account nearly any day of the year. There was no doubt that she had more of them packed away in the suitcase Bryce had sent.

Steven looked bored and irritated. It was the same expression Kate remembered seeing on his father's face far too often. He glanced up at the clock on the wall, then compared it to his watch. He shook his head and mumbled.

But Hannah was talking animatedly with the woman behind the help desk. She was young and black, her hair cut short and elegantly styled. She wasn't old enough to have children of her own, Kate thought, but from the way she reacted to Hannah, the way she really listened to her, she must have had younger brothers and sisters.

"My mom does all kinds of things like that," Hannah was

saying. "Sometimes, when people get lost in the Everglades—in the swamps and stuff—she goes out and gets them. She fights snakes and wrestles alligators—"

"She doesn't wrestle alligators," Steven interrupted angrily.

"Does too," Hannah said, putting her hands on her hips even though she was sitting down.

"She's never wrestled alligators," Steven said. "You're confusing her with the guy on television."

"Does too," Hannah said. Whenever she got into an argument with Steven, she generally stayed with one tack because it drove her brother completely crazy.

Kate knocked on the door.

Steven and Hannah swiveled their heads toward her. The young receptionist looked up and said, "Can I help you?"

"I'm—" Kate began, but then Hannah was up out of her chair, dress flying as she ran across the room.

"Mommy!" Hannah called.

Kate knelt on one knee and caught her daughter, holding on to her tightly as she felt Hannah squeeze her. It had only been a few weeks since they'd seen each other this time, not months the way it usually was, but she was so glad to see Steven and Hannah that it felt the same.

Steven stood up stiffly and reached down for one of the bags beside his chair.

"Ms. Garrett, I presume?" the receptionist asked with a smile.

"Yes," Kate said, "but I really don't wrestle alligators."

"Told you," Steven said sullenly.

Hannah stuck her tongue out at her brother. "'Told you,'" she parroted.

"You're the same Kate Garrett that stopped for the prison bus? The one that saved that guard's life?"

"I don't think his life was ever in danger," Kate said, standing and feeling a little embarrassed.

"What prison bus?" Steven asked.

"It's been all over the news," the receptionist said. She pointed at the small television set mounted on the wall.

Stock news footage of the overturned bus was showing, interspersed with footage of Raymond Jolly and the Desiree Martini kidnapping. She saw a clip of Clyde Burris talking about his exclusive with Kate. At least they're not interviewing me, Kate thought.

"Your mom's a hero," the receptionist told Steven.

Looking at the television, Steven frowned. Evidently his dad hadn't prepared him for his mom being a celebrity.

Temporary celebrity, Kate told herself.

"You stopped for a prison bus that had broken down?" Steven asked, looking displeased. "That sounds really stupid. You could have been hurt."

Not as much as you just hurt me. Kate tried to let the worst of his insult pass over her, but it was hard. Steven didn't approve of many things she did.

"If your mom hadn't stopped," the receptionist said, looking at Steven, "a lot of people could have gotten hurt. That bus was on fire. She saved a lot of lives."

Steven looked away from her and at Kate. "Can we go? We've been sitting here a long time."

"Not so long," Hannah said. "Charlotte has been good company."

"Why thank you, Hannah," the receptionist said. "That's very kind of you to say."

Steven rolled his eyes.

Kate wanted to correct him, but she knew it wouldn't do any good. Steven had his father's backing. Anything she said to him about his manners—or lack of them—rolled right off him like water off a duck's back.

"I do need to see some proof of ID, Ms. Garrett," Charlotte said.

Kate held on to Hannah, shifting her to her hip, and dug her ID out of her jeans pocket.

"Why don't you carry that in a purse?" Steven asked.

"I do," Kate said, looking at him and making full eye contact. "When I need to."

Steven dropped his eyes and didn't say anything. His rudeness bothered Kate. When he was younger, it hadn't been like that. He hadn't been so judgmental. But he more than made up for it now.

"Thank you, Ms. Garrett." Charlotte handed the ID back, then lifted the phone. "Let me get you a skycap to help with that luggage."

"Thanks," Kate said, looking at all the luggage. There was more of it than normal, and she wondered what that meant. And why Bryce had sent the kids to her so unexpectedly.

"Just put everything in the back," Kate said, pointing to the pickup bed. There was no way the luggage was going to fit even in the truck's extended cab.

The two skycaps quickly offloaded the luggage. Kate tipped them, then buttoned down the cargo tarp so none of the luggage would blow away during the trip. She loaded Hannah into the back and belted her in.

"You don't have a safety seat for Hannah," Steven said as he crawled in on the other side.

"You're right," Kate said. "I don't." She was determined not to let his father's tone and recriminations touch her. She'd been given extra time with them—for whatever mysterious reason—and she was going to make the best of it. "Do you need help with your belt?"

"No. I can do it." Steven sat in the other seat in the back and snugged the safety harness. "Where's your Jeep?"

"It was stolen."

"By the prisoners you helped?"

"By the ones that escaped, yes." Kate slid in behind the wheel and started the engine. She was thankful for the air-conditioning. With Hurricane Genevieve fast approaching, the air was turning leaden and turgid. The sky to the southeast was turning black. The storm was only hours away, and even the meteorologists were starting to say it was gathering more strength than they'd thought it would.

"Big mistake, huh?"

Kate slid her sunglasses into place. Don't react. It's just a phase. He'll grow out of it. But she was afraid that he wouldn't. Bryce never had. "Yeah," she said. "I guess it was."

"I bet you won't do that again."

It's not like there are opportunities to do that every day, Kate thought, but she didn't say it.

Navigating the traffic, Kate pulled out through the airport exit ramp to follow the route out of the city. When she spotted the golden arches of McDonald's only a little out of the way, she decided to stop.

"Anybody want a soda?" she asked.

"Can I have a McFlurry?" Hannah asked.

"Sure, baby girl." Kate looked in the rearview mirror at Steven. "What about you? Want a McFlurry?"

"Dad says they're not healthy."

"Not everything has to be healthy. Sometimes it's okay to splurge a little."

Steven was reluctant, but she knew he liked ice cream. She

didn't like thinking that they didn't get much of anything like that when they were with Bryce. There was excess, but they were kids too.

"All right," Steven said.

As she changed lanes, Kate noticed that a black Lexus moved over at about the same time, cutting off the car behind them. Then she had to watch the entrance at McDonald's.

She drove through the drive-thru and ordered the treats and three waters, telling Steven and Hannah that after the ice cream they could concentrate on being healthy.

Back on the street, she turned on to Dolphin Expressway, west on US-41, then north on Tamiami Trail for a straight shot to Everglades City. The trip was going to take about an hour and a half.

"Aren't you going to miss school while you're gone?" Kate asked.

"I'm going to miss school," Hannah said, then spooned more ice cream into her mouth. "I like school. We're getting to finger paint."

"Very cool," Kate said. "You should paint me a picture."

"I will."

"But that's not exactly what I meant," Kate said. "Won't you get behind in your classes, Steven?"

He was looking out the window. "Not really. It's a private school. The teachers do whatever Dad tells them to do."

"Oh." Kate sipped her water. She changed lanes again, watching the traffic closely. Although the truck handled a lot like the Jeep, it was different and she was conscious of the difference.

Glancing back through traffic, she thought she saw the same black Lexus again, then realized there were a lot of Lexuses on the road.

"You know," she said as conversationally as possible, "your dad never did tell me why he wanted you to come stay with me for awhile. Or even how long you're going to be here." She smiled at the rearview mirror. "I guess with all the luggage back there, it could be for some time." Please let it be for a long time.

But even as she hoped for that, she knew that it was a double-edged sword. The longer they stayed, the more she would miss them when they were gone.

"Dad just said it was business," Steven said. "He didn't say how long we were going to be down here."

"Well," Kate said, "your grandpa is excited to see you. I think he's got some new video games to play."

"Great!" Hannah cheered.

"He wins all the time," Steven protested.

"Then beat him."

"I can't."

"You can if you try hard enough."

"He doesn't have to play so hard."

"One thing I learned from your grandpa," Kate said. "He's never going to give you anything you don't work for. If you want it, you're going to have to try to take it."

Steven frowned but didn't say anything.

Kate switched on the radio and concentrated on driving. Traffic was thicker than normal, what with everyone preparing to hunker down and wait out the storm or evacuate. There were only two kinds of people along the Florida coastline when it was storm season: those who stayed and those who left.

"The weatherman said a storm was coming," Steven said.

"Her'cane Genevieve," Hannah added.

"There is," Kate said.

"I've never been here during a storm."

Kate suddenly realized that was true. With them only coming down during the early summer, Steven and Hannah had never weathered a tropical storm. Maybe that's what's got Steven so irritable, she thought. He's scared. She felt badly then about her own feelings.

"Don't worry about it," Kate told her son. "You're going to be with me. Everything's going to be all right. This'll be cake."

"What if we lose power?" Steven asked.

"I've got a generator," Kate said. "We won't lose power long."

Kate's house was a two-story farmhouse with a screened veranda on two sides. When she'd been small, she'd lived there with her dad and brother and sisters. After she'd returned to Everglades City—actually, outside Everglades City—she'd lived with her dad in his other house, one that was a little larger than this one with its small three bedrooms.

He'd kept the old house, though, as a rental property. After Kate started working for Epperson's Contracting and Building, her dad had quietly closed out the rental agreement and given her the house. She'd tried to pay him for it, but he'd just pointed out all the work they'd done on it when they'd lived there while she was growing up. It wasn't much of an investment, but it held so many memories.

The house sat back in clumps of cypress trees in a yard that flooded during the wet season and got overgrown in the dry season if she didn't stay on top of the mowing. It had been painted white for years and needed a new coat now. But the roof kept the rain out and the screen doors and windows kept out the mosquitoes.

She pulled off Plantation Parkway and on to the shell-covered driveway that led to the house. The shells crunched under the tires. She parked under a copse of cypress and magnolia trees where the rope swing that Hannah loved hung. Steven's tree house still occupied the lower branches, but he'd largely outgrown that these days.

While Hannah occupied herself with a favorite DVD and Steven took over the PlayStation 3 in one of the other rooms, Kate went around the house and made sure all the shutters were locked up tight. The storm warnings said there was going to be a lot of wind. Flying debris was always a problem.

As she walked around, a sleek black car drove by the front of the house. She was just coming up from the backyard when she saw the vehicle. It stood out at once in the neighborhood.

An unexplained fear ripped through Kate. The black car slowed just for a moment, the ruby taillights gleaming in the gathering darkness of the storm. Then it sped up again and disappeared around a corner.

For one insane moment, Kate felt certain whoever was driving the car was watching her. But that didn't make any sense.

Unless it's Bryce, she told herself. Her ex-husband was totally into playing sadistic little mind games with her. He'd proven that over the last few years.

Maybe the whole unexplained visit from the kids was some kind of test, designed solely so that she would fail somewhere along the way. Maybe he was even now plotting some way to take away the meager summer visitation she had with Steven and Hannah.

Panic tore through her and she leaned weakly against the side of the house. She hated feeling helpless, and that was all she was whenever Bryce started playing his games.

After a few minutes, she managed to force the crippling paranoia away and regulate her breathing, then she finished her inspection of the house. She was satisfied she was as prepared as she could be, but the best thing would be if the storm changed course and never came to Everglades City. Looking at the dark skies, she doubted that was an option. They'd just have to survive whatever it handed out.

Kate prepared spaghetti and garlic bread in the same tiny kitchen where her mother had prepared so many meals. They also had salad, which she pointed out to Steven, was a definite healthy choice.

Hannah had two servings of spaghetti.

"I guess you didn't hurt your appetite today with the McFlurry, did you?" Kate asked.

"Nope," Hannah agreed. "But you always make the *best* spaghetti. Not even Consuelo knows how to make spaghetti as good as you."

Consuelo was the live-in cook.

"Well," Kate said, "I take that as high praise indeed." She took up her daughter's plate as well as her own and put them in the two-compartment sink where she'd already washed, dried and put away the preparation dishes.

Steven added his own, then helped her quickly clear the table without being asked.

"Thank you," Kate said.

"Sure," Steven replied. "I knew I couldn't play video games unless I helped."

All right, Kate thought, go with it. At least that's a step in the right direction. "Thank you anyway. It's nice to have help cleaning up."

"You should get a maid," Steven said. "Like we have. Then there's a lot of things you don't have to do any more."

Kate had to agree with that. When she'd been married to Bryce, she'd never had to lift a finger to do a household chore.

Some days she missed that. "That may be true, but there's a lot of things you need to learn to do for yourself."

"Like clearing the table and washing the dishes?"

"Yeah."

"Grandpa already knows how to do that. Why do you have him help you with the dishes when he eats with us?"

"Grandpa helps because he wants to help." That was just one of the things Kate cherished about her dad.

"Why does he help? He already knows how to do all that."

"Because there are some things you should never forget. Knowing how to take care of yourself is one of them."

Steven shrugged. "I'd rather have a maid. Clearing the table and washing dishes is boring. Can I be excused?"

"Sure," Kate said, and wondered again how wide the gulf was going to be between herself and her children as they grew.

Steven turned to go.

"Hey," Kate said, "wait up."

At the doorway, obviously in a hurry to get back to whatever game he was playing, Steven looked at her.

Kate turned the water on and let it fill the sink. Steam rose from the hot water. "I've got to go out later."

"Why?"

"I have to make sure the camp sites are taken care of. With this storm coming, the people there are going to need plenty of water and food in case they get stuck out there for a few days. I've got Megan coming over."

"Okay."

With the storm coming on, Kate would have preferred to have her dad there, but he either wasn't answering his phone or didn't currently have service wherever he was. Megan was a seventeen-year-old who worked at one of the bait shops in town. During the summers when school was out,

Kate hired her to help run supplies out to clients during heavy bookings.

"At least I can beat Megan," Steven added, then drifted off back to the bedroom where he was playing.

Kate turned her attention to the dishes, shutting off the water and quickly washing them, putting them in the drainer to dry. Even though Steven looked down at the work, she took a certain sense of pride in it. Washing dishes was necessary and there was a lot of satisfaction in doing it right. With the storm closing in, simple tasks offered a safe emotional harbor.

Megan arrived a few minutes after seven, bundled up in a rain slicker that dripped water. "Wow," she said. "It's really getting bad out there. The meteorologists say we should expect some really bad wind, and maybe some flooding. There's even talk that the storm is going to change directions and hit us now."

"That's what I'd heard." Kate had been watching the news on the living-room television. The storm had already shut down the satellite hookups, but the local channels were still occasionally operational. When that failed, there was the radio. "They don't know how bad it's going to get."

"They never do."

Kate silently agreed. With the storm changing directions, leaving her clients out in the wilds hunkered down was no longer an option.

Storm season in Florida was always dangerous. Over the years, Everglades City had been flooded a number of times. The Okeechobee Hurricane of 1928 had caused storm surges of twenty feet and more, and had killed twenty-five hundred people. Hurricane Andrew had struck in 1992 and devastated the Everglades area. In 1999, Hurricane Harvey flooded a lot of coastal Florida and storm surges of two and a half feet were reported at Fort Myers. The county airport in Everglades City was closed when a portion of the runway was flooded. In 2005, Hurricane Rita became the fourth most powerful Atlantic storm in history, with sustained winds reaching one hundred and eight miles an hour. A month later, Hurricane Wilma caused serious flooding in Everglades City, with wind gusts up to ninety-five miles an hour, and killed seventeen people in the Caribbean before finally exhausting itself.

"Where are the kids?" Megan peered around the house. She was young and slim. Her brown hair reached her waist in the back. She had a few tattoos that her dad didn't know about yet—she'd confided in Kate—but she was a good person. And good with Steven and Hannah, able to be firm as well as giving.

"Video game and DVD," Kate said.

"Ah," Megan replied, smiling. "The 'stuff that rots their brains.'"

"According to my ex-husband, yes."

"What he doesn't know—" Megan said.

The comment made Kate remember the black car that had cruised by the front of her house. There probably isn't much Bryce doesn't know, she realized. And she wondered again why her ex would send the kids down with a tropical storm about to hit the coast.

"What about bedtimes?" Megan asked.

"Whatever you think," Kate said. "Though with the plane flight today, you may find they both go down pretty quickly." She gathered her storm slicker.

After she'd finished in the kitchen, she'd gone back to her bedroom, taken a quick shower, then she'd dressed in jeans, a black sleeveless T-shirt and her hiking boots, and she'd pulled her hair back through her baseball cap. She didn't bother with makeup. The storm would only have smeared it anyway.

"Until the storm blows itself out," Kate added, "keep them in here if they go to sleep or you have to switch over to the generator."

"Sure."

"I'll be back as quick as I can."

"No problem," Megan said. "With the storm coming in so strong, my dad wanted me to spend the night here. If that's okay with you."

Kate smiled at her. "You're always welcome here." Then she called Steven and Hannah to her, telling them to mind Megan till she got back.

Steven acted put out, but Hannah hugged her mom and told her to hurry back.

"Be safe," Kate told her kids.

"You always say that," Steven grouched. "Why do you say that? 'Be safe.'" His tone mocked her.

Kate felt the familiar mix of anger and frustration and hurt that came with her son's attitude. "Because," she said, "I want you to be safe. It's what my dad always told me."

Steven rolled his eyes and said, "Whatever," then headed back to his room and the video game.

Not knowing what else to do to address the situation, Kate was out the door and into the rainstorm Hurricane Genevieve was offering as an hors d'oeuvre.

Tyler was waiting at the convenience store/bait shop when Kate arrived. He was dressed in a rain slicker and had gear rolled up in a sleeping bag slung over one shoulder. During storm season, it was better to be safe than sorry. Carrying gear back out if it wasn't needed was much easier than needing gear and not having it.

Kate parked at the pump, topped off the gas tank, then

went inside, struggling against the high winds. They had to be at least fifty miles an hour, and the storm hadn't even reached them yet.

"The woman of the hour," Marty Dillworth said. He was a big man with fuzzy black hair and a scruffy beard. He'd gone away to Florida State University for a computer degree or film degree. No one could ever settle on one story or the other when they were talking about Marty. He wore sweat pants and a superhero T-shirt.

"What's that about?" Kate asked. They were the only ones in the store. Wind and the big plate-glass windows didn't mix and no one wanted to be around them.

"The prison bus," Tyler said. "I didn't know about that."

"And I didn't know about the dentist you opened up a can of whup-ass on."

"Anesthesiologist," Kate corrected automatically.

Marty grinned and shrugged. "Whatever. We were just catching up on our favorite Kate Garrett stories."

"You two," Kate told them, "have *way* too much time on your hands if that's how you're spending it."

"It gets more interesting," Marty said. "Turns out the *anesthesiologist* had an arrest warrant out for his butt."

"Why?"

"I heard improper conduct with a patient or two. Homer, over at the sheriff's office, mentioned something about digital pictures of those patients in his possession."

Kate felt a little better about the confrontation she'd had with Dr. Darrel Mathis. It was better to incapacitate by force a sleaze rather than a drunk.

"Tyler showed me the video footage of you kicking that guy's ass." Marty shoved out his thumbs. "Two thumbs up. *Way* up."

"Not exactly the career choice I had in mind," Kate said.

"And the prison-bus thing is adding a new wrinkle," Tyler said, pointing to the small television set that kept fading in and out on the local channels. "Seems one of those prisoners turned up dead."

Kate's thoughts immediately turned to the blond man she'd seen with Jolly. The one who had taken her keys from her. "Which one?" She hoped it wasn't the blond man. According to the news reports, Shane was the only one of the escapees who hadn't been part of Desiree Martini's kidnapping and disappearance.

"Some guy named Phil," Tyler said.

Phil Lewis, Kate remembered. She didn't remember much about him other than he'd been one of Jolly's gang. "What happened to him?"

"The police aren't releasing that information at this time." Tyler grimaced. "They're only confirming that he's dead. Oh, and they found your Jeep."

"Where?"

"Not far from the campsites we're heading to tonight. Evidently those guys didn't try to get too far. Or maybe they wrecked your Jeep during their getaway. Sheriff Bannock and the FBI aren't saying."

"The FBI is involved? Why?"

"They originally handled the kidnapping thing," Tyler said. He shrugged. "Maybe they just want to take care of old business. Clean the slate. Something like that." He paused. "Either way, we're going to have to be careful out there."

Kate silently agreed.

"Don't know," Marty said as he rang up Kate's gas and the supplies she'd ordered from him. "With this storm coming, I'm not sure if I'd want to face the storm or those escaped cons."

Neither, Kate thought, but she knew that was too much to hope for. But she wondered about the dead man. How and why had he died?

Chapter 4

The storm hit southern Florida's coastline when Kate was only a few minutes away from the campsite. The black, roiling heavens opened up and poured forth a deluge of biblical proportions. The windshield wipers were hard-pressed to keep up with the torrent. Lightning seared the sky, followed by thunder that came closer and closer. The wind hit seventy and eighty miles an hour. The truck jumped viciously across the road, making driving hard.

Anyone with sense is at home, Kate thought. She fought the steering wheel again, pulling the truck back into a straight course when it wanted to go sideways.

"Damn!" Tyler swore after a particularly close lightning strike. "That one seemed to have our name on it." He sat in the truck's forward passenger seat and stared out at the storm.

Already, small waves of rain swept across the highway, propelled by the surging winds. Debris filled the ditches and channels on either side, surely no more than moments from pouring out across the highway and causing all kinds of hazards. Two emergency vehicles, a fire truck and an ambulance, had roared past them.

Kate had to concentrate on driving. Conditions had turned worse than she'd imagined. Even though she had four-wheel drive on the truck and good road beneath her, she knew she couldn't trust the road.

She went east off Plantation Parkway, toward Everglades National Park. She turned back south on one of the dirt roads that led to a campsite she'd set up for two brothers from Missouri and their three teenaged sons. They were a good group, the kind of clients she wanted to keep. But they were inexperienced with Florida's weather and the sudden, aggressive nature of tropical storms. She'd used Tyler's cell phone in an effort to reach them but hadn't been successful. She would have been in touch with them before if it hadn't been for getting the kids, the bus wreck and the problem with Mathis.

The road had turned to soup under the driving rain. A firm foundation existed beneath the mud, but the tires had to chew through a few inches to reach it. Even then, the rain would soak down into those levels too. In years past, lumberjacks, hunters—of both game and rare orchids and other plants—and residents had used all the dirt roads in the area. The state and federal government didn't provide for much more than grading, which didn't even begin to solve the pothole and drainage problems.

Kate used the lower gears, slowing to a crawl. The headlights barely reached through the driving sheets of rain that looked silver-gray in the glare. Also, the innumerable potholes provided a deadly minefield of potential strut-busting bangs and bumps that could tear the truck's front end out and leave them stranded to ride out the storm.

"—record high amounts of rain and wind," the newscaster droned on over the radio. "The Coast Guard is already reporting thirty- and forty-foot swells in the Gulf of Mexico. Meteorologists are continuing to upgrade the storm as conditions worsen. People living in the low areas and in Everglades City are advised to seek out high ground as Hurricane Genevieve comes roaring into the coastal areas."

Another white-hot dazzle of multi-veined lightning ripped across the sky, followed by a cannonade of thunder that vibrated the truck and caused Tyler to jump. He cursed as he shifted and tried to relax.

"Did I ever tell you that I don't like storms?" he asked.

Kate looked at him, seeing the fear and nervousness in him. During the confrontation with Mathis, Tyler had been totally calm and collected, even with drunken men and weapons potentially in the mix. But the storm had him stressed. Kate knew it was like that for a lot of native and long-time residents who had survived the big ones.

"Yeah," she replied. "I think you've mentioned it before."

"Well," Tyler said. "I really don't like them. In case there was any confusion."

A gust of wind slammed the truck and forced it off the road. Kate kept calm and guided the steering rather than fight it. The passenger-side tires dipped down, falling off the road entirely, picking up water and creating a jetstream against the truck's side that sluiced the window with muddy water. Kate brought the truck back up on to the road through steady effort.

"Damn," Tyler groaned. He looked pale in the darkness.

"Maybe you should have stayed home," Kate suggested.

"It's a little late for that now, isn't it?" Tyler asked.

"Don't you throw up in my truck," Kate warned, trying to lighten the moment.

"Ha, ha," Tyler said dryly. "I'm not going to throw up. But I can't guarantee that the seats are going to stay dry."

Despite the tension of the moment, Kate laughed. Tyler joined her, but it sounded strained. "I appreciate you coming along," she said a moment later.

He shrugged, like it was no big deal. "There's nothin' on television, and Dad has a fit when I use the generator to run the X-Box. I mean, what the hell else can you do when it gets like this?"

"What's your dad doing?"

"Watchin' the weather. Like all the old guys do. Keeps wanderin' out to the front porch, standin' there nursin' a cup of coffee an' a cigarette, shakin' his head, an' talkin' about the big ones he's seen in the past an' how this ain't gonna compare to them. Like all that's gonna do something toward preventin' what we got goin' on here now."

Another lightning strike hit a dwarf cypress tree ahead and on the left. For a moment, the tree's crown ignited in flames and sparks, and the Spanish moss stood out stark and mysterious. The flames blazed for a moment, then the tree fell over into the deep slough on that side of the road and extinguished in the black, running water that cascaded deeper into Big Cypress Swamp.

"Damn," Tyler sighed. "We're gonna need a rowboat to get out of here."

Nearly an hour later, they reached the campsite. The area was primitive, holding only four screened chickees. Tyler had referred to them as "chickees on steroids" because the original designs hadn't included walls, which these had.

Kate had built the shelters, modeling them on the small, elevated cabins the Seminole people had lived in.

As a little girl, she'd seen them in the Seminole Camping

Village on the Big Cypress Reservation near Fort Lauderdale and had fallen in love with them. She'd even built one in back of the house where she now lived. That one was more traditional, without walls and with a rush roof that sometimes leaked. Hannah loved going there for picnics with her mom and to "look for dinosaurs."

A massive SUV sat under a bald cypress tree. Water and mud were already creeping up the tires. If it didn't move soon, it was going to get mired where it was. Kate knew she didn't have the room she needed to haul the men and their sons back to Everglades City. They needed to get moving now, while they still could.

Electric lanterns glowed inside two of the chickees, tearing holes in the darkness and offering shelter from the storm. The hiss of rain sluicing into the earth deafened Kate for the most part, but she still heard the *chuckatapop-chuckatapop-chuckatop* of the gasoline-powered generator she had there for emergencies.

Water already covered most of the land, several inches deep in places. Kate's hiking boots kept her feet dry, but mud clumped up on the tread, adding weight. She pulled her poncho tightly around her but knew it was a situation she couldn't win. No matter what, she was going to get wet tonight.

She pointed Tyler to one of the chickees and she took the other. Climbing up the slightly inclined ladder, Kate knocked on the door. "Mr. Iverson," she yelled, hoping he could hear her over the rain.

Rock-and-roll music blared from inside the chickee. They were watertight. She'd made certain of that when she'd constructed them, and when she weather-stripped them right before each rainy season. Maintaining the cabins, chickees and campsites was a lot of work, but it was work she felt good about.

She banged on the door again. "Mr. Iverson!"

This time the door opened. Clarence Iverson, the older brother, peered out at her. He wore thick glasses and had ginger-colored hair. He was in his late forties and had the kind of relationship with his two boys that Kate wished she had with Steven and Hannah. It was, she'd reflected a few times since dealing with the brothers over the last three years on their annual guy-trips, the kind of relationship she had with her dad.

"Ms. Garrett," Iverson greeted. Since the chickee was so low, he had to stay on his hands and knees.

Behind him, two young teenagers sat up in their sleeping bags. There was little room for anything else in the shelter. Luxury was never offered or even mentioned when renting the chickees out. Both boys looked slightly worried.

The gale winds slammed against the chickee, causing it to sway a few inches. Then thunder exploded again and Kate felt it vibrate through the wood beneath her hands.

"You know I'm not one to complain," Iverson said, "but you've really got to do something about these noise levels. I mean, blaring rock-and-roll at this time of night?"

Both teens rolled their eyes and yelled, *"Dad!"*

Iverson grinned at them. "Told you that you'd get in trouble playing music that loud. Man, your mom's going to hate it when I have to leave you here in prison."

The mention of prison reminded Kate of her earlier encounter with the DOC bus. And the fact that the escaped prisoners, except for the dead one, were still in the area.

Despite the situation, Kate grinned. The Iverson brothers were firefighters from St. Louis. They were good men, solid men. Men like her dad. If Kate was still interested in pursuing— or better yet, being pursued by—a man, that was the kind of man she'd want. Unfortunately, all the ones she knew were taken.

And it wasn't like she was looking. The last thing she needed was a man in her life breaking her stride. Steven and Hannah came first.

"Mr. Iverson," Kate said, "you're going to have to leave."

Iverson looked at her then. Concern etched his face. "The storm?"

Kate nodded. "Hurricane Genevieve. It turned. We're right in its path."

Iverson shoved his head out into the rain. The chickee swayed threateningly again. "Looks worse than they were expecting."

"It is," Kate agreed, having to raise her voice over the howling wind and the rumbling thunder. Lightning danced naked in the sky, flip-flopping like a centipede. "And it's going to get worse before morning."

"What do you recommend?" Iverson asked.

That was why Kate loved having clients like the Iverson brothers and their sons; they were never a problem and they always listened. She was slowly building her client base, weeding out the problem ones like Mathis. Unfortunately, she still needed high rollers like the anesthesiologist to keep Garrett Guides comfortably in the black while managing to fund custody pursuits.

"There are hotels in Everglades City," Kate said. "I'll refund your money for tonight."

Iverson shook his head. "That won't be necessary. You can't control the weather. I'm glad you came out all this way to check on us. I thought we could just sleep through it. Give us a second to get squared away."

The two boys high-fived each other. "A hotel!" one said.

"Beds and television!" the other one said. "Now that's a vacation!"

Iverson glanced back at Kate. "As you can see, Ms. Garrett, the boys are heartbroken."

Kate laughed and retreated down the ladder. "Just toss your gear down. I'll keep it out of the mud."

The Iversons, the boys' excitement at spending the night in the hotel notwithstanding, were expert campers. They had their gear packed in minutes. Iverson dropped the rolled sleeping bags down. Kate caught them and slung them over her shoulder.

Tyler was already ferrying equipment to the SUV, wading through water that was up over his ankles now. It's getting deeper, Kate realized. Fast. Fear rose in her then as the winds hit the extra surfaces created by the sleeping bags over her shoulder and nearly swept her away. She walked deliberately, leaning into the shifting winds, having to move constantly.

Within minutes, they were packed and loaded into the SUV.

"Do you know the way to Tamiami Road?" Kate asked, shouting through the noise of the storm.

Willard Iverson, the younger brother, sat behind the wheel. "Yeah." He closed his eyes tight against the lashing rain. "We've been to Everglades City a couple times since we've been here. Had to get movies for the tenderfeet."

"Yeah," one of the boys yelled from in the back. "Gross, gory zombie movies. Our moms won't let us watch them at home."

"Just our way of communing with nature and the unnatural," Clarence Iverson said, grinning. "We had to throw in pizza to swear them to secrecy."

Kate smiled, wondering what Steven would think about watching zombie movies. Those had been a staple of her brother's, and she and her sisters had raided his popcorn and joined him on most nights that he didn't have one of his buddies over to spend the night. Everything had been so simple then. Zombies had been monsters with rules, not attorneys.

"Are you going to be all right driving in this?" Kate asked.

"I drive a fire truck in St. Louis, Ms. Garrett," Willard Iverson said.

"This isn't St. Louis," Kate reminded, "and I don't think you've ever had a hurricane there." Lightning flashed and thunder boomed.

"No, ma'am. Just mentioned that so you'd know I was trainable."

Kate smiled again. "Stay to the middle of the road. Flood-waters are going to mask the potholes. Go slow. You break a strut or screw up the front end, you're stuck. Emergency services are going to be out, but they're only going to known sites, not cruising for people needing help. Certainly nowhere out this far. Their orders are to help when they know they're needed and when they know they can."

"I can appreciate that."

"If a disaster is declared," Kate said, "emergency services are going to take over all the cell phone frequencies. You might be able to get through on 911, but that's not a guaran-tee either."

"Are you going back to Tamiami Road, Ms. Garrett?" Clarence Iverson asked.

Kate shook her head. "Tyler and I have got two more sites to check on. If you don't have any trouble, you'll be back at Everglades City before we finish up out here."

"We'll wish you good luck then." Willard Iverson of-fered his hand.

Kate took it and shook.

"Tyler," Willard Iverson said, offering his hand to him. "You two be safe."

"Yes, sir," Tyler said, shaking hands. "We'll do that, sir."

Kate headed back to the truck, holding the hood of her

poncho down. Without warning, the wind rose up again and
knocked over one of the chickees. Damn, Kate thought,
watching as the structure was blown away and shattered
against a copse of cypress trees.

She settled in behind the truck's steering wheel, grateful
for the slight warmth pouring from the heater. The warmth
was more a psychological comfort than anything. Tropical
storm conditions weren't cold; they were just wet, awfully,
awfully wet.

"I bet Hank Coolidge is already gone from his site," Tyler
said. "He's been through this a couple times. He knew to
clear. And Dinali changed his plans and was supposed to be
gone this mornin'."

"Were you out there to make sure Tomkins left?" Kate asked.

"Not with everythin' goin' on with Mathis this mornin',"
Tyler said. "Then you dropped me back home. Couldn't get
much done while I was afoot."

And that was another problem that was waiting for her
tomorrow. To get everything done with the clients she'd still
have in the field tomorrow, and to check on the sites and
make sure they were cleaned up, they needed another vehicle.
She sighed. Tomorrow, she promised herself. I'll deal with all
of this tomorrow. I just need to get through tonight.

She waited till the Iversons rolled slowly forward, then
followed them. Willard Iverson drove sensibly, which relieved
Kate tremendously. She trailed behind them for four miles,
then took another dirt road to the north. The next campsite was
only a few miles away.

"Authorities in Everglades City and outlying areas continue
to report power outages," the radio broadcaster announced.
"Folks, seriously, you should *not* be out tonight. Stay home

and kick back. Those of you who still have power, just listen to the radio as I take you back to Buddy Holly and the Crickets. People that don't have power are going to miss out on—"

Lightning stretched ropy veins across the dark sky. Thunder boomed almost immediately.

The broadcaster's voice departed, leaving only the hiss of white noise in its wake.

Kate held on to the steering wheel and continued to drive slowly. Her eyes burned from staring through the rain. The wipers labored at high speed, but did little to increase visibility. The tires were several inches deep in the water now.

According to the news, Hurricane Genevieve was throwing everything at the coastal areas. Several swamps were already under water. And the tide was rising, sweeping inland. It had been nearly a hundred years since Big Cypress Swamp had flooded to this degree. And this storm promised to be a record-breaker on several fronts.

Coolidge had already packed and gone when Kate and Tyler had arrived. The chickees there so far promised to weather the storm because they were tucked more closely into a hammock of hardwoods. But the land was lower there. Flooding was going to be a definite issue.

She turned in at the dirt road that led to Dinali's campsite. The old naturalist was a favorite client of Kate's. She'd known him as a little girl when he'd hired her dad as a guide. Once she'd started doing business under her own name, after her dad went to find his fortune in marine salvage and possible pirate treasure, Pietro Dinali had returned.

"He's gone," Tyler said, rubbing at the fog on the windshield caused by the humidity of their bodies in the cab. Leaving the heater on had made the truck's interior too hot to bear.

Relief filled Kate as she looked at the empty campsite.

"Told you he had to go," Tyler said.

"I know, but it's better to be safe than sorry."

After another lightning flare and the cascading thunder, Tyler shook his head. "Hate to be the one to break it to you, but we ain't exactly safe out here."

Kate put the truck in Reverse and backed at an angle. "We'll be home soon." But when she put the transmission into first gear, the tires spun through the mud and refused to grip any solid traction.

"Oh man," Tyler said.

"It's okay," Kate said confidently. "The incline's just a little steep here. We'll back up and get a running start at it." She backed up more, trying to think of what she'd do if that didn't allow them to power up the grade. There wasn't another way out.

She put the truck in gear again, then eased out on the clutch and started the vehicle forward as slowly as she could. Once the tires found purchase, she added speed. Her heart stopped for a moment when they slipped, then started beating again when she gained the top of the hill.

I just want to be home with my kids, Kate thought. The reports of the damage and flooding to the lower areas of Everglades City—where her house was—had her concerned. Thinking of climbing into bed with her son and daughter and listening to the storm pass sounded like the best thing she could ever do. She also worried about her dad, wondering where he'd gotten off to and if he was all right.

Tyler's phone rang, startling her.

He scooped it up from his belt holster. "Speak," he said gruffly. The greeting, if it could be called a greeting, was something that he'd gotten from his father.

The elder Jordan was a painter by trade, and a heavy drinker by choice. His social skills weren't important to him because he was good enough that people always wanted him for one job or another.

"*Who* is this?" Tyler demanded, as if totally surprised.

Then he shoved the phone out to Kate. "For you," he growled, grimacing like he'd just bitten into something sour. "Your ex."

Bryce? Kate couldn't believe it.

"Says he got the number from Megan," Tyler added.

A yawning pit of despair opened up in Kate's stomach. Bryce calling her couldn't be good. She made herself take a quick breath, forcing herself to remember that the last time Bryce had called had been to offer to let her keep Steven and Hannah for "a few days." Then there'd been all that luggage.

She took the phone when Tyler shook it. "Hello."

The connection wasn't good, but it worked. Popping and crackling sounded over the line.

"Kate?" Bryce asked. Usually he sounded cultured and distant, too good for most of the people he dealt with. She'd never noticed that tone till after she'd married him, though her dad had told her it was always there.

"Yeah," she said. Then said, "Yes," because he'd corrected her diction often after they married. He'd claimed the way she'd talked had "embarrassed" him in front of his friends. The way Kate had remembered it, many of Bryce's friends—the ones that came equipped with functioning personalities, at least—had enjoyed her stories of Florida and her guide experiences.

"There's something I haven't told you about the kids coming to visit you," Bryce said.

No joke! Kate didn't say anything because she knew that any time she attacked Bryce, he retaliated in ways that usually cost her more money than she could afford at the attorneys' offices.

"You know I've got enemies," Bryce said with all the self-indulgent, self-importance that she'd come to loathe. "A man like me, the kind of business I do, I'm going to make enemies."

Kate let the comment pass. She knew her ex had enemies. She was one of them. And their number is legion.

"I had to send Steven and Hannah away," Bryce went on, "to protect them. I need *you* to protect them."

That got Kate's attention. "Bryce, what's going on?"

"There's a man," Bryce said. "His name is Hugh Rollins. I helped engineer a hostile takeover that cost him a lot of money. He had a company he was about to take public."

That made vague sense to Kate. She knew her ex dabbled in all kinds of businesses, usually with ruthless abandon that left destruction—and twice, suicides—behind. Bryce had taken particular pride in those deaths; one before the divorce and one after. Kate knew that if she ever gave up and did something stupid to herself, Bryce would no doubt take pride in that too. It was one of the things that kept her motivated to stay strong.

"What does that have to do with Steven and Hannah?" Kate asked.

Lightning flashed and thunder blasted, and the phone connection went away.

Kate stared at the phone, powerless to call back because she didn't know what number Bryce was calling from. There were several. Please, she thought, staring at the phone.

It rang.

She answered and pulled it to her ear again. "Bryce?"

"I appear to have lost you," he said calmly. "From the Weather Channel, I see that you people have a storm down there that's doing quite a bit of damage."

"We do," Kate agreed. "Genevieve. What does this man have to do with Steven and Hannah?"

"His name is Hugh Rollins," Bryce said, his voice sounded thin and far away. "As it turns out, he wasn't just a computer mogul. He is, apparently, something of a common criminal. My attention to divesting him of his company has placed him in an awkward position with certain personages at the organized crime task force."

Organized crime task force rolled through Kate's mind like something she'd heard in a movie. She couldn't believe something like that could actually touch her life, not even through Bryce. It was all just too—*unreal*.

She made herself take a deep breath.

"Kate?" Bryce asked.

"I'm still here," she said.

"Rollins is a dangerous man. A very devious man." Bryce sighed, something Kate had rarely heard him do. "I underestimated him, it seems."

Or maybe you overestimated yourself, Kate thought unkindly. Not everyone is afraid of you, Bryce. Some of us just don't have the power to strike back the way we'd like to. She turned her thoughts to Steven and Hannah. Then she remembered the black car she'd seen at the airport, then again on the way home.

"What does Rollins have to do with Steven and Hannah?" Kate asked.

"There is the possibility, a remote one, I assure you, that Rollins may choose to get to me through them." Bryce said that as calmly as though a dermatologist had told him he might get a rash.

Kate wanted to scream. More than that, she wanted to be home. She *needed* to be home—with Steven and Hannah.

"That's why I wasn't happy to learn, when I called your house, that you weren't with them."

Some of us have to work for a living, Kate thought, but she didn't say that. Bryce would have considered it too inflammatory and would have retaliated at once.

"I had to check on clients," Kate said. "Make sure they'd taken shelter before the storm hits."

"Surely to God, Kate, even those bumpkins down there know to come in out of the rain!"

Kate cursed inside, dangerously close to losing control. She forced herself to stay calm. Bryce wasn't Dr. Darrel Mathis. She didn't have her ex over a barrel legally, nor could she take away his size advantages with a collapsible baton.

"If I'd known about this other problem," Kate said, "I'd have handled things differently."

"I thought you'd be happy to see the kids," Bryce accused. "Normally when they come down you've got things better in hand."

Normally I'm planning on them coming down. When Steven and Hannah visited in the summer, Kate generally had other people dealing with the clients on a day-to-day schedule, leaving her own schedule open for spending time with her kids. That hadn't been the case this time.

And she sure hadn't planned on Genevieve.

"I'm working things out," Kate said.

"Good. I'll be in touch as things on this end progress."

"There was a car at the airport," Kate interrupted. "I noticed it at the time, but I didn't think much of it."

That caught Bryce's attention. "Do you know who was driving?"

"No. But I'm pretty sure the same car drove by my house when I got home with Steven and Hannah."

Bryce cursed. It wasn't something he often did, but when he cut loose he was brutally efficient. "You need to be home with them, Kate!" he blustered. "Do you hear me? This man Rollins is a killer! If he decides to get at me through them, I don't know what he—"

Another flare of lightning filled the sky. The thunder was on its heels, filling the truck's cab with fury. White noise hissed in Kate's ear, letting her know the phone connection had once more been disrupted.

Ring! she thought at the phone. Ring!

But it didn't.

"Do you have Caller ID?" she asked Tyler.

"Yeah. Do you want me to—"

Kate thumbed through the menu. The last two phone calls to Tyler's phone were listed as Unknown. She sat helplessly. The only phone numbers she had for Bryce were Steven and Hannah's numbers, and the numbers for his legal firm. Bryce wouldn't answer either of those.

"Look out!" Tyler yelled.

Glancing up, the phone still in one hand, Kate saw a man jump from the line of cypresses and swamp water in the slough beside the road. He ran out in front of her with a pistol in his hands.

Chapter 5

Instinct made Kate ram her foot down on the brakes. The cell phone tumbled from her hand as she reached for the steering wheel. Unable to stop in the mud, the truck coasted sideways, totally out of control.

"Son of a bitch!" Tyler yelped.

Raymond Jolly stood savage and unmoving in front of Kate. The pistol was large and shiny. His mouth moved as he yelled.

Kate couldn't hear the man over the sound of the rain. Lightning blazed, gleaming along the pistol's barrel. When the thunder sounded, for a moment Kate felt certain the escaped convict had fired.

Then he dodged out of the way as the truck slid past.

Kate fought the steering wheel, trying desperately to find traction. The tires juddered through potholes, jerking the truck around, bouncing them against their seatbelts.

"That was that convict!" Tyler had hold of the handgrip beside the window with one hand and his other braced against the dash. "That guy that kidnapped that rich woman!"

Kate eased off on the clutch, dropping the transmission back down into low. C'mon! she pleaded. Catch! Give me something to work with!

Instead, the truck came all the way around, till it was facing back the way it had come. The headlights flared through the darkness. The rain was so heavy and so relentless in the glare of the headlights that the world seemed yellow.

Raymond Jolly and four other men, one of them the blond-haired convict Kate had seen in the bus window, ran through the rain, speeding toward the truck. The pistol in his hand bloomed.

The truck window suddenly spider-webbed and chunks of safety glass flew over Kate and Tyler. The bullet passed within inches of them, then—flattened by the initial impact—smashed through the rear window, leaving an even bigger hole.

"Son of a bitch!" Tyler exclaimed.

Kate tried to get the truck moving. The tires spun, tearing through the mud. The escaped convicts, still wearing their orange jumpsuits, came at full speed.

Another man fired just as the sound of the first shot rolled over the truck. The side mirror outside Kate's door disappeared in an explosion of reflective splinters.

"Out of the truck, Tyler! *Now!*" Kate opened her door and slid out. She grabbed the Asp from under the seat, thankful that she'd left it there after dealing with Mathis.

Another shot ricocheted from the top of the truck's cab in a shower of sparks. Metal whined.

Glancing across the truck bed, Kate saw that Tyler was out of the vehicle and running. "Here!" she cried. "With me!" Maybe all they want is the truck.

She ran to the roadside and plunged through the fast-moving slough. They'd been dug to help manage the standing water that gave the wetlands their name so much of the year. Ghost orchids grew in them, pollinated by the giant sphinx moth whose larvae grew fat on the leaves of pond apple trees.

She plunged through the eco-system, hoping the water wasn't deep enough to halt them.

"Could be snakes!" Tyler shouted.

"Snakes don't shoot at you," Kate said, and tried to hang on to that thought as she plowed through the chest-deep water. She glanced over her shoulder, spotting Jolly and the other men as they passed the stalled truck. The convicts kept coming.

"They're not stoppin'," Tyler shouted.

"Then we're not stopping." Kate redoubled her efforts, reaching the other side of the slough slightly ahead of Tyler. "Run, Tyler!"

Together, they plunged into the brush.

"Stop shooting!" Shane shouted as he ran with Jolly and the other members of the kidnapping team that had taken Desiree Martini seven months ago.

But it was like trying to call off a pack of wolves that had the scent of blood in their nostrils. Raymond Jolly led them, and wherever Jolly led them, Shane had discovered over the past couple months, that's where they went.

It still didn't explain how Phil Lewis had turned up dead earlier that afternoon.

Shane stared at the woman, watching her charging through the water-filled ditch. The young man was at her side.

"Get them!" Jolly shouted to the others. "We don't want any witnesses!"

Witnesses, hell! Shane thought. Jolly just wants to kill somebody! It had taken Shane months to get to know Jolly in

Everglades Correctional Institution. Months of working his way up the food chain in the prison and staying alive. Then even longer to maneuver Jolly into a position where the man had to depend on him.

Even after he'd arranged the escape from the prison bus, despite the "premature" explosion that had ripped out the bus's side and left them overturned on the highway, things hadn't gotten any better for Shane. He was tired and worried, and no closer to his ultimate goal than he'd hoped to be.

He was an FBI agent working undercover to bring some closure to the Martini family. When Raymond Jolly had kidnapped Desiree Martini seven months ago, beginning long, torturous days and nights for the family, Jolly had promised Gabriel Martini that he wouldn't kill her.

Martini hadn't trusted Jolly and had called in the FBI. Shane hadn't worked that investigation. But when the Bureau decided to try this last-ditch effort to turn up the heiress's body—there was no doubt in anyone's mind that Jolly had killed her—the Director wanted to go outside the original team of agents for the talent.

The Director had called Shane in and asked him to go to prison. Again. Prison was one of the things Shane did best. The rules were simple. Everybody got along—or Shane busted someone's head. And there was really no way to screw up an assignment on the inside.

Except to get killed, of course.

That had almost happened twice. But Shane had gotten what he was after both times.

Working outside an undercover assignment, in the largely white-collar world of the FBI, left Shane cold. He didn't like playing the political games and kissing ass. He was blunt and confident, and those were things he liked about himself. Not exactly career-building personal skills, to be sure, but they got him by and lowered the daily dose of crap leveraged his way through administration channels. The level he worked at, the things he was willing to subject himself to and be cut off from, bought him leeway and room to maneuver. It also made up a lot for the lack of polish he felt he was missing.

Some days Shane thought he would have been better off staying in the army. But he knew he would have gotten tired of being told what to do every day. In fact, most of the time, if asked, Shane would have replied that he didn't know what he was looking for. His world was all about the hustle and flow, the adrenaline-laced edge of life or death as he conned or outsmarted everyone he was in the room with.

He was getting close on this case, and he knew it.

Everything he'd learned before going to the Everglades Correctional Institute, everything he'd overheard afterward, had indicated that they were somewhere close to where Jolly and his fellow kidnappers had stashed the ten million dollars they'd demanded from Gabriel Martini, Desiree Martini's wealthy father. The FBI had captured Jolly and his men, but the young woman's body and the money had never been recovered.

"Deke!" Jolly yelled. "Stay with the truck!"

Of them all, Deke was the only one who didn't seem to operate off bloodlust. He was young, nineteen, a cousin to Ernie Franks, who had been a career criminal for the last twelve years since he'd gotten his start knocking down banks.

Shane wasn't even certain that Deke belonged in prison with the others. Shane had never been as innocent as Deke was. During his early years, Shane had been in and out of juvie, a misguided boy who was looking at the long fall till he landed in prison for the rest of his life. A judge had pitched him toward the army, telling him he had a choice to make.

Shane had made the choice, then gotten a taste for police work while he was in the Criminal Investigation Division arm of the military police.

Lengthening his stride, Shane pulled even with Jolly. That was hard. The guy was a monster. In Cell Block D, Jolly had held the record for the most weight lifted, and he ran on a daily basis. Shane had only gotten close to him through Jolly's latest interest in prison basketball, playing two-on-two. Basketball was something Shane had played all his life, too.

He paced Jolly, breath burning the back of his throat. "You don't want to kill them, Ray."

"Why not?" Jolly demanded. "I'm in prison for life."

"Yeah, but you ain't strapped down in Ol' Sparky, man. Not even for capping Desiree Martini. You take these two people out, you could be. That mouthpiece you got that talked the jury and the judge into giving you life won't be able to pull off a miracle twice in a row."

"I ain't going back to prison, man," Jolly vowed. "I had me a bellyful of that."

Doing time in prison wasn't easy. Shane agreed with that. It was a lot different than juvie. But he'd understood the edgy ebb and flow of criminal life.

"Then let's get the hell out of here," Shane urged. "Get in the truck and get gone, man. That's what we should be doing."

"I got unfinished business here," Jolly said. "I need time to work it and bring it to a close."

That gave Shane heart. Jolly hadn't said anything about going after the ransom money, but he would try for it if he thought he had a chance to get it while he was outside prison walls. That was what Shane was hoping for. A chance to finally bring Desiree Martini's body home and give her family some peace.

But he said, "Chasing these people is a mistake. We're wasting time we could use to get the hell out of here."

"I like you, Shane," Jolly growled. "Really I do. I like the way you handle yourself. But don't try to tell me how to run my business." He poured on more speed and plunged into the rapidly moving water.

Shane followed him, hoping the two people they were chasing got away. He didn't know what he was going to do if they didn't. There was still a lot of his plan that he was working out, so many things he hadn't taken into consideration. Like this damn storm. He ran, spotting the shadows of their prey ahead of them.

Kate kept her hands and arms lifted ahead of her, using them to fend off the smaller branches and brush and keep it from her eyes. She ducked or dodged the bigger ones, twisting and gliding through them. Her hiking boots bit deeply into the mushy ground.

Tyler ran only a few short feet away, keeping to his own path. The rain and the intermittent lightning flashes made the already treacherous ground almost impossible to navigate.

She glanced over her shoulder again, knowing she shouldn't have. Two of the men chased her. Two others chased Tyler. She didn't want to split off from Tyler and leave him alone, but their paths took them in different directions. Tyler had chosen a course along a creek, swamping through the shallows as fast as he could go.

Kate chose the high ground because it favored her higher muscle to mass ratio. At five-feet-ten, a hundred and fifty pounds, lean and in shape from exercise and an active life, she knew she could charge up the hill easier than the two men following. Both of them were carrying in excess of two hundred pounds. Even if that weight was from lifting and working out every day, it was still fifty-plus more pounds than she had to carry up the hill.

Her strategy was sound. She just wished that Tyler wasn't off to himself and that her breath wasn't already coming short. She ran on.

"Over there, Shane!" someone yelled. "Head over to the left! I've got her on this side!"

Kate tried to lengthen her stride. At the top of the hill, she cut back to the right, hoping to split up her pursuers and maybe get a chance to find Tyler. There was no way she was going to leave him out here alone.

The thing that bothered her most was the fact that the convicts weren't slowing down. By rights, they should have grabbed the truck and gotten gone.

So what do they want?

Tyler's pain-filled scream brought Kate up short.

"Oh my God! Kate! Kate! Help me, Kate!" Tyler screamed again in pain.

Kate drew up against a bald cypress, distinctive because of its straight trunk and brown bark. The feathery needles brushed at her face. She stood in the middle of eighty-footers who still had some growing to go before they reached their optimum of a hundred and twenty-five feet.

She drew the Asp and pressed the button. The length extended with a metallic snap that she didn't think could be heard over the constant hiss of the rain and the thunder.

"Kate! God! Kate! Help!"

Quivering, so scared she thought she was going to be sick, Kate stood in the shadows of the tree and listened to the thudding footsteps of one of her pursuers getting closer. The man was heading for Tyler's voice too.

Tyler kept crying out, panicked and in pain.

Kate bit her lips and made herself wait. The big man ran by her and looked out across the cypress forest. Then he turned unexpectedly and a big, cruel smile split his face.

"Playing hide and seek?" he asked.

Kate didn't answer. She kept the Asp hidden behind her thigh. Maybe he'd found her, maybe she hadn't been as hidden as she'd hoped, maybe a stray flicker of lightning had given her away, but she was going to keep one surprise.

"Why don't you come on out here where I can see you, pretty lady?" the man invited in a low voice that he probably thought was sexy. He held out a hand. "C'mon now. Don't be shy."

Kate didn't move.

The smile dropped away from the man's face. He held up a broad-bladed hunting knife. Lightning flickered along the keen edge. "You better come on out of there if you know what's good for you. Otherwise, I'm going to come in there and get you. Take you out piece by piece."

Renewed fear clawed through Kate.

Tyler continued yelling for help. Only that kept Kate nailed to the spot, because there was room to run and she could have been gone again.

"Out. Here," the man ordered.

Slowly, Kate took a hesitant step toward him. She kept her eyes down, as though she was afraid to look at him or the knife. What she was really doing was watching his body movement, looking for an opening.

"*Kate!*" Tyler sounded like he was going into shock or about to pass out.

Kate thought maybe he'd fallen and broken his ankle or his leg. In the darkness, on the broken terrain, that was the most likely. She kept moving toward the big man.

Up close now, she saw that he was in his early thirties. Years of weightlifting showed in the broad shoulders and muscular neck. He came close to being a rhinoceros. His hair was cut short. Tattoos covered both arms. He'd torn the sleeves off his jumpsuit, and Kate suspected it was to show off the ink work.

"That's right," the man growled in a voice filled with anticipation. His eyes raked Kate. "Is that poncho hiding some kind of body?" He laughed. "I bet it is. A tall girl like you, I bet you are one fine-looking woman." He gestured with the knife and smiled. "What say you take off that poncho and show me what you got. Treat me to my own wet T-shirt contest."

Kate pulled the Velcro loose with her free hand. If she was going to fight the guy, she didn't want him to be able to grab hold of the poncho easily. She shrugged out of it, and then let the sleeve leak down the hand holding the baton, still hidden behind her leg.

He smiled bigger, then reached down and rubbed his groin with his free hand. "Now that's what I'm talking about. I haven't had a woman in over seven months. You're in for a treat." He shrugged. "Then I suppose I'll have to share you with the others." He reached for her.

When Kate felt his fingers close around her wrist, she struck. Her instructor in the dojo had told her that was the primary time to go to work with the baton, the time when she could cause the most immediate damage. She didn't hesitate, listening to Tyler in the distance and knowing that others were closing in on him.

She swung the baton, whipping it up at the man's head. She didn't hold back the way she had with Mathis. In that situation she'd aimed to incapacitate, not truly injure. At the moment, not knowing what had happened to Tyler and feeling responsible because she'd brought Tyler along, she wanted to cripple the man. She didn't want him to cut her with the knife.

The baton smacked into the man's forehead, staggering him backward. But it didn't put him down, and it was her fault for not following up immediately. By the time she realized the man wasn't going down, he was roaring in rage and slashing at her with the knife.

Shane pulled up short when he saw the woman fighting Monte Carter. The man was a monster, a steroid freak even in prison, trading sexual favors for his drug of choice. Shane didn't know why Jolly had Carter along, except maybe as the wild card if things had to turn bloody.

When Shane saw the woman hit Carter with the baton, it stunned him but he knew she was going to trigger a murderous rage in the man. Carter wouldn't quit now until the woman was dead—or begging to die.

Carter slashed at her, attacking again and again. Shane ran toward them, slipping and falling on the loose ground, tripping over a log concealed by the tall grass. He pushed himself up, watching in disbelief as the woman took Carter apart.

She blocked the knife and the rasping metal on metal sound reached Shane's ears. Even as he registered that, the woman disengaged, stepping to the side. Carter wheeled and tried to lunge at her, but his greater weight tore the ground loose and caused him to stumble.

Just as she was counting on, Shane realized. His estimation and respect for her rose like mercury on a hot day.

Turning, the woman set herself and slammed the baton into Carter's temple. He staggered and remained on his feet through an effort of sheer will. Her second strike hit Carter's wrist. The big-bladed hunting knife dropped from Carter's numbed fingers. He staggered back and lifted his hands to protect his face.

The woman kicked him in the groin. Carter dropped to his knees, catching himself on one hand. Moving to the side, the woman slammed the baton against the back of Carter's neck.

The man went down like a poleaxed steer. Considering the steroids and Carter's size, maybe the comparison was really fitting, Shane thought. By the time he'd registered what had taken place, she was running toward the plaintive voice.

Instead of catching up to her, Shane trailed along behind her, wanting to see what was going to happen next.

"Kate!"

Pausing to listen again, thrown off by the constant sound of the rain, Kate got her bearings on Tyler's voice. She tracked him to a rise and looked down at the creek twenty feet below.

Tyler stood in the middle of the rushing water, up to his chest. He held his hands over his midsection.

At first, Kate couldn't see what the problem was. Then, when lightning chased across the sky, she saw the line tied tightly between the trunks of two cypress trees on either side of the creek.

"Oh God," Kate whispered, knowing what had happened then.

Bait-hook alligator traps were the chosen weapons of hunters trying to keep alligators from their land, or of poachers. Normally a size 12, barbed fishhook was suspended two feet above the water level, attached to a strong rope or cable, and baited with nutria, beef lungs, fish or chicken. Once the alligator took the bait, usually swallowing it whole, the hook became embedded in the stomach and it was stuck there till the hunter came back and put it out of its misery with a bullet through the brain.

In the darkness, probably running at near full speed, Tyler had run into one.

Kate didn't even want to think about the possible damage the barbed hook had already done. She looked for a way down. Then she heard something move behind her.

Whirling, she brought up the baton, seeing the man-sized shape rise out of the shadows behind her. She saw then that the hair was blond, and she recognized the man in front of her. Shane. Something. She couldn't remember what it was from the fragments of news stories she'd caught on the radio and television. But she did remember that he hadn't been one of the men who had kidnapped Desiree Martini. He was a drug-dealer and a cop-killer, though. Not the kind of guy to get caught alone in the dark with.

She lifted the baton, but he caught her wrist. She tried to knee him in the groin, but he caught her knee and slipped inside the kick, pulling her up close against him so that his thigh slid neatly between her legs.

He grinned at her for some stupid reason that she couldn't understand. She felt the hard planes of his body against hers, felt the strength of him.

"I don't want to hurt you," he said.

Kate almost believed him. He had sincere down pat. She reared her head back and slammed her forehead into his face.

"Damn!" he said.

Shifting quickly, Kate tried to free her wrist. Instead, he wrapped his leg more tightly around hers and threw her to the ground. He landed on top of her. Shane outweighed her by a good sixty or seventy pounds and was four or five inches taller than she was. This was exactly the situation her dad had sent her to the martial arts dojo to learn to avoid. She tried to head-butt him again. He smacked her forehead with his open palm. Her senses spun.

"Stop it!" he told her. "I don't want to hurt you!"

You've got a strange way of showing that, Kate thought, and kept wriggling to escape. His long hair hung down in her face. He kept his head against hers so she couldn't head butt him again. His hazel eyes stared into hers.

All at once, Kate was struck by the intimacy of the situation. Shane lay plastered against her like another skin. It had been years since she'd had a man that close to her. She'd only had a physical relationship with a man once, two years after she'd gotten divorced.

Bryce had found out about the affair. He'd hired a private detective to make the man's life hell for a month or so, informing her lover's employer about indiscretions he'd made in past jobs and money he'd hidden from the IRS. Kate hadn't known about his problems beforehand, but it didn't matter either way. He got the message and stayed away from Kate. In fact, everybody got the message and stayed away from Kate.

She stared up at Shane, feeling helpless and pissed and scared.

"Over here!" someone shouted in the creek below. The sound of slogging footsteps echoed up from the lowlands. "He's over here! Got himself hung up!"

"Hey," Shane said.

She looked at him, refusing to respond.

"When I let you go, I want you to promise not to hit me," he said. "Then I want you to get the hell out of here."

She studied his face, trying to figure out what his game was. "What?"

Voices sounded down in the creek, but Kate couldn't understand them.

"These are bad men," Shane said. "They won't think anything of killing you." His hazel eyes bored into hers. "I don't want to see you get hurt."

"Why?" It didn't make any sense.

He smiled at her, looking like a little boy with a secret. "Because I'm not like them. And you've been unlucky enough to cross paths with us twice today. Nobody deserves that much bad juju."

So he recognized her. That made Kate feel a little more vulnerable.

"Do we have a deal?" Shane asked.

"Sure," Kate said after what she deemed a proper hesitation.

Gradually, Shane got his knees up under him and lifted his face from hers. She promptly headbutted him in the face and brought her leg up into his groin.

"Damn!" he swore as she pushed him off her. He lost control of her baton wrist. She levered it up under his throat and pushed, rolling over on top of him, her knees straddling his hips and locking him to the ground.

Kate kept the baton against his throat, choking him down as he struggled. She got a fistful of his hair, too, then drew back the baton and prepared to strike.

"Kate!" a man's voice boomed from below.

"Hold still," Kate ordered, pressing the baton's end against Shane's throat. *He knows my name.* Then she realized that Tyler had been yelling for her by name.

Shane froze, but he looked sad. "You should have gone."

I couldn't, Kate thought. *Tyler's down there.*

"Kate!" the man yelled again. "If you can hear me, listen up! I've got your friend down here! If you don't answer me by the time I count to three, I'm going to put a bullet through his head! One!"

Kate was torn, not knowing what to do.

"Jolly will do it," Shane said. Blood leaked from his nose and split lips, staining his white teeth.

"Two!" Jolly yelled.

"All right," Kate said loudly. "I'm coming down." She let go of Shane and stood.

Shane lay there on his back, staring up at her. Then he did the strangest thing. "Sorry," he whispered.

Chapter 6

Kate stood at the top of the hill and looked down. "Here I am."

Jolly, the big man with the scar that cut through his eyebrow, aimed his pistol at her. The other, a thick man with an Elvis haircut and thick sideburns, had a shotgun. Both of them, she supposed, were from the prison bus. Her immediate impulse was to try to hide. She forced herself to stay where she was.

Raymond Jolly looked up at her. A smile split his savage face as lightning arced across the sky and the wind howled through the branches. "Good," he said. "Your friend should live a little longer. But he's in a hell of a fix." He gestured with the big pistol. "You might want to come down here and see for yourself."

"Kate," Tyler said softly. His eyes were glassy.

He's in shock, Kate realized. She pushed away her own fear and thought about Tyler. Carefully, she made her way down the incline, slipping from tree to tree, till she reached the creek's edge.

The weapons remained pointed at her.

"Can I help him?" Kate asked.

"Sure," Jolly said. "Gutted on a fishhook like that, should be interesting to watch."

Kate waded out into the water. "Tyler. Hey, Tyler." She dug in her pocket for the mini-Maglite she carried. She switched it on. "It's going to be okay," she told him gently. "You're going to be okay." *Please, let him be okay.*

Tyler looked up at her. Tears leaked from his eyes, mixing with the rain. "Son of a bitch, Kate. Look what happened." His voice sounded thready and weak.

Looking down between his cupped hands, Kate saw the hook—as big as her curled forefinger—embedded in his stomach. The tear was already two or three inches long. So far he'd been lucky, the membrane holding his intestines in hadn't ruptured. Otherwise he'd have spilled all over the creek.

For a moment, Kate thought she was going to throw up. She steeled herself. She'd taken fishhooks out of other people before. Just never one this big.

"We can do this, Tyler," she told him. "Just stay with me."

"I didn't see it, Kate. I didn't see it."

"I know," she told him.

"What are you going to do?" Jolly asked. "Clean him?" The men laughed at that.

"I could use some help," Kate said. "He can barely stand. He needs to be still while I get this out."

"I'm not much into helping other people," Jolly said. "In fact, my better judgment tells me I should kill you—and him—right here. Right now." He lifted the pistol and took dead aim at her.

"I wouldn't do that," Shane called from the hilltop.

"I'm not you, Shane."

"Don't you recognize her?" Shane asked.

Jolly squinted at Kate. "Not really. Should I?"

"This is the woman at the bus crash," Shane said, making his way down the hillside. "The one we took the Jeep from. She's been in the news. We saw her on television at the house where we stole the truck. Kate Garrett."

Jolly laughed. "Damn, some people do have a run of bad luck, don't they?"

"I just want to help Tyler," Kate said. "Please." It was all she could do to keep from breaking down. Shaking, she held Tyler in her arms, helping support his weight so the fishhook wouldn't accidentally penetrate more deeply.

The pistol didn't waver from her head. She stared back at Jolly without flinching. More than anything, she wanted to wake up and find out this was all a nightmare, that she was in bed with Steven and Hannah and they had waffles to look forward to. Waffles didn't include potentially gutting Tyler Jordan.

"You want to keep her alive." Shane reached the creek bank, then waded out to join Kate and Tyler.

"Why?" Jolly challenged.

"Remember the Jeep? Her business cards?"

"Wilderness guide," Jolly said.

"That's right," Shane said, walking up behind Tyler and taking the younger man's weight easily despite the fast-running creek. "She's a wilderness guide. Now that Mother Nature has decided to open up the heavens and let all hell break loose, you might look at it like *we're* lucky. Do you know anybody else who would know where everything is around here?"

Jolly didn't say anything.

"I know you've got some unfinished business around here," Shane said, "but don't you think a wilderness guide will come in handy tonight?"

Kate resented that, but it was foolish to do so. Still, she didn't like the idea of helping the man. "Can you hold him?"

Shane nodded. "I've got him."

"I've got to cut the hook out." Kate reached into her pants pocket and took out her utility knife.

"'Cut?'" Tyler echoed. He tried to move but he was weak.

"You won't feel a thing," Kate said. "I promise." She transferred the mini-Maglite to her mouth and opened the shortest blade, only two inches long. If she penetrated the membrane, she was afraid it would rip completely and Tyler's intestines would be exposed to massive infections. Gangrene would be the least of his worries.

"Maybe you're right," Jolly said. He lowered the hammer on the big pistol and dropped the weapon to his side.

Looking over Tyler's shoulder into Shane's hazel eyes and speaking around the mini-Maglite, Kate asked, "Ready?"

"Yeah."

"How's your stomach?"

"We're about to find out, lady," he growled.

Tyler whimpered and pleaded.

Steeling herself, knowing she couldn't leave Tyler out there, Kate slipped a finger into the wound in Tyler's stomach. Fat and blood allowed her to slide right through and find the end of the hook.

Groaning, Tyler briefly tried to fight, then went slack.

"He's out," Shane growled. "Do what you have to do. He's not going to feel a thing."

Crimson blood dripped to the top of the murky water but was immediately torn to threads and carried away. The water was rising. During the short time she'd been standing there, it had risen at least two inches. And the current was getting stronger.

Kate found the end of the barbed hook and turned it outside, away from the protective sheath that held Tyler's insides inside. She pushed and twisted till the barbed end popped through Tyler's flesh in another spot. More blood dripped into the water.

There's too much blood! Kate felt panic well up inside her. She concentrated on her breathing, focusing on that and letting her eyes guide her fingers.

"Just do what you have to do, Kate," Shane said softly. "Get it done. You can do this."

Kate resented the confidence he gave her. He didn't know her. He didn't know anything about her other than she was a wilderness guide. That was nothing.

"It's going to be all right," he said.

No it's not. We're being held by a group of murderers. And you're one of them. Kate used the knife to slit Tyler's stomach, cutting through fat and muscle. If she'd had a pair of wire cutters, she could have snipped the barb off and withdrawn the hook. That wasn't an option now. She pulled the hook out and threw it away, then took the mini-Maglite from her mouth.

Blood dripped into the water.

"There's too much blood," Kate whispered.

"You did good, Kate," Shane said. "You did good."

She felt lightheaded and almost fell.

Shane started toward shore.

"Wait," Kate said. "You're going to rip him open. I need something to bind the wound."

"Hold him for a second."

Kate took Tyler's weight and watched as Shane shucked out of the top of his jumpsuit, then took his undershirt off. "This work?"

"Yeah," Kate said, staring at his torso.

Two ugly bullet wounds marred his chest. A knife scar was carved into his left deltoid. Kate recognized both wounds from scars she'd seen other hunters and fishermen around Everglades City display.

"Not too sanitary," Shane said as he pulled the jumpsuit back on.

"It'll work. That's what matters right now." Kate ripped the shirt into strips, then wrapped Tyler's skinny middle and tied it together. Blood soaked the material at once. But it looked like it would hold.

Together, each holding one of Tyler's arms over a shoulder and one of his legs, they carried him to the bank.

"I have to tell you," Jolly said smugly, "I'm impressed, Kate. Maybe what we needed was a wilderness guide on this little jaunt."

Go to hell! Kate thought. But she didn't say a word.

Kate was almost ready to drop by the time they carried Tyler to the truck. Several times, they had to stop and rest, though Kate got the impression that Shane could have continued on without interruption.

The storm's fury continued to escalate. Dark clouds swirled overhead. The wind howled through the swampland, pushing up vicious sprays of water.

"Hey," the young man back at the truck called, lifting the tarp over the back. "There's food back here."

"You got food in the truck, Kate?" Jolly asked.

"Some supplies for campers," Kate answered.

The men quickly crowded around the back of the truck and started going through the food.

"Take it into the truck," Jolly ordered. "You're going to get it all wet."

They claimed their prizes and retreated into the truck.

"You too, Kate," Jolly said. "Get into the truck."

Kate looked at the sodden mess covering Tyler's stomach. Mercifully, he was still unconscious, though his color didn't look good.

"Tyler won't survive the trip," Kate said.

Jolly's eyes tightened. Whatever was driving him, it was harsh. "You're getting awfully bossy, Kate."

"I don't want him to die." Kate tried to make her voice as non-threatening as she could, talking the way she did to Bryce, but she had to speak loudly over the noise of the storm. Since Jolly had a pistol he could put to her head at any moment, the act wasn't really a stretch for her.

"Then what do you propose?"

"I've got a first-aid kit in the truck," Kate said. "There's a surgical needle and thread. I can sew the wound. I've had to do it before for clients that cut themselves or got wounded on a wild pig hunt. It'll hold till a doctor can do a better job."

"Wilderness guide *and* seamstress?" Jolly laughed mirthlessly. "You're going to make some guy a great little wife."

Black anger filled Kate. Bryce had said something like that when she'd been his guide. But compliments like that had just been chumming the waters.

"Shane," Jolly said, locking eyes with Kate, "go get the first-aid kit."

"I didn't sign on to be a nurse," Shane complained.

Jolly looked at him. "That's right. You were the guy who was going to get us out of prison."

"I did."

"The explosive didn't exactly detonate where it was supposed to, 007," Jolly said.

"Hey," Shane said angrily, "you can just back it up right there. If it hadn't been for me, your ass would be in your old cell by now. Maybe the explosive didn't come off exactly as planned. Maybe the guy that was supposed to pick us up wasn't there. But that wasn't his fault. The explosive detonated too early."

Had it? Kate wondered. She remembered how she'd seen Shane through the window of the bus. He'd been looking at his watch. Expecting the blast? Or looking to see how long it would be before it happened?

Shane continued, "And I don't blame him for not hanging around to watch us get arrested again. Especially since there was the possibility that he could get arrested with us."

Jolly just stared at Shane for a moment.

"I'm still the guy that can get us out of Florida and down to Cuba," Shane said. "Unless you're not interested in that any more." The challenge was in every word.

"Deke," Jolly called after a minute of standing in the driving rain with the lightning flashing and the thunderous booms all around.

"Yeah, boss," Deke yelled back.

"Lady says there's a first-aid kit in the truck."

"I already found it. Took inventory while you guys were gone."

"Bring me the kit," Jolly ordered. After Deke gave him the first-aid kit, he looked back at Kate. "Clock's ticking, Kate. That truck's only carrying the living."

Shane marveled at Kate as she set to work by the light of an electric lantern under a plastic tarp that had been in the supplies on the truck. They'd laid the young man on a blanket beneath a towering bald cypress hammock so that he was out of the rain and the wind.

On her knees, hands shaking a little, Kate threaded the curved surgical needle.

"You've really sewn people up before?" Shane asked, thinking maybe small talk would help her relax. He didn't know if he could do what she was about to. It didn't help that he had to practically shout over the noise of the storm.

"Yeah," she replied, looking at him. "You ever killed anybody before?"

That irritated Shane. It was one thing to act tough to get through a bad situation, but he was trying to help her. He didn't have to do that. Except you can't do any less.

"I have," he answered, mirroring the same dead tone she had. It wasn't something he was especially proud of, but he had. He locked eyes with her, wanting to scare her enough that she would run the next time he was able to give her an opening. He hoped that it would come soon.

She was the first to look away. But Shane didn't take any special glory in the feat. He knew there was every possibility that she simply couldn't stomach the sight of him.

"I can sew up a cut better than the person who did your arm," Kate said. She leaned in and pushed the edges of the wound together. Thankfully, most of the bleeding had stopped. Despite the ripping nature of the laceration, the edges of the wound met pretty much cleanly. Shane knew that was important.

Satisfied, Kate leaned down and pushed the needle through the young man's flesh, quickly pushing through the other side and looping back around to pick up the first side again.

"Aren't you supposed to make individual stitches?" Shane asked.

"Sometimes," Kate agreed. "When you're doing plastic surgery or something else where you care about the scar that's left. At the moment, I just want to try to save his life. When

Tyler gets proper medical attention, the doctor will probably re-open the wound to make certain all the infection's washed out." She continued working, slowly and steadily making her way across the four-inch gash.

"My granny didn't see so good," Shane said.

"What does that have to do with anything?"

"She's the one who sewed up my arm," Shane explained. "Thought maybe you'd understand it better if you knew who did it. My granny was seventy-three. Her best sewing days were behind her." He still missed talking to her. She'd been the gentlest person he knew, and she was experienced at sewing up knife and gunshot wounds. He hadn't had a normal childhood or family.

The silence stretched out between them for a time. Shane was conscious of the rain beating down on the tarp and the voices of Jolly and his buddies talking in the truck. Monte Carter had finally arrived back at the truck. He was bruised black and blue, promising revenge on Kate when he found out she was still alive. Shane knew the man was going to be trouble if Kate stayed with them.

"My dad sewed me up twice," Kate said after a while.

Shane thought maybe she did need to talk. "Twice, huh?" he prompted.

"Once when I was nine I cut my hand while we were out in the swamp on an orchid hunt with a group of professors. It was too far to come back. And once when a wild pig gored me. I was fifteen then."

"How did you get gored by a wild pig?"

"We were hunting wild pigs. I went into the brush to drive it out, got drove out myself. The pig was faster than I was."

"Given a choice between hunting orchids and hunting pigs?" Shane laughed. "I'd have stuck with the orchids."

"In my life I don't get a lot of choices."

In that moment, Shane almost felt a connection between them. His life hadn't exactly come equipped with a lot of choices either. Crime had been in his blood from day one. His father had died in a shoot-out in front of a bank in Mobile, Alabama. Most of the time Clayton Warren had been a confidence man, pulling down just enough to live on. But he liked to watch the horses run, and sometimes he got behind on the vig he owed the bookies. Shane had grown up around murderers and thieves and drug runners.

"I didn't have a lot of choices either," Shane said. "My dad was a professional con artist and sometime bank robber. It was the bank robbing that got him killed. My older brother got crossways with a Colombian drug cartel in Miami. I buried him about five years ago." That had been the hardest job he'd ever done. But in the end he'd gotten revenge on Alex's killers when he'd infiltrated their organization and set them up to go away for a long time. There were still death threats on his head. The good thing was, those threats were on the false name he'd been wearing then, not his real name.

Kate didn't say anything, just kept that looping stitch going.

"I'm not like these men," Shane said. Somehow, it seemed important to say that and to let her know. And he was surprised to find that he even wanted her to believe him. He *was* different.

"When you're helping your friends hold us captive," Kate said, "I don't see a whole lot of difference."

Shane couldn't argue with that, so he didn't. He just hoped he could find a way to get Raymond Jolly to let Kate and the wounded man go before Jolly decided to kill them. Shane had no doubt that Jolly would do exactly that if he had to.

And Kate Garrett already seemed like trouble. Just enough to get herself killed. And maybe him with her.

* * *

Less than an hour later, whipsawed by the wind, Kate rode in the back seat of the truck cab sandwiched between Deke Hannibal and Ernie Franks. From their conversation, she'd learned that they were cousins, and that Ernie was the career criminal while Deke was young and hadn't even really taken part in the Desiree Martini kidnapping.

Deke was young and sallow, shy and backward. He sat stiff as a board against Kate's right side. Ernie was the heavy guy with an Elvis haircut and sideburns. While Deke was quiet, Ernie was a blusterer, always talking about jobs he'd done with Jolly or on his own. With everything he'd claimed to have done, Kate thought he'd have needed his own wall at the post office.

Monte Carter, the man she'd knocked out with the Asp, sat in the front seat between Shane—who drove—and Jolly. Tyler, who was still unconscious, rode in the truck bed by himself. At least the tarp had been replaced and the rain was kept off him, but Kate knew he was taking a beating from the rough road.

"When are we gonna go after the money?" Ernie asked after he'd finally stopped telling one gruesome story after another. Even Deke seemed a little put off by them.

"Soon," Jolly said. He kept flipping through the radio stations, trying to find one that would come in.

Is that what this is about? Kate wondered. The missing ransom? Over the last few months, any number of treasure hunters, insurance agents, and law-enforcement officials had been out roaming Big Cypress Swamp looking for the ransom money. No one had ever turned up a thing. As far as anyone knew, the money was still sitting out there waiting to be found.

Unless the rats or nutria had gotten to it. Or it had rotted, which sometimes happened in the southern Florida climate.

"Man," Ernie complained, "the whole time we were locked up, the only thing that got me through was the idea of that cool ten million waiting on us." He absently stroked the barrel of the shotgun he held.

"After all this time," Shane said, "you can't even be sure it's still there." He glanced up in the mirror, a mocking smile on his bruised and swollen lips.

Kate took a little satisfaction in his looks. She was even more proud of the job she'd done on Monte Carter, who—Ernie had stated—looked like a reject from a freak show.

"It's still there," Jolly said. "Don't wind them up like that."

"Why wasn't the money ever found?" Shane asked.

"Because," Ernie retorted sarcastically, "we hid it. Got a lot of things we hid. Even a few bodies over the years."

"Is that what happened to the heiress?" Shane asked. "What's her name? Dierdre Something-or-Other?"

"Desiree Martini," Jolly said.

"Why don't you know her name?" Ernie asked. "It was all over the damn news."

"Because seven months ago I was finishing up a shot in Huntsville."

"That's in Alabama, ain't it?" Ernie asked.

"Yeah."

"What were you in prison for?"

"That time?" Shane shrugged. "Some damn thing or another."

That caught Jolly's attention. "Most guys doing a stretch know what the stretch is for." The menace was inherent in his tone.

"Is it that important to you, Raymond?" Shane asked.

"Yeah," Jolly said. "It is."

Shrugging again, Shane said, "Receivership."

Kate vaguely knew that receivership had something to do with stolen properties. Some of the guys she'd interviewed for guide positions had had that on their applications. Plus, the charge was one that was on a lot of the guys she'd worked with on the construction sites.

"PD detective in Mobile had a grudge against me," Shane said. "Bastard planted evidence on me, took out a storage space in my name, and let me take the fall. I was in almost a year before my attorney got me out."

"Then you were in Everglades Correctional Institution," Deke said.

Shane gave the young convict a good-natured grin. "Took a fall for a drug shipment. I screwed that one up, trusted too big, and got nailed by an undercover policeman. One of the guys got killed. I took the long fall for a homicide. I wasn't going to get out again. I'd just gotten out of Huntsville. Decided I'd try my luck here. The problem was, I was flat broke. Too eager to do business and not on my home turf."

"Why were you in Miami?" Jolly asked.

"Because that's where the action is," Shane said, "and I was too well-known on my home turf. I had to get out of Mobile."

On the other side of the spiderweb of cracks running across the hole, torrential rain continued to batter the countryside. Two and a half hours into the storm, Genevieve didn't look close to blowing herself out yet. Or to breaking apart.

At the top of a rise, a radio station decided to come through. A faint voice issued through the speakers.

"—in Everglades City and Broward County need to take precautions now," the announcer was saying in a tense voice.

"The United States Coast Guard has confirmed the existence of a thirty-foot storm surge that's heading for the coast now. We've lost all contact with even the emergency agencies in that area. Genevieve is proving she has a few nasty surprises to show us, folks, and—"

As Shane headed down into the lowlands on the other side of the rise, the radio signal faded out again.

"Dammit!" Jolly hammered the dash with a big hand.

"Did he say, 'a thirty-foot storm surge'?" Deke asked in a small voice.

"Yeah," Ernie said. "Now don't get your panties in a bunch. Them news people have habits of making things out worse'n they seem. Makes people keep listening."

A rumble, this one different than any the thunder had made so far, sounded off to the left.

Even scared as she was, Kate was on the verge of going to sleep when she noticed it. She also thought the ground was vibrating, too, though she felt certain that was more from the lack of sleep than anything else.

When she looked, leaning forward to see around Ernie, Kate couldn't believe what she was seeing. A wall of water at least twenty feet high was rolling through across the land, barreling and crashing through the cypress trees. There was enough momentum behind the thousands of gallons of water that nothing stood before it. Genevieve had turned churning destruction loose on the land.

And they were directly in its path.

"Look!" Monte yelled, pointing at the storm surge.

The water was moving fast, coming at them hard.

"Drive!" Jolly ordered.

Shane cut the wheel instantly, bringing the truck around in

a mud-slinging one-hundred-eighty-degree turn as he tried to power back up the high ground. But it was too late.

The wave hit them and lifted them from the road like a child's toy.

Chapter 7

Water didn't immediately flood the truck. The closed windows prevented that. But the truck sank all the same, and every second in a vehicle that had gone down under water counted against the survival rate. Kate knew that from stories she'd been told by her dad, who had salvaged sunken vehicles.

Her first thought after the shocking realization that she was being tossed in a storm surge over twenty feet high was for Tyler Jordan. Her only hope was that the tarp over the truck bed had held and he was still with the vehicle, not lost somewhere out there in the floodwaters.

As the truck turned over with surreal slowness, Kate unsnapped the seatbelt and pushed up. Several inches of water sloshed across the floor, then ran up the side of the truck cab and across the roof. Lights in the instrument panel flickered and shorted out.

"Son of a bitch!" Ernie squalled. "We're underwater!" He had his face pressed up against the window.

Kate grabbed the sliding window that overlooked the truck bed. With the outside water pressure working against it, the sliding glass was hard to move. But she managed. As she opened it, water poured into the truck cab.

"What the hell are you doing?" Ernie demanded, reaching for the window.

Kate fought the man off, elbowing him in the face and drawing curses. Jolly pointed the pistol at her from the front seat. Water continued to cascade into the cab.

"Stay in the truck and you're going to die," Kate shouted.

"She's right," Shane said, rolling down the window and letting more water in. That seemed to act as a control for the truck, sending it down like a diving submarine. "We've got to get out now!"

Kate caught the edges of the window and heaved herself through. Grabbing the tarp, aware that suddenly submerged trees were on all sides of her, she struggled to hang on. Then the truck hit a tree and spun sideways lazily in the water.

Peeling the tarp back, she located Tyler by feel and hooked her fingers in his shirt. He floated up easily. Lightning flared across the sky and looked strange through the murky water. Kate tasted the salt of the ocean and felt it burning her eyes and nostrils.

She held on to Tyler and grabbed an orange life vest from the toolbox. She never went anywhere without them. Too many fishing clients forgot them, or simply decided they didn't need to wear them. The law required they wear them, and Kate kept them on hand to provide.

Swimming strongly, Kate kicked for the surface, still struggling with the concept that this had once been dry land. The coastal areas had been underwater before. In 1960, Hurricane Donna had sent six-foot floodwaters four miles inland, well past where they were now. Andrew, Wilma, Charles and others had all slammed Florida over the years.

But Kate had never seen anything like this outside of the levees breaking in New Orleans. If something like this hit Everglades City—

She made herself not think about that. Steven and Hannah were there. *The flooding only looks this bad because we're so close to the coast and because we're in a low area.* She wanted desperately to believe that, but she knew her house was in a low area, too.

Then she was above the water's surface, glancing back toward the incoming tide in time to get hit with another cascade of water. Wind howled above the storm surge.

If this isn't a Category Five storm by now, Kate thought, *they're going to have to reinvent the scale.*

She held on to Tyler, feeling him slack and loose in her grip but feeling his breath warm on her cheek as well. Getting the life vest on over his head while keeping him afloat was hard work, but she managed. When it was in place, securely tied, she activated the compressed air cylinder and the vest filled almost instantly. As soon as the vest was inflated, a bright red light beacon activated, blinking to attract attention.

"Hang in there, Tyler," she told him. She wished she'd been able to grab a second vest. She was a strong swimmer, but there were several trees all around them that posed hidden dangers. If she got knocked unconscious or broke an arm or a leg, she could still drown.

Holding on to Tyler, Kate rode the rush of water and steered toward a towering bald cypress. She caught hold of the tree and stopped their movement, anchoring them to the tree. Kate held on against the swirling rush of water. She didn't know if she was calm or if her senses were just so overloaded that nothing made sense any more. But the panic felt removed from her, as if it was an alien thing that couldn't touch her.

Lights blinked in the dark sky. A moment later, Kate recognized the wasp-like shape of a helicopter. The aircraft jumped and jerked in the high winds, but the pilot had definite control as it scooted along just a few feet above the water.

Working quickly, she held her breath and slipped underwater long enough to take the lace from one of Tyler's boots. Surfacing again, she used the lace to tie Tyler to the tree through the metal rings on the life vest. In seconds, he was securely held and she could manage her own position with two hands.

Looking out at the water, Kate wondered if Shane or Jolly or any of the others had survived. Then something grabbed her left foot, unleashing the panic that she'd been holding back.

Her first thought was that an alligator had gotten hold of her. Fear thudded through her. She jerked her feet up, hoping that whatever it was would go away or get pushed along by the incoming water. Above, the helicopter had started to come in their direction. It was possible the pilot or the spotters had seen the blinking beacon on the back of Tyler's life vest. She hoped so.

A hand closed around her ankle. She knew what it was then. But before she could fight against it, the grip tightened and pulled her under. The current moved her along rapidly, whipping her through branches and against trees. Finally she grabbed a tree and climbed up, pulling herself out of the cold, churning water up to her waist.

She coughed and choked for a moment, then looked around wildly for Tyler, spotting the life vest's flashing beacon nearly a hundred yards away. She breathed a sigh of relief. The helicopter *was* a US Coast Guard Craft. It descended now, homing in on Tyler's beacon.

A hand clamped around her ankle again. Whoever had hold of her climbed her, hand over hand.

Monte Carter surfaced behind Kate, spitting water as lightning blazed overhead, wrapping an arm around her neck and jamming his forearm up under her chin. Kate didn't have the strength to fight him and try to stay out of the water. Panic kept her fingers locked around the branch. Then he grinned at her, his face lumpy with swelling and bruises.

"Hey, bitch," he snarled, leaning in close so the stink of his breath flooded her nostrils. "Guess who's about to get hers?" He grabbed her head in one meaty hand and shoved her under the water.

Kate tried to get free but he had a fist knotted up in her hair. Then she remembered the big hunting blade he carried on his hip. She felt around his waist and found the handle, having to work by touch in the darkness.

She pulled the knife free and shoved it in the closest lethal direction—between his thighs. Turning the edge sideways, she cut deeply into the inside of his thigh. The blade grated against bone, letting her know she'd sliced through the femoral artery where it lay along the inside of the bone. That deep, she couldn't have missed.

Monte Carter was a ticking time bomb, a dead man waiting to happen. With the femoral artery cut, he would bleed out in less time than it would take her to drown. She could already feel his grip weakening and wondered if he knew he was dying. In the cold water, he might not have even recognized the knife slash.

Lightning flickered again, and when it did Kate saw a shadow swim through the water above her. It seized Carter around the neck and wrapped its legs around the man's waist.

Carter released Kate and concentrated on his newest opponent, flailing with his fist as he fought to stay above the roiling sea. Kate swam up and sucked in a breath, holding on to a tree limb as she watched Shane grab Carter's forehead in one hand and his chin in the other. Then, with a sudden wrench, Shane snapped the big man's neck, separating the skull from the spine the way hunters did to end the suffering of an animal they'd found in a trap or had shot but didn't immediately kill.

As Carter died and went limp, Shane grabbed the tree. He looked after the big man's corpse as it floated away. Kate was surprised to see sadness in Shane's eyes. He had killed without mercy, but not without regret.

The rotor wash of the helicopter overcame the sound of the storm for a moment. As Kate watched, a Coast Guardsman came down in a rescue basket right beside Tyler and started shifting him aboard.

Kate released her hold on the tree and swam, driving herself through the storm surge. She didn't know if she had enough strength to reach the helicopter, but she intended to try. She shouted out to be heard. "Over here! *Over here!*" but knew that her voice couldn't possibly overcome the helicopter's own noise or the fact that the Coast Guard team would be wearing helmets.

"No." Shane caught her foot, stopping her progress.

Kate flipped over and kicked at him with her other foot, scoring on his already battered face and snapping his head back.

He cursed in pain but didn't let go. Kate bent at the waist, lifted the knife and prepared to plunge it into Shane's chest. She hesitated for just a moment, remembering how he had helped her with Tyler.

Then Kate felt cold metal press against the base of her skull and a much larger body bump into hers.

"Drop the knife, Ms. Garrett," Jolly whispered into her ear. He wrapped an arm over her breasts and held on tight.

Stubbornly, Kate held on to the knife for a moment. She stared straight at Shane, who was only then recovering from the kicks she'd administered.

"If you don't drop the knife," Jolly whispered in her ear, "I'm going to blow your brains out in one big, fat puddle."

"He means it, Kate," Shane said. Lightning flickered in his hazel eyes as he implored her. "Drop the knife. Please."

Jolly shook Kate roughly. "One wrong move," he declared, "and you're dead right here."

Slowly, Kate released her hold on the knife. Little more than a hundred yards away, the Coast Guard helicopter reeled the rescue basket back in. The chopper hung in the wind for a moment, swaying wildly from side to side, then began searching the area with spotlights. Kate wished that it had a FLIR, a Forward-Looking Infrared Searchlight that could read body heat in the cold seawater.

"Back with me, Ms. Garrett," Jolly said, pulling her deeply into the shadows of the cypress grove where they'd be hidden from sight. "If they find us, you'll never live to be rescued."

Helpless, scared and cold, Kate watched the helicopter search for a few more minutes, then it broke off the search pattern and flew east, probably toward Miami. Either it had gotten a call or Tyler Jordan's condition was too bad to stay and risk.

Tears filled Kate's eyes as the fear came crashing down on her. She looked at all the water that had surged in over Everglades National Park. If it was this bad here, this deep, she couldn't imagine what it would be like in Everglades City.

Where Steven and Hannah were.

Then she realized Jolly was talking to her. She focused on him, swallowing and pushing the panic away from her as far as she could for the moment. If she was going to help her children she had to stay alive.

"What?" she asked.

Jolly frowned. "I said, we need somewhere we can go to get clothes and some kind of transportation."

Kate thought. The storm surge had to be fifteen or twenty feet deep even after it had leveled off. There weren't many that had ever reached that depth.

"Do you know somewhere we can go, Kate?" Shane spoke in a calm voice, almost cordial. He didn't act like the guy who'd only a few minutes ago kept her from swimming away.

"Yeah," she said. "It's about a mile from here."

Jolly cursed, looking at the huge expanse of water all around them. "We can't swim a mile in this."

The alternative is to drown, Kate wanted to tell him. And she thought about adding that she'd stay and watch him when he did.

"Jolly! *Jolly!*"

Looking around, Kate spotted Ernie and Deke swimming through the water. The cousins made their way through the trees, swimming a short distance, then catching hold of the next tree and resting for a moment. In minutes, they'd joined them, looking like bedraggled rats. Both of them were scared, but Deke looked terrified.

"There's 'gators in this water," Deke said, climbing out of the water to sit in the tree where they'd all gathered. "I kept expecting one of them to get me any minute."

"The 'gators won't be doing much right now," Kate said. "With the water this active, they'll seek out a dry place and wait till it calms a little. Then they'll hunt. Even then, they won't have to hunt much. The water's going to be full of dead birds, deer, pigs and other animals."

She'd seen similar circumstances before. Floodwaters killed everything in their path, and a lot of the casualties were wildlife. If the brackish water stayed too long, the salt could kill the freshwater trees and plants too. It would take Everglades National Park a long time to recover from the flooding.

"We've still got to swim a mile," Jolly said.

Deke shook his head. "Not me. I can't swim no more."

"You'll swim," Jolly ordered, "or I'll leave you here." He paused. "And I won't leave you alive, Deke."

The young man nodded and looked away. "Okay, Jolly. Okay. I'll swim."

Feeling compassion for the young man even though she knew she shouldn't, and feeling exhaustion set into herself, Kate said, "We can fashion a makeshift raft."

"How?" Shane asked.

Kate pointed at the trees. "We'll top the trees. Take branches we can cut off and weave them together in a bundle."

Shane tested the branches. "Tying a bunch of branches together that are no bigger than our fingers is going to take all night."

Kate looked at Ernie. "You took my camp knife." Actually, Deke had been the one to find it under the truck's seat, but Ernie had claimed it from his younger cousin. "I'll need it back." She held out her hand.

Ernie grinned like he knew he was getting tricked. "You ain't gettin' no knife."

"I need the knife," Kate said. "It's got a saw cord in it." She kept her hand out and stayed patient.

After a moment, Jolly said, "Give her the knife."

Ernie scowled but did as he was told.

The knife was a serviceable survival knife in a thick-bladed Bowie style. For just a moment, Kate thought about diving under the water and taking her chances on swimming out in the darkness of the storm.

"You'd never make it," Jolly told her, grinning.

Letting out a tense breath, Kate opened the knife's handle and took out the metal saw cord and the tiny compass. She quickly attached the two rings, one at either end so she could pull the saw, then handed the knife back to Ernie.

Turning her attention to the tree, Kate picked the nearest good-sized limb—a little thicker than her wrist because they needed the flotation capabilities—and started sawing. Wet sawdust looked white and stark against the dark bark, and it fell to the swirling water in clumps.

She concentrated on the task at hand, but her mind kept reaching for an escape route.

Almost forty minutes later, knowing she was losing body heat to the water, Kate tossed down the last branch. She'd taught Shane how to weave the limber branches together, forming a roughly flat rectangle in the water. They'd had to jam it into the tree to keep the heaving tide from taking it.

"Can we ride on it?" Deke asked as Kate climbed down out of the tree.

"No." Kate lowered herself into the water and didn't like the fact that the water felt warm after being out in the wind. Her wet clothing had contributed to that. The warmth of the water was a dangerous illusion because the elements were still at work leeching her body heat. Continued exposure might kill them all. "It's not that kind of raft."

"What the hell are you sayin'?" Ernie demanded.

"It's a flotation aid," Kate answered. "We can swim with it. Hang on to it and rest in shifts while everybody else swims. If we do this right, we shouldn't lose anyone."

"Enough jabber," Jolly said. "We're wasting time. Is this thing ready?" He slapped the clump of tree branches with the pistol.

"Yeah," Kate said. "It's ready."

"Then you take the lead. A mile to this guy's house, you said?"

"About that," Kate replied.

"I thought you knew."

"I know how far it is when this area isn't flooded," Kate responded. "Things look different with all the water." She walled away the fear and confusion, dealing with the convict like he was one of her dissatisfied clients. Until he pulled the trigger or destroyed the flotation raft, she was going to claim the leadership role.

That would change, she knew, as soon as Jolly felt safe again. But by then she'd have time to think and plan.

"About a mile," Jolly repeated.

"That's my best guess," she told him, sticking to the answer she'd given.

Jolly frowned, started to say something, then just nodded.

Kate took the tiny compass out of her pants pocket, grateful that it was waterproof, got her directions straight, then grabbed hold of the flotation raft and started swimming. She thought about Steven and Hannah, and hoped that Megan had had enough warning to get them out of the house before the storm surge hit. She had no doubt that Everglades City was at least partially submerged.

Chapter 8

"That's it." Kate lifted an arm out of the water and pointed at the trailer house moored high in the trees. The winds rocked the tree and the house back and forth, threatening to spill it into the churning water. She was surprised at how happy she was to see the home. After swimming nearly an hour in the floodwaters, dodging displaced snakes and shoving aside drowned deer, rabbits, rats and other wildlife, the trailer in the trees looked inviting.

Thankfully, the windows were dark.

Kate felt a knot in her stomach loosen. Woodrow Barnes was a true swamp rat. He'd made and run moonshine out in the swamp for years, and he poached as often as he hunted legally. Over seventy years old, Woodrow was one of those men who looked like he'd shrunk inside his own skin over the years. But he'd been a friend to Kate and her dad.

The fact that the lights were off suggested that Woodrow

wasn't home. More than likely, he'd be in Everglades City keeping track of all the excitement with the volunteer disaster relief crews.

"I still don't see why in hell anybody would stick a mobile home in the trees," Ernie grumbled.

"You're looking at the reason," Jolly said. "We're near to drowning, and that trailer looks as dry as can be."

"Yeah, well, all I'm saying is it's a long way to fall if it ever does."

"It's still there despite this storm," Kate said. "It'll be all right for a little while longer." She turned the flotation raft in the mobile home's direction and kicked out again.

The sign in the window beside the mobile home's front door said: Premises Guarded by 12-Gauge Shotgun 3 Nights Out of the Week. Do You Feel Lucky?

Kate grabbed hold of the doorknob and started to twist it.

"Wait," Jolly directed, taking a step to put himself behind Kate on the narrow porch. "Knock on the door."

"Woodrow's not home," Kate said calmly as she could.

Jolly put the pistol barrel to the base of her skull. "Knock on the door," he repeated in a slow, deadly voice.

Kate knocked.

There was no answer.

At Jolly's direction, Kate knocked again and called out the old man's name. The house remained quiet. Only the gurgling of the floodwaters ten feet below them sounded. Knowing how high the mobile home was, Kate guessed that the flood level had reached about twenty-five feet. There had never been a storm like Genevieve in Floridian history.

After Katrina and Andrew, the evidence of the escalation of the storms and the predictions of meteorologists and storm chasers, Kate knew she shouldn't have been surprised. But she was. It was always astonishing to see how merciless nature could be when it wanted to be.

"Okay," Jolly said, "open the door."

Kate did. It wasn't locked. Woodrow always claimed that he took everything of worth with him whenever he left. That included whatever cash money he had, his guns, and his bloodhound, Ike. The dog had been his constant companion for the last twelve years.

She started to walk in but Jolly grabbed her arm. She briefly considered trying to break away from the big man and take her chances inside the house. Maybe Woodrow had taken his guns, but there were knives in the kitchen—if she could find them in the dark—and there was a back door that led to the boat landing behind the trailer that the convicts hadn't found yet. Woodrow always kept three or four boats with outboards and an airbuggy or two around in the creek that ran behind his place. All he had to do was climb down and get in a boat.

That was all Kate thought she had to do, too. But that was if they weren't flooded and sitting on the bottom now. And if she could tell which ones were operational and which ones were in a state of disrepair. And if she could get one of them started before Jolly killed her.

She let out a tense breath and waited.

Jolly pulled her back out of the doorway. "Ernie," Jolly called.

"Yeah." Ernie came forward.

"Check out the house."

Ernie balked. "Why do I have to check out the house?"

"Are you just carrying that scattergun to balance out?" Jolly asked. "Or can you use it?"

"I can check out the house," Shane volunteered. He reached for Ernie's shotgun.

"Ernie can do it." Jolly waved Shane back.

In that second, seasoned by a nearby lightning strike that hammered sparks from the crown of a bald cypress a short distance away, Kate knew that Jolly didn't really trust Shane. That was something to know.

Back at the trees, Jolly had asked about Monte Carter. Shane had spoken up at once, saying that neither one of them had seen the man. Kate had agreed.

At first, Kate had thought Shane had said that to protect her from Jolly's wrath. Or maybe to protect himself. But now, realizing the two men were each relying on the other only as much as he had to, a whole new and ugly thought entered her mind.

Phil Lewis had turned up mysteriously dead. Shane had chosen to kill Monte Carter, not realizing Kate had already done that very thing. Just maybe, her new line of thinking told her, Shane was killing his way to the ransom money Jolly claimed to be after.

Ernie took out one of the flashlights he'd gotten from Kate's truck and entered the house. He returned a few minutes later. "Nobody's home," he announced. Then he wrinkled his nose. "It's dry inside, but this damn place smells like wet dog."

As the convicts tore through Woodrow's home, Kate sat on the threadbare couch and felt guilty for bringing them here. The old man didn't have much, and Jolly and his men ransacked thoroughly what Woodrow did have. The prize Jolly seemed most excited over was a GPS unit.

Since the GPS unit had a map of the area, there was some discussion as to whether Kate was still necessary to their escape. She listened, their quiet voices more threatening than the storm partially blocked by the trailer's thin walls.

The Global Positioning Satellite unit could access twelve of the twenty-four geosynchronous satellites orbiting above the earth at any given time. With it, Jolly would know where he was. However, Shane pointed out that none of them knew the area, and even if they did, the flooding would make everything different.

In the end, Jolly decided to keep Kate along.

The mobile home was only twelve feet wide and had a seven-foot ceiling. Jolly looked like he filled up the living room all by himself. Ernie found the small generator Woodrow used to power the trailer on the back porch and fired it up. Within minutes, the lights were on and they weren't in the dark any more. The vibrations of the generator warred with the jerky swaying set up by the high winds Genevieve continued to bring.

Ernie and Deke stuffed themselves on the dry goods and junk food Woodrow kept. There was milk in the small dorm-sized refrigerator in the tiny kitchen, and some deer meat Woodrow had evidently taken lately. In minutes they had a frying pan going on the propane stove and were cooking deer steaks.

"Do you want anything to eat?" Shane asked. He offered her a can of peaches.

Kate just looked at him. Her stomach rolled at the thought of eating. She didn't know if Steven and Hannah were all right, didn't know if Tyler Jordan was still alive, and she didn't know if she would even live to see morning. What she did know was that she did *not* want to eat, and she despised the men that had taken her.

Of them all, she thought she despised Shane most. She realized it was because he was the one she would most likely believe wasn't involved in a life like this, even with the bullet-hole scars and the knife scar his granny had sewed up. It didn't help that she couldn't forget how lean and hard his body had looked when he'd taken his T-shirt off to make bindings for Tyler. Bryce had gone to the gym, but he'd never looked that cut.

"You need to eat," Shane said, pushing the peaches at her.

"No," she told him, ignoring the proffered can.

"You've got to keep your strength up."

She returned his level gaze. "I want to go to the bathroom."

Shane took the can of peaches back. Deliberately, he stuck a fork in a peach half and popped the fruit into his mouth. He chewed, then smiled.

The smell of peaches and Shane's natural musk filled Kate's nose. Both were wonderful, and both made her hungry.

"Raymond," Shane said.

"What?"

"She needs to go to the bathroom."

Jolly didn't say anything for a time. He'd been lost deep in his own thoughts, barely responding to Deke and Ernie's comments about how they were soon going to be living it up on the ten million they were going after.

"All right," Jolly said finally, comfortable in the role of commander. "Take her."

"Let's go," Shane said gruffly, nodding to the back of the mobile home.

Kate stood and walked back to the miniature bathroom. It was tiny, the sink, toilet and shower stall rusted from hard water, and foul in ways that she didn't even want to think about. But it was dry.

Shane stepped inside and surveyed the bathroom's contents. He took the straight razor next to the shaving soap cup and slipped it into his pocket. "Don't want anybody getting hurt, do we?"

Kate didn't respond. When he pulled back out of the bathroom, she looked at him. "I'm going to wring my clothes out, so it's going to take a while."

Shane speared another peach. "Okay." He stepped back out and closed the door.

Kate quietly slid the small latch closed. She knew Shane could easily break it, but just that slight movement made her feel like she had some privacy.

At the sink, she looked into the mirror. Dark hollows showed under her eyes. She looked tired. She looked, as her dad had told her once lately, "like a woman who didn't smile too much." He'd apologized at once, saying he hadn't meant to tell her that. At the time, she hadn't known what he meant, but looking at her somber reflection, she thought that she did.

Then she threw up. Her stomach churned and emptied itself in a rush, leaving her shaken and weak.

"You okay?" Shane asked through the door.

Kate wiped her mouth with a tissue, but the sour taste of bile haunted her. "I'm fine," she replied.

"Sounded like you were getting sick."

For a moment, Kate thought she heard concern in the convict's voice. Then she remembered how easily Shane had snapped Monte Carter's neck and let the floodwaters take the body. But he'd also shown regret, hadn't he? She wasn't certain.

"If you're sick—" Shane began.

"I said I was fine," Kate told him more forcefully. Angry now, she turned the faucet on and washed the vomit down the sink. She found a bottle of mouthwash and used it to rinse her mouth.

She emptied her bladder, then unlaced her boots and took them off. She took off her socks next and wrung them out as best as she could, then quickly followed with her pants and her T-shirt, draining them all into the shower stall. She did the same with her panties and sports bra. Then she toweled herself off, including her hair, and luxuriated in the feeling of—*finally*—being dry again.

She turned on the propane space heater and used the self-contained striker to light the flame. Then she hung her clothes on the towel bar above it and hoped they'd dry a little more. Maybe they were only going back outside in the rain, but Woodrow had rain ponchos in the house that would help keep them all dry. Deke was the only one who could wear Woodrow's clothes. Shane and Jolly were stuck with the orange jumpsuits for a while longer.

Looking at herself in the mirror, Kate found she had a multitude of bruises and scrapes, most of them she couldn't even remember acquiring. Thinking about the propane space heater made her realize the water heater was powered by propane as well and might even be on. Checking the hot water, she discovered it was warm.

She found a fresh bar of soap and stepped into the shower. Maybe it was foolish to shower with the convicts just outside the door and down the hall, but she knew she wouldn't take any time at all and her clothes were going to take even longer to dry.

Not only that, but a plan on how to further split Jolly and Shane started to form in her mind. The fewer people she had watching her, the better her chances were of escaping and getting back home.

She stood under the weak stream of warm water and lathered up, developing what she had in mind, knowing it was risky on several fronts.

None of the men truly seemed to trust each other. She'd

seen hunting parties deal with the same kind of competitive jealousies.

She knew she could use that against them.

Shane stood outside the bathroom door with his can of peaches and continued eating. Unfortunately, remembering the way Kate Garrett, Wilderness Guide, had looked down her pretty little nose at him while he was trying to fill his hollow stomach, the flavor seemed somehow off.

He grew more irritated at her as he thought about her. She should have left when I gave her the chance, he thought. Putting the fork back in the peach can, half the contents untouched, he stared out the window of the back door.

Genevieve continued to dump rain over the Everglades. Buckets and buckets of it poured on to the new oceanfront property the storm surge had temporarily created.

And you really expect to find Desiree Martini's body out there in all that? Shane growled in disgust. The plan he'd made had been simple. Okay, maybe a little complicated by the whole make-friends-with-Raymond-Jolly aspect—especially since the guy turned out to be more of a cold-blooded killer than Shane had thought. But it should have worked.

If it hadn't been for the damned storm. By the time the Bureau knew Hurricane Genevieve was coming, everything had been put into play. Raymond Jolly's trust hadn't exactly been unwavering, but delaying the "escape" might have ended the possibility of getting the woman's body back altogether. After seven months, there was no telling how much of it was left out there to find.

And, on top of the damned storm and managing Raymond Jolly's "escape," Shane was now struggling to juggle Kate Garrett into the volatile mix. Not only that, the miniature communications device "guaranteed" to connect him with the rest of the FBI team wasn't working. His communications were infrequent, interrupted, and not totally accurate on the Global Positioning Satellite systems.

For just a moment, Shane closed his eyes and tried to imagine what it felt like to be rested. And warm. He briefly considered telling Kate Garrett the truth, that he was an undercover FBI agent on special assignment. Only how the hell was he supposed to do that now? He hadn't made a terribly great impression on her so far. The comparing scars shtick that had worked for Mel Gibson hadn't driven her crazy.

Not only that, Shane didn't trust her to keep her mouth shut, to know when to speak and when to shut up, or to see that her interests dovetailed his. The true problem was he didn't trust anybody outside his own skin. Judging from the tight-lipped way she acted around him, maybe they both shared that trait.

Hell, even Jolly played things close to the vest. Maybe all of them had been betrayed somewhere along the line.

Shane sighed, tired and cold from the long swim in the invasive ocean waters. He thought about Kate Garrett. Who hurt you? he wondered, because he was certain someone must have. Whoever it was had done a good job of it too. They hadn't broken her, though. She was too confident in her own abilities for that to be true. She was hanging on to whatever safe ground she'd found.

He thought about her again, the way she had taken out a steroid monster like Monte Carter with the baton—and been prepared to do it again in the water when she'd taken Carter's knife, and the way she'd taken the kid off the 'gator hook and sewn his stomach up.

She'd even saved the young man out of the back of the

truck before Shane could get free and get back there. He'd followed behind her, astonished at how she was able to get her charge to the surface and throw the life vest on him.

All in all, she was damned amazing.

He frowned, listening to the water inside the bathroom. It didn't take much to imagine her naked under the shower. Maybe she wasn't beautiful by Hollywood standards, but she was a striking woman. Shane liked the way she looked and the way she moved.

He even liked the way she sat quietly paying attention to everything going on around her. That could be dangerous, though, he admitted. If she had the chance to think too much, she could probably stir up all kinds of trouble.

Shane wiped a hand over his chin and felt the beard stubble there. The last time he'd shaved had been at 3:00 a.m. that morning, before the bus had taken the prisoners to East Naples.

The cover story had been that one of the "fish"—new arrivals—in the cell block had carried in some kind of variant of the Asian bird flu. Several of the prisoners, supposedly a cross-section of the general population, had been bussed out to different clinics. They'd had to arrive there before the physicians' normal business hours, then get in and get out.

That had provided Shane the opportunity to spring Jolly and his crew. He'd deliberately chosen the Tamiami Highway, knowing they were only a few miles from where the FBI team had run them to ground seven months ago. If things hadn't gotten so crazy, Jolly would have already led the way to Desiree Martini's mortal remains.

Now Shane just hoped that her body wasn't buried out there under all that water. Maybe that was what was had Raymond Jolly so lethargic about making a move.

Then there was the mystery of how Phil Lewis had gotten

himself dead. Shane still wasn't clear on that. Lewis had ended up with a bullet through his head. No one claimed to have been around him, but Jolly had been the first man to arrive. By then Lewis was way past talking.

Unless the FBI gets a direct line to Mistress Cleo or one of those other 1-800 psychics. The mystery actually wasn't that deep. Jolly and Ernie had been the only two armed with firepower, which had been taken from the prison guards, and Ernie was carrying a shotgun.

Phil Lewis hadn't been shot with a shotgun.

No one contested Jolly's innocence, though.

But why kill Lewis? Shane's only answer was that maybe even ten million dollars didn't look like all that much after seven months in lock-up.

Shane yawned, a real jaw-creaker. And his imagination returned to Kate Garrett naked under the shower. He tried to shake it off, aware of the physical response his imagination was triggering in him.

Standing under the water, Kate knew she wasn't going to have a better chance to set her plan into motion. She glanced longingly at her clothes. Or at least the towel. It had been years since a man had seen her nude.

Get over it, she told herself. This is what it's going to take.

She steeled herself, pushing aside all thoughts of what Shane might think. It was what the others thought that mattered.

Taking a breath, she tried to speak. Couldn't. Her throat was too tight. She took another couple of breaths, then tried again. "Shane."

No answer.

Kate tried again, speaking louder. *"Shane."*

"Yeah?"

"I need some help. Can you come in here?" She stared at the door, waiting, knowing she was only going to have this one chance. But all she had to do was drive a wedge among the men. That might give her just enough room to escape.

Can I go in there? Shane's imagination went into overdrive. He started to ask her if she was decent, then he pushed that out of his mind, telling himself not to be stupid. Surely she was dressed. Otherwise she wouldn't call for him.

He opened the door and went inside.

And found Kate Garrett in the shower, holding her hair up with both hands.

Shane froze, hypnotized by the full-bodied curves naked before him. She had great shoulders, slightly freckled, full breasts that held their shape and poise, a taut waist that led down to generous hips. A woman's figure, not some waif's, not one of those women Shane figured would break at the slightest touch. Her legs were firm, muscular, her calves sculpted from working out or maybe just hard work in her chosen field.

The sight of her *au natural* made Shane's breath catch in his throat. The baggy, wet jumpsuit suddenly felt too tight.

If she was modest, she didn't act it. Instead, she came across as a woman comfortable with her body. There was no screaming, no frantic covering up, no quick grab for a towel.

She looked at him frankly, her dark-green eyes challenging. Her striking features remained composed. If she was scared or surprised or pissed, she didn't show that either.

Without a word, she turned off the water and reached for one of the towels sitting in a built-in cabinet. Without hurrying, she wrapped the towel around her torso, hiding her body only a little, because the thin towel somehow emphasized her figure. Memory filled in everything he couldn't see.

Somewhere in there, Shane's heart kick-started in his chest again. He suddenly felt dumb and awkward. He hadn't often felt that way.

"Sorry," he mumbled, and started to back out of the room. "Guess you weren't ready."

She surprised him totally by reaching for him, dropping a hand on his shoulder and moving toward him. He stood as though paralyzed, totally mesmerized by her beauty and the unmistakable eroticism of the moment.

"Wait," she said. "I need you to look at something for me."

"Sure," he said, but he really didn't know what the hell to expect.

Then she leaned in close, turned her face up to his, and pressed her mouth to his lips that she had bruised during their fight out in the swamp.

The kiss was hot and electric. Before he knew he was going to do it, Shane had his arms around her, holding her close. He felt the strength of her, the coiled muscle that lay just beneath the soft-as-velvet skin. She smelled clean, a mixture of rainwater and soap, and a hint of primitive feminine mystique that woke the sleeping savage inside his mind and drove him crazy.

He kissed her back, locking his left hand behind her head, cupping the base of her skull as he felt the length of her body pressed into him. He tightened the arm he had around her waist, pulling her even closer, molding her body with his own.

Desire swept over him with a ferocity he'd never before experienced, like it had been smoldering since they'd fought and she'd pinned him to the ground with her body, straddling him with her hips in a manner way too suggestive and pleasant.

Then she broke the lip lock and looked up at him with those dark-green eyes. Her voice was hoarse and low when she spoke.

"Tell me again about the ten million dollars in ransom money," she said.

When he heard the triple click of Raymond Jolly's .357 Magnum behind him, knew that the man had heard what she'd said, Shane knew how treacherous Kate Garrett had been in setting him up.

Damn.

Chapter 9

"What the hell is going on?" Jolly demanded.

Kate slid away from Shane, breaking out of the embrace like she was scared or embarrassed. Truthfully, she was both.

Shane seemed at a loss for words as he stared down the length of Jolly's pistol. Jolly glared at her as well.

Working quickly, Kate kept the towel around her and pulled on her panties—dry, thank God—then stepped into the still-damp jeans without endangering her modesty. Both men stood silent and still while they watched her, their argument temporarily on hold. What was it about a woman getting dressed—or undressed, for that matter—that locked a man up like a deer in headlights? She shoved her head through her T-shirt and pulled it down over her breasts before dropping the towel to the floor. She was all too aware that the shirt's wetness didn't completely disguise the chill she'd gotten.

But it isn't just the chill, is it, Kate? she chided herself.

She'd gotten more into the kissing than she'd intended. There was something about Shane that awakened a hunger in her that she'd tried to keep buried these last few years. When dealing with her ex-husband, desire equaled vulnerability. He found out what she wanted just so he could take it away from her.

She turned her thoughts from those old losses to the new battle she had on her hands. With her semi-seduction of Shane, she'd exposed a few weaknesses in the players she was surrounded by. She also felt the hard length of the straight razor in her pocket that she'd swiped from Shane while she'd had his mind on other things. With any kind of luck, Shane would have to work so hard on his own survival that he wouldn't remember the straight razor.

"I said," Jolly repeated, "what the *hell* is going on here?"

"Take it easy, Raymond," Shane said calmly.

Jolly pointed the .357 Magnum at the center of Shane's face.

Sour sickness twisted inside Kate's stomach and she thought she was going to throw up again. She choked back the response. Any weakness on her part was going to devalue the wedge she was trying to drive between the two men.

"What were the two of you talking about?" Jolly demanded.

"Nothing," Shane responded. "We weren't talking about anything." He held his hands up, but Kate could tell by the way he shifted his body that he was thinking about making a try for the pistol all the same.

Another quiver of fear trembled through Kate as she realized that if Shane did try to take the gun away, she was going to be directly in the line of fire. Great plan, she told herself.

"What are you doing in here?" Jolly asked.

Slowly, Shane shook his head. "It was a trick. She asked me to come in."

"I saw you kissing her. You were talking about the ransom money."

"*She* kissed me," Shane protested. "I didn't kiss her."

Liar! Kate thought. She hadn't been the only one who'd gotten caught up in the moment. His excitement had manifested itself hard enough and big enough that she hadn't been able to miss it. Or maybe it hadn't been able to miss her.

"That's not how it looked to me," Jolly said.

Shane cursed and shook his head. He took a step forward, daring Jolly to act. "Then shoot me, Raymond! Do it!" He tapped his own forehead. "Right here!"

For a moment, Kate thought Jolly was actually going to do it. She knew the big man thought about it. She'd seen that in his face and in those hard predator's eyes. With everything she'd done, she might as well have put the pistol against Shane's head and pulled the trigger herself.

"Hey," Ernie said out in the hallway behind Jolly. "Hold up there a second, boss."

"Stay out of this," Jolly snarled.

"Can't," Ernie said. "Got an interest in how this turns out myself. Shane says he can get us out of the country. Down to the Grand Caymans. That's something we can't do, an' we can't just stay around here after we get that ransom money."

"We can hire a boat." Jolly didn't waver.

"Can you, Raymond?" Shane pressed. "Can you really? Do you know who to hire?" He snorted derisively. "You can't just go around asking anybody that has a boat to take you to the Grand Caymans. Hell, half the people you ask are going to be undercover agents for the DEA or Coast Guard. You'll get nailed before you ever make it out of Miami."

"Shut up!" Jolly ordered.

"No," Shane said. "To hell with that. You come over here,

see me with that woman, and you jump to the first conclusion *she* wants you to."

Jolly looked at Kate. She returned his gaze full measure.

"Think!" Shane tapped his head. "Think, Raymond! You outsmarted the cops and the FBI when you took that heiress and slipped off with that ransom money. Don't make a dumb mistake now."

"Don't call me dumb," Jolly warned.

Shane pointed at Kate. "Do you think I'm really going to blow sweet nothings in this woman's ear? Take a chance on screwing up getting my percentage from you?"

"Maybe you're thinking about taking it all," Jolly suggested. "You and your partner."

"My *partner?*" Shane laughed derisively. "When the hell did she get to be my *partner?*"

"She was there," Jolly reminded. "When the bus blew up. Kind of suspicious now that I think about it."

"Maybe," Shane said. "But how could we have planned that? The explosive device detonated early."

Jolly stared at Shane. "Could be it didn't," Jolly said. "Could be you arranged that."

"So we could steal her Jeep?" Shane shook his head. "Then why didn't she go with us?"

"I don't know," Jolly replied. "But she's here now."

"Son of a bitch, Raymond!" Shane exploded. "You were the one telling me where to go. How could I tell her how to find us?"

"He's right about that," Ernie commented.

"Shut up, Ernie," Jolly ordered.

"After we dumped the Jeep," Shane said, "we got lost. Wandered around for hours. Then the storm hit. Do you really think I could have given her precise directions on how to find us? The fact that she's here now? That's just because she's having the same rotten luck we've been having since this storm hit."

Kate silently agreed with that.

Jolly thought about that. The silence that descended over the men and the situation was interrupted by the creak of the tree limbs, the muffled throbbing of the generator, and the sound of thunder that was finally starting to sound more distant.

"How did she know about the money?" Jolly asked finally.

"It's been on the news," Shane said in a calm tone. Damn, but she was good. She'd done a hell of a job on the frame. Her act had tripped every paranoid feeling inside Jolly. "Every station on the radio was running it. Probably all the local television stations too. And Ernie and Deke have been spending it every time they've thought about it. Which has been a lot. Or don't you remember those conversations?"

Finally, after another long, tense moment, Jolly reached into his pocket and took out a pair of handcuffs. "Cuff her somewhere where she won't get into trouble." He tossed the cuffs to Shane. He looked at the shower. "That water warm?"

"There wasn't any steam," Shane said, "but she didn't look like she was freezing."

"Good. Get her out of there. I'm going to take a shower, then I'm going to eat me one of those steaks Ernie and Deke are fixing. After that, we're all going to get a good night's sleep and see what tomorrow brings."

Shane took Kate by the elbow and led her back to the living room. Meat was sizzling in the frying pan on the propane cook stove. Deke and Ernie were debating culinary skills, talking about cooking shows they'd seen on cable TV at prison and arguing about how best to prepare the meat.

Kate didn't look at Shane while he closed one of the cuffs

around her left wrist and the other around a boat anchor he'd had Deke bring in from outside. They'd found Woodrow's little flotilla and were evidently hopeful about the boats they found there.

"You can probably pick up the boat anchor and carry it," Shane told her. "But you'll have a hell of a time swimming with it."

Kate just stared at him.

"You get the couch," Shane told her, "but I'll be here." He sat in the overstuffed chair on the other side of the room.

Knowing her escape was temporarily foiled, Kate made herself comfortable on the couch. The semi-wet clothing made that almost impossible, but she tried anyway. If she lived through the night, tomorrow would offer more possibilities. That was one thing she'd learned while fighting Bryce. She needed to rest if she was going to make the most of them.

Closing her eyes, she pushed her breath out and tried relaxation techniques she'd learned about while dealing with the anxiety problems Bryce's legal attacks had caused. Even then, she could feel Shane's eyes on her.

Worse than that, she could still feel his kiss. The sensation of his lips against hers followed her right into oblivion.

Kate woke early the next morning. She didn't move for a while. Snoring sounded to her left. Turning her head, she found Ernie and Deke asleep on the floor. Pillows cushioned their shaggy heads.

Dim sunlight shone on the window above her, promising better weather than the day before. She took hope in that. The storm season could last for months, but there were occasional days of perfection.

Shifting, Kate readied herself to get up, gripping the handcuff chain to keep it from making noise. Her arm was asleep from the uncomfortable positions she'd been forced to sleep in to manage the cuff, and her wrist was chafed from the rough contact.

"Don't get up," Shane said, his eyes opening. He was still seated in the overstuffed chair. "We're not going to get out of here till later."

"I've got to go to the bathroom."

Shane was quiet for a moment, then he sighed and pushed up from the chair. "Let's go."

Kate walked down the hall. In the bathroom, she discovered the propane space heater's controls had been wrecked. Disconnecting the unit from the gas line was beyond her present ability without tools. She'd woken up with the idea of turning the mobile home into a raging bonfire, saddened that she hadn't had the chance and hadn't thought about it last night.

Afterwards, she washed her face then rejoined Shane out in the hallway. She thought about trying to talk to him, but she had no idea about how to approach him.

In the living room, she put the boat anchor back on the ground beside the couch and sprawled again. At least during the night her clothing had dried. With the sun bright and shiny outside the window, she hoped she'd get to stay dry.

Rolling over on to her side, she closed her eyes and found sleep once more.

By noon, after a breakfast of sausages, bacon, hot biscuits and gravy, they were ready to move. Unfortunately, the storm had moved back in, bringing echoes of the power and fury back, and a steady light rain as well. Tropical storms had a tendency to gather in an area for days and linger, petering out, and strengthening periodically.

Only one of Woodrow's boats left tied to the tall pole next to the mobile home was operational. As the water from the storm surge had come in, the boats had floated up, secured to the pole by large metal rings and chains. Woodrow had always been prepared for flooding.

One of the boats didn't float. It sat midway down in the murky depths, barely visible as it shifted and turned at the end of its tether.

Clad in a poncho, Kate carried a cardboard box containing food they'd raided from Woodrow's meager supplies to the waiting boat. She had to climb down the ladder to reach the boat. She couldn't be certain, but she thought the floodwaters were already starting to recede.

The craft was a twenty-foot johnboat equipped with a powerful outboard motor. Shane had had to work on it for a little while to get it operational, but the motor ran steadily and sounded powerful enough at the moment.

Kate put the food in the center of the boat, then took a seat in the prow at Shane's direction. Jolly stood watch on the porch above, using a pair of binoculars that Woodrow had left behind.

Ernie and Deke were finishing the scavenging.

For the moment, Kate was alone in the boat with Shane.

He spoke to her in a low voice. "You got two kids, right, Kate?"

Bile rose in the back of her throat. If you threaten my kids, you bastard—

"I saw their pictures in your Jeep," Shane said. "They're good-looking kids. You should be proud."

Kate made herself breathe out and not be sick. The hard lines of the straight razor were still in her pocket. She was tempted to try her luck at overpowering Shane and stealing the johnboat.

Everglades City wasn't far away. It was possible, barring an accident, that she could reach the town in a few hours.

But Jolly remained only a short distance away. She didn't think he would miss with the pistol at close range.

"What I want you to think about," Shane said quietly, "is getting back to them. Safe and sound. You want to live long enough to do that, right?"

After a moment, she nodded. She still didn't know how badly hit Everglades City was. The admission seemed to give her focus and lift a million pounds off her shoulders.

"I want to see you get the chance to do that, Kate," he told her. "Don't do anything stupid and lose those kids their mother." He paused. "Let me do my job and we'll get out of here."

My job? The words sounded strange and it was hard to put any real meaning to them when she thought about Shane. Guys like Shane didn't have real jobs. They just cruised through life like nothing could ever touch them.

"I'm sure they want you back, too, Kate," he said. "All you have to do is wait a little longer."

Kate swallowed the lump in her throat.

"Do you hear me?" he asked.

Unable to speak, she only nodded again. But she slid her hand across the straight razor in her pocket. He was a damn fool if he thought she was going to put her future and that of her kids in his hands.

Looking out at the flooded swamplands, Shane felt as though the world had suddenly turned apocalyptic. It seemed that there was nothing left alive for miles around. He was tired and edgy, constantly trapped between Kate Garrett and Raymond Jolly. Both of them had their own ideas about what they were going to do, and it was totally screwing up Shane's agenda.

He had a job to do, but he was feeling more protective of Kate. The woman had surprised him with the shower scene. There was cunning in Kate Garrett that he hadn't seen, and when she went for something it was obviously no-holds-barred. He respected that about her.

But it was making everything he had to do even harder.

He peered through the rain, looking at the deliberate set of Kate's shoulders. All during the day she'd maintained vigilance, ready to seize any opportunity that came her way. He saw that in her, and so did Jolly. That was why Jolly had handcuffed her to the boat.

Shane hadn't liked that, but Jolly hadn't given him much choice. If the boat turned over, Kate's chances of survival turned slim. And maybe if Jolly hadn't handcuffed her, she might have decided to jump from the boat and take her chances in the water when they got around some of the thick groupings of trees.

If he wanted to escape, Shane knew that's how he would have done it. He manned the tiller, going slowly so they wouldn't hit any submerged obstacles that could rip out the bottom of the boat.

"When are we gonna get the ransom money?" Ernie asked.

Shane listened quietly, knowing Jolly was watching him. Even though Jolly wasn't pushing the issue about Kate's comment last night, Shane also knew the man hadn't forgotten it. If Shane hadn't dangled the Get-Out-of-Florida-Free card in front of Jolly—complete with a savvy sea captain who was totally fictitious at this point—he was certain he'd never have made it off the bus.

"We'll get it soon," Jolly said. He consulted the GPS unit as he'd been doing all morning. "We need to make a trip into Everglades City first."

"How soon?"

"Tonight or tomorrow." Irritation sounded in Jolly's voice. "Be patient, Ernie. You've already waited for months. Another day won't kill you."

Unless we get caught by one of the emergency agencies, Shane thought bleakly. Then we're all dead in the water. Twice during the day they'd seen Coast Guard helicopters flying overhead.

Shane stared at Jolly's back as the man looked out over the floodwaters and took another reading. Up till now, Shane had thought Jolly was looking for a landmark. But a landmark didn't explain the need to go into Everglades City.

So what are you looking for, Raymond? Shane wondered.

Near dusk, Jolly spotted another mobile home in the trees. The rain continued to fall as the sky rumbled and lightning flickered.

Kate was relieved to see that this trailer was dark too, meaning, she hoped, that none of the residents were home. She pulled reflexively at the handcuff securing her to the longboat. All day long she'd had to fight the constant terror of drowning if the johnboat flipped over on a submerged tree.

Shane guided the johnboat in and they tied up at the ladder leading up to the mobile home twenty feet above.

"Stay with the boat," Jolly said. "We'll check out the house."

Nodding, Shane pulled at the orange jumpsuit under the poncho. "See if they have anything my size."

"Sure."

Kate noted that the relationship between the two men remained strained. She thought she'd probably have taken more satisfaction in that if she hadn't been in harm's way too.

"Thinking about your kids, Kate?" Shane asked from the stern.

She turned to him then, anger boiling over in her. "Listen, you sick son of a bitch, I may not have much of a choice about the company I keep at the moment, but I can tell you that it's generally a whole lot better. I don't want you talking to me. Don't mention my kids again."

He looked at her and he looked apologetic. "I'm sorry," he said. "I just need to know what you're thinking. The last thing I need is for you to go off half-cocked. It's the last thing you need too."

Kate shook her head. "I don't understand you at all."

A small smile flirted with his bruised lips. "I'm a simple man, Kate. You just caught me in a really complicated situation."

"You," Kate told him distinctly, "weren't the one who got caught."

"I don't know about that," Shane said. "Getting stuck out here in the middle of a hurricane with Raymond Jolly probably wasn't the brightest move I ever made. But there's a reason for it."

"What?" she dared him.

"You know about the Martini kidnapping?"

"Yeah. The ten million dollars in ransom money gets mentioned frequently around here."

Shane smiled a little. "Ernie's got a one-track mind just about big enough for a BB to roll through. But the money wasn't the only thing that went missing during that kidnapping. Mr. and Mrs. Martini didn't get their daughter back either."

"She's dead," Kate said before she realized how crass that sounded.

Nodding, Shane said, "I think you're probably right. But Mr. and Mrs. Martini haven't gotten the chance to bury their daughter. That's why I'm here."

Kate looked at him more closely then. What makes the daughter's missing corpse your business?

Just then, Jolly, Ernie and Deke reappeared on the porch and climbed down carrying boxes and plastic bags. Jolly and Ernie wore street clothes now. Jolly handed a bag to Shane, who stood in the johnboat and stripped off.

Kate turned away, but it was difficult. In the waning sunlight he looked robust and fit, and she had the terrible impulse to run her hands over his body. Heat warmed her face. Get a grip, she told herself. This is ridiculous.

But ridiculous or not, proper place or not, those feelings and thoughts insisted on surfacing.

"I need to go to the bathroom again," she said as Shane continued to dress. If he was putting on a show for her, she was going to pass.

Jolly unlocked her cuff and instructed Ernie to take her.

Climbing up the ladder, Kate felt the man's eyes on her the whole way. She didn't like the idea of being in the house alone with him. The straight razor in her pocket made her feel a little safer.

After she'd finished in the bathroom, she stepped back out into the hallway. That was when Ernie made his move. He slammed a big hand against her throat, leaned in against her to pin her against the wall with his weight, and fumbled for the front of his pants.

"I think it's time me an' you had a little fun, girlie," Ernie said, grinning wolfishly. "The way you got Jolly an' Shane riled up at each other, I'm thinkin' maybe somebody needs to teach you a lesson."

His stale breath pressed against her face. She started to scream, but his other hand came across and covered her mouth. She tried to pull the straight razor from her pocket but couldn't get to it.

Lifting her left arm, she swept it across her body as hard

as she could, knocking both his hands off her face and throat in a martial arts move she'd learned while training with the Asp. Then she bunched her right hand into a fist and punched him in the eye.

Ernie cried out, putting his hands to his face.

Kate turned and ran, but she hadn't taken two steps before her attacker jumped her from behind and dragged her down to the floor. She struggled to roll free, struggled to get a hand free to go for the straight razor, but he was all over her. He kneed her legs apart and reached for her belt.

Then a flashlight beam fell over them.

Ernie went still at once, lifting a hand to shield his eyes from the brightness.

"Dammit, Ernie! Don't do that! C'mon, now! Get off her!"

Kate took the opportunity to drive a palm into his nose, hoping that she hit him hard enough to break it. He screamed and his head snapped back.

The light shifted and Kate saw that it was Deke. For a moment she was afraid that he was going to help his cousin. Until he pulled his cousin off her and helped her to her feet.

Deke led the way to the door, obviously leery of his cousin's wrath. He went down the stairs quickly. "I'm sorry, Miss Garrett. I should have gone with you. I should have known he might try something like that. He's my cousin, but he's one rapist son of a bitch when he gets the chance."

The young man sounded so worried and distraught, Kate felt the need to tell him that everything was going to be all right.

"I never did any of that," Deke was saying as he reached the bottom of the ladder. "I know people thought I did, but I never did. I—"

Below the young man, the water roiled and shifted. Something hit the johnboat where Jolly and Shane stood staring at

Deke at the bottom of the ladder and at Ernie above. When the boat tipped, almost lifting out of the water, Kate knew exactly what was about to happen.

But it still surprised her when the alligator leaped up out of the water, opened its jaws to expose its pink-white throat, and tore Deke from the ladder.

Chapter 10

Deke vanished into the murky water without even an opportunity to scream.

Above, Ernie yelled hoarsely after his cousin. In the boat, still rocking from the collision with the alligator, Jolly and Shane stood stunned.

Kate reacted at once, knowing that there wasn't much time. She could still see the alligator below, Deke still in its mouth. Bubbles exploded across the surface. Reaching into her pants pocket, Kate took out the straight razor and opened it. Then she stepped from the ladder and plummeted into the water.

Sinking at once, Kate hoped there was only one alligator. Sometimes there were more. With the flooding in the park, though, she thought maybe they might have gotten scattered. Otherwise she'd just dropped to her death.

The murky water reduced visibility dramatically. She barely saw the giant lizard cruising silently with its prize struggling in its jaws. Normally an alligator took a prey down into the water and started turning over and over, letting its sharp teeth tear its victim to pieces.

Slipping in, the straight razor tight in her fist, knowing that Deke would be dead in seconds once the alligator started turning, Kate swam down on top of the alligator and wrapped her left arm under its chin while she laid her cheek on its neck and held on.

The alligator's powerful body writhed at the unexpected contact, trying to shake her off. She held on tightly, then shoved the straight razor into the flesh of the alligator's neck just beneath her left arm, and cut the creature's throat. She slashed as deeply and as quickly as she could.

For a long moment, the alligator simply glided through the blood-darkened water. Kate was afraid to let go, and equally terrified by what she'd done. If she'd actually stopped and thought about what she was about to do—if she hadn't just been attacked—she wouldn't have gone into the water.

It had been reflex, pure and simple. Her predicament reminded her of what Shane had said. *I'm a simple man. You just caught me in a really complicated situation.*

Now look at the situation she was in. Afraid to stay, afraid to let go.

Then, abruptly, the alligator went limp. Deke still struggled, but his efforts were weaker. A lot of the blood darkening the water was from him.

Kate let go of the alligator's neck and took hold of its snout. She jammed a boot against the alligator's lower jaw— *Still not the most foolish thing you've done tonight!*—and grabbed the upper jaw in her hands. She pulled and pushed at the same time and the alligator's mouth opened.

Deke floated free.

Before Kate could reach him, Shane was there. He grabbed the young man by the shoulders and hauled him toward the surface. Already trembling from adrenaline overload, Kate swam after them.

They surfaced only a few feet from the johnboat.

"Help me," Shane called.

Wary of the water, Jolly reached down and caught the back of Deke's shirt. Kate joined them as Ernie leaped from the ladder and dropped into the boat, mewling in fear for his cousin.

Jolly pointed the pistol at her. "I'll take that straight razor, Ms. Garrett."

Only then did Kate realize she still had the blade in her hand.

Jolly waved to the bottom of the johnboat. "Just throw it over there."

For a moment, Kate thought about dropping back into the water and swimming for it. Then she knew that was stupid. If there weren't other alligators in the nearby water, there would be soon. The blood smells—man and alligator—would draw them.

Still, she couldn't bring herself to just do what Jolly ordered. She held the straight razor over the water, feeling Shane's eyes on her, and dropped the blade into the water.

"Okay." Jolly smiled. "That'll work too."

In the end, they had to take Deke back into the mobile home. Continuing on with him in the johnboat would have been tantamount to homicide. Jolly hadn't wanted to stay, but in the end he hadn't had the heart to leave Deke behind or subject him to a night in the boat when the empty mobile home was right there.

If Jolly had chosen either one of those courses of action, Shane knew he would have fought him over it. From the grievous nature of Deke's wounds, though, Shane didn't hold out much hope for a recovery.

She jumped in the water to save him, Shane realized, knowing that she was risking her life. He still couldn't believe he'd actually seen her do that.

Kate worked by candlelight. Whoever had put this mobile home high in the trees had chosen to leave the generator somewhere below, probably off the ground, Shane reasoned, but definitely not out of reach of the storm surge. During a second search of the house, they'd found candles and a fairly complete first-aid kit.

Deke lay in one of the beds, the sheets already covered with blood.

Going to be a hell of a crime scene for someone, Shane thought. He stood at Kate's side and helped her as much as he was able.

Deke's waist was covered in lacerations. Some of them were just cosmetic, but it was hard to know which was which until Kate probed with her glove-covered fingers.

Shane respected what she was doing, just as he had done when she'd dealt with Tyler Jordan. When Kate was finally finished, hours later at 2:00 a.m., she looked pale and exhausted. They took time to transfer Deke to another bedroom where the bed wasn't soaked with blood. The whole time, Ernie had stood worried outside the door, asking questions and dreading answers.

"Is he going to be all right?" Shane asked quietly out of earshot of Ernie.

Looking at the young man lying unconscious on the bed, almost a pale imitation of himself, Kate sighed. "I don't know. I'm not a doctor."

"You ever heard of somebody surviving something like this?"

"Yeah. People do." Kate took another deep breath and let it out. "And people don't. He's lost a lot of blood that we can't replace."

"What about a blood transfusion?"

She looked at him as if he'd just sprouted a second head.

"I could give him blood."

"That's awfully generous."

Sarcasm. Shane got angry enough to react before he knew it. A harsh response was on his tongue before he curbed it. He made himself let it go. If anybody had the right to act somewhat antisocial, it was Kate Garrett. "It was a sincere offer."

She looked away, and maybe she looked a little ashamed. "Do you know what blood type you are?"

"O," he said, remembering that much from the times he'd been shot and had been in surgery.

"O what? Positive or negative?"

Shane thought about it for a moment, then shook his head. "I don't know." Evidently blood type wasn't one of those useful bits of information that stuck with someone like a social security number.

"I bet you don't know Deke's blood type either," she went on.

Standing, Shane went outside the room to where Ernie sat on the floor with the shotgun standing between his knees.

Ernie looked up, worry and fear etched deeply into his big, broad face. In the darkness, he looked like he had a new bruise by his right eye, and his nose appeared swelled. Shane didn't know when that had happened, but he suspected it was when Ernie and Kate Garrett were in the mobile home alone. Before they had both come down the ladder so rapidly

"Is…is he okay?" Ernie asked.

"He's still alive," Shane said. "Thanks to Kate."

At least Ernie had the decency to look a little ashamed.

"Good. I don't want to have to go back an' tell his momma he passed on."

Going back would be a bad idea in general, Shane couldn't help thinking. *The police and the FBI will be waiting for you there.* Then he blew out a breath and tried to force away some of the hostility he felt. Maybe Kate wasn't the only one with an anger-management problem at the moment. "Do you know Deke's blood type?"

Ernie's eyes widened in panic, gleaming in the candle-light. "No," he answered nervously. "Don't know my own."

That makes two of us, Shane thought.

"But we're cousins," Ernie went on. "We share blood. It's probably the same. I can give him what he needs. Ever' drop if I have to."

"Doesn't work like that," Shane said. "Just because you're cousins doesn't mean you're the same blood type. And if we give him the wrong blood—if we were even able to find a way to transfuse blood—giving Deke the wrong kind could kill him."

Ernie leaned his head back against the wall. "Just let me know what you need me to do. Until then, I'm gonna sit right here outside his door an' pray for him. Might help if y'all prayed for him too."

Quiet, derisive laughter came from the living room. Glancing in that direction, Shane barely made Raymond Jolly out in the darkness. A cigarette ember glowed orange-red for a moment, highlighting Jolly's harsh features. In addition to another .357 Magnum and ammunition and food and clothing, they'd also found a carton of cigarettes.

Jolly let a stream of gray smoke out through his nose and didn't say anything.

Shane couldn't imagine Raymond Jolly praying. Despite how he felt about Ernie, Shane dropped a hand on the guy's shoulder in support, then turned and went back into the bedroom where Kate sat with Deke.

"Ernie doesn't know Deke's blood type," Shane said.

"Surprise," Kate said bitterly. "It wouldn't have mattered. I've never transfused blood before. I could kill him just as easily as help him."

Shane stood next to her. Everything in him screamed out to take her into his arms, hold her and tell her that everything was going to be all right and that she'd see her kids again soon. But that would be a lie. The one thing FBI Special Agent Shane Warren knew was how uncertain life could be. A person never knew where a road was going to take him. Or her. Hell, none of them might live to see morning.

Deke's labored breathing filled the room. Lightning danced outside, slicing the shadows inside the room to pieces while it lasted.

Kate sat quiet, contained. Shane watched her, calm—at least on the outside—where most other women he knew outside of female FBI agents would be falling apart.

And the way she'd jumped into the water was nothing short of amazing. Despite what he thought of her as a strong individual, he kept remembering how she'd looked in the shower the night before. The gleaming curves of her body had haunted his dreams.

Lost in the quiet of the moment, Shane wondered if telling her that he was an FBI agent would help. But he decided against it. Knowledge was power. She could use that against him, turn the tables between Jolly and him and make the situation even worse. He still couldn't take the chance.

"If he was in a hospital," Kate said softly, "he'd get better care."

"I know," Shane said. "But that's not going to happen tonight." He rubbed his face. "Maybe if he makes it through the night, we can do something like that."

Her dark-green eyes turned hard and distant. "Sure," she said.

He knew she didn't believe him, but that was the real crux of the problem. When the Director had given him the assignment to gain Jolly's confidence and break him out of prison, the stipulation was that no one would get hurt. Now Phil Lewis was mysteriously dead, and Deke had a foot in the grave and the other on a banana peel.

Not one of your more inspiring performances, Warren, Shane told himself.

Thunder woke Kate. Or maybe it was the cramped position she was sleeping in. She'd curled up as best as she could in the armchair that overfilled the bedroom. Mobile homes were designed for Spartan living at best, and whoever lived here was pushing the envelope.

A blanket covered her. She frowned. She hadn't put it there. It bothered her that someone had touched her—Almost touched you, she corrected herself to ease the paranoia that slammed into her—and she hadn't known it. The blanket, instead of providing warmth, was a further indication of how vulnerable she was.

Memory of the rough treatment she'd had at the hands of Monte Carter and Ernie Franks had made her restless. She'd also felt the hunting knife bite deeply into Carter's thigh again, and had relived the horror and guilt of knowing she'd killed the man even though it had been him or her. And she'd kept seeing Deke in the alligator's jaws over and over. Only this time the young man hadn't escaped and bits and pieces of him kept floating up at her. Sometimes it had been Tyler Jordan in the alligator's jaws and not Deke Hannibal.

She pushed the blanket off, resenting its implied accusation that she couldn't take care of herself. Then, chilled because her clothes were still damp although no longer running with water, she pulled the blanket back on.

Shane Warren lay in the middle of the floor. He had his shoes and socks off, probably to prevent foot rot. She'd done the same thing. He had his hands behind his head and was snoring softly.

He had a different appearance in the jeans, T-shirt, and flannel shirt he'd buttoned up to stave off the cold. Watching him sleep, Kate felt that he was somehow softer and more vulnerable. As though somehow he didn't belong with Jolly and Ernie any more than Deke did. Her conflicted feelings about Shane Warren annoyed her. If she had the chance to escape and could get away without him, she wondered if she'd feel guilty leaving him behind. Then she put that out of her mind.

He's a convict, she told herself. He's killed people. Sold drugs. He's not out here because he's innocent.

She looked back at Deke, lying so silent and still in the bed. Of all the escapees, Deke was the innocent. Going by how he'd acted, how protective of her he'd been, as well as how reluctant he'd been to take part in any violence, Kate felt that maybe Deke had gotten trapped with his cousin in a manner not too unlike her own situation.

Listening to his ragged breathing, she worried about Deke. He was going to die, she knew, if he went untreated. Allowing that went against everything Kate believed in. On her trips, she took care of people. When she had Steven and Hannah, she took care of them too.

Thunder continued to boom in the distance. Rain pelted the mobile home's tin roof in a constant staccato of sound. The home swayed gently in the trees instead of being tossed.

Deke shifted a little then, mumbling, "No, Ernie! Don't kill her, man! She's begging you!" His face knotted in pain.

At first, Kate thought Deke was remembering the earlier events before the alligator attack. But she hadn't begged. And, Deke hadn't asked his cousin not to kill her; he'd only—

"Listen to her! She's *begging*. I know you don't speak Spanish, man, but I do. She's askin' you not to kill her!" He twitched, quivered and moaned. "You shot her, Ernie! You shot her in the face!"

Then he went still for a long time and Kate thought maybe the nightmare had killed him. A moment more passed, then Deke took a long, slow, wet breath.

Breaking out of the hypnosis the story had instilled in her, thinking that maybe she knew how Desiree Martini had met her fate, Kate glanced at her watch and saw that it was 4:47 a.m. If she moved now, maybe she had a chance. Otherwise she was certain she was going to end up just like the missing heiress.

Tonight, no one had secured her with the handcuffs. Easing up from the chair, she hooked her fingers through the shoe-strings of her hiking boots, tucked into them the dry pair of socks she'd taken for herself from the home, and moved slowly across the floor.

Out in the hall, she crept to the living room, ignoring the side door because Ernie had complained it was stuck when he'd tried to go out it. Her best chance was the front door in the living room.

Ernie was asleep on the couch, the shotgun cradled in his arms like a lover. She didn't feel too wicked for hoping that the man rolled over wrong and blew off his own head. But she knew she'd never be able to get the shotgun from him without a fight.

Raymond Jolly slept in the big easy chair, his bare feet splayed out before him. The .357 Magnum was tucked between his hip and the chair arm, his hand resting lightly over it.

At the door, Kate took a deep breath and put her hand on the doorknob. Her fingers trembled and she felt weak. *Please,* she thought. *I just want to get home.* Nightmares about Steven and Hannah getting caught in the flood, or getting hurt by some faceless criminal named Hugh Rollins that Bryce had betrayed had plagued her waking thoughts and her sleep.

She didn't know Hugh Rollins. But if he was a career criminal, and if he was no worse than Jolly and Ernie and Monte Carter, Kate knew her son and daughter were in danger.

If Bryce had told her the truth of what was going on, Kate knew she wouldn't have left that night. Or, at least, she wouldn't have left the children there at her house.

She worked hard to tell herself that Megan had gotten the kids to safety or that her dad had come by and taken them to safety.

She steeled herself and turned the doorknob.

The knob ratcheted only slightly.

That wasn't enough noise to wake anyone! she told herself desperately. No one could have heard that!

Then the menacing triple click of a revolver being drawn back to full-cock echoed inside the small room.

"Don't, Ms. Garrett," Jolly said softly.

Kate froze. Her body trembled, waiting to be released and spring into action. She made herself remain still.

"Good," Jolly went on. "Now come away from the door before I make those kids of yours orphans on their mother's side."

Hot tears of frustration and fear burned Kate's eyes. The hiking boots felt like lead weights at the end of her arm. She turned toward the man, hating him with every fiber of her being. Her throat was locked tight in inarticulate rage.

Don't cry, she told herself. Whatever you do, *don't* you let him see you cry.

"You move very quietly when you want to." Jolly stood, towering above her. "You might even have gotten away."

Kate knew Jolly said that to taunt her, to let her know how close she'd come to getting away. Biting her lips, she didn't react.

"What's going on?" Shane stood in the hallway, his blond hair in disarray, looking windblown and tired.

"We almost lost our guide," Jolly said laconically. He held up his hand and let the handcuffs dangle. "See that it doesn't happen again. I don't fancy trying to swim out of here in alligator-infested waters. She makes another attempt, I'm going to cuff her hands behind her back, tie a beefsteak around her neck, and drop her into the water. We'll see how well she does at alligator-wrestling then."

The pop-pop-pop-popping of an outboard motor sputtering to life woke Kate. Blearily, she gazed around the dark room and listened to the sound of rain. With the storm continuing, she didn't know if it was early or late. The handcuff on her wrist held her securely chained to the nearby window mechanism.

Raymond Jolly stood in the doorway. The .357 Magnum was thrust through the waistband of his pants. He smiled. "Good morning, Kate."

She didn't say anything, centering herself so that nothing he did could touch her.

Outside, the outboard engine stuttered and died.

"We seem to be having a little trouble with the engine this morning," Jolly told her. He sounded hard and distant, as if preoccupied by another matter. "I don't think it's anything Shane can't figure out. He's pretty handy with things. Escapes. Boats to the Grand Caymans. That kind of thing. But I have to admit, I liked him a hell of a lot more before you came along. He was more...tractable. Like his interests went along with mine." He shrugged. "Which they did. After all, he was cutting himself in for part of the ransom money."

Kate watched the man. She didn't know why he was talking so much, but the experience was unnerving.

"When a man's greedy," Jolly said, "you can count on him to do exactly what he says he's going to do. Or what you know he's going to do. Which is, whatever he has to in order to get the money."

On the bed, Deke moved weakly. The young man was still alive. Kate felt a bit hopeful. If Deke could make it through the night, there was a good chance he could live long enough to get to a doctor who could finish what she had started.

The outboard engine surged to brief life again before fading out.

"Then you entered the picture," Jolly said. "Not just once, which I could understand, but *twice*. Like some kind of damned albatross."

"I don't believe in luck," Kate said.

"Neither do I," Jolly said. "Which means I have to wonder what the hell you were doing out on that road when Shane's escape plan came apart."

"Getting my day started," Kate said. "I was on my way to a campsite—" She was talking because she was getting afraid that if she didn't he'd kill her due to his own paranoia.

"Shut up!" Jolly ordered. His face turned red and he spat when he spoke.

Kate read the anger in the man then, and knew that it wasn't any of her doing. Jolly's own personal demons were getting the best of him. Maybe he was tired and scared, starting to think he wasn't going to get out of the swamp, much less the state of Florida.

"As if having you along screwing with Shane's head wasn't bad enough," Jolly went on. "Now I've got to deal with this!" He pointed at Deke.

A bad feeling coiled restlessly in Kate's stomach.

"If we'd been on our own when that damned alligator jumped up and got Deke, he'd have been gone," Jolly said. "In a heartbeat. But you had to jump in with him, with just a damned straight razor. And you somehow *saved* him." His chest rose and fell rapidly.

Kate shifted on the chair, drawing in her legs so she could defend herself against him if it came to that. Of course, if it came to that, arms and legs weren't going to stop a .357 Magnum round.

"To make matters worse," Jolly said, "this poor, dying bastard won't have the decency to go ahead and die."

"Deke made it through the night," Kate said calmly. She named the young man, hoping to make him more of a human being than a problem for Raymond Jolly. "He's young. He's strong. There's the possibility that he can make it." She paused, hoping to get through to Jolly. "If he gets medical assistance."

"But that's the rub, isn't it, Kate?" Jolly showed her a cold smile. "We can't exactly take Deke to a hospital, can we? I mean, we just got out of prison, we've got money to get, and I don't plan on going back." He stepped in close to the bed and looked at Deke. "So we have to come up with a new plan. Something that frees us up a little."

Cold menace filled Kate in a way the rain and the sea surge hadn't. She tried to think of something to say, but before anything came to mind, Jolly picked up a pillow from the bed and held it over Deke's face. Jolly leaned on the pillow as Deke woke and tried to fight back.

Leaping up, Kate ran toward the bed. The handcuffs brought her up short, biting into her wrist. Jolly and Deke remained just out of reach.

Chapter 11

"*Shane!*"

The ragged cry came from the mobile house stuck in the trees above Shane. He stood in the stern of the johnboat, the carburetor partially disassembled so he could clean out the debris that was choking it down. Blue plastic tarp covered him so the rain wouldn't get into the engine and cause even more problems.

"*Shane! Shane!*"

Adrenaline laced Shane's system as he pulled out from under the tarp and turned toward the ladder. They'd moored the johnboat to the nearest tree.

"*Shane!*"

Leaping from the johnboat, feeling it slide across the smooth water away from him, Shane clawed at the rope ladder leading up to the covered porch. He didn't make the distance, dropping into the water and sinking immediately.

Panic gripped him as the water closed over his head, and

he thought about the alligators he'd seen only that morning. They'd evidently been drawn to the area by the one Kate had killed. The corpse had gotten tangled up in some branches beneath the mobile home.

He heard Kate's cry again, sounding more distant while he was underwater. Kicking out, he swam to the surface and caught the rope ladder. He climbed rapidly, hands and feet moving together as he hauled himself up.

His breath was short by the time he reached the landing where Ernie was thumbing shells into the shotgun after cleaning it.

"What the hell?" Ernie asked, racking the slide to chamber a round.

Shane resisted the impulse to rip the shotgun from Ernie's grip and knock the big man into the water. That would have been overplaying the hand that he'd been dealt and would have cost him the opportunity to find Desiree Martini's body when cadaver dogs and search teams hadn't been able to do it.

Kate's yelling, he told himself. *That means she's all right.*

He raced through the mobile home to the bedroom where Deke was and where Kate had been left handcuffed. After she'd almost escaped last night, Shane hadn't tried to fight for her freedom from the cuffs.

In the room, Jolly stood by the bed, looking bored and a little put out. He jerked a thumb at Kate, who stood straining at the end of the handcuffs.

"Man, she's gone totally psycho," Jolly said. "Screaming and yelling and carrying on."

Shane looked at Kate, who was staring at Deke on the bed. Tears flowed down her cheeks and she looked more scared than he'd ever seen her.

"He killed Deke," she accused. "He put a pillow over his face and smothered him. Deke was still alive."

Crossing to the bed, Shane looked down at the young man. Deke stared up sightlessly, his eyes glassy in death. Shane picked up one of Deke's arms and let it drop. The young man hadn't been dead long.

"Do you know CPR?" Kate asked. "Maybe you can do CPR."

Shane shook his head. "It's too late."

"Get these cuffs off me!" Kate ordered. "Get them off *now!* Maybe it's not too late!"

Turning to Jolly, Shane said, "Give me the key, Raymond." He held out his hand.

"It's a waste of time, man," Jolly said. "That boy's done passed."

"It hasn't been long!" Kate cried. "There's still a chance!" She looked at Shane with those dark-green eyes. "Let me try!"

"The key," Shane said, with more force in his voice. *"Please."* But he wasn't asking; he was telling. And Raymond Jolly knew it.

For just an instant, Jolly's hand slid dangerously close to the .357 at his waistband. Then he smiled and took the handcuff key from his shirt pocket. "Sure, Shane. You just don't let her get away while she's going through all these theatrics." He tossed the key into the air and left the room.

Shane caught the key and crossed to Kate.

"Sorry about your cousin, Ernie," Jolly said as he passed the big man. "He was a brave young man."

"Thanks," Ernie choked out, wiping tears from his eyes. "He was, wasn't he? The salt of the earth."

As Shane watched, Kate threw herself on the bed, on top of Deke, and put her hands on his chest after measuring where she wanted them to go. She pushed on his chest for a moment, then slid off, pinched Deke's nostrils, opened his mouth and breathed into his lungs a few, measured breaths.

Then she went back to the chest and started shoving again. Tears rolled down her face. She was crying the whole time she was striving to bring life back into the young man, as if his death were all her fault and she hadn't tried everything she could do twice last night to save him.

She worked at it for over five minutes before Shane walked over to her and put his arms around her from behind. Holding her, even then, during such an emotionally charged time, felt like the most natural thing in the world.

"Kate," he whispered in her ear as she fought to get him off her.

"Let me go!"

Shane hung on, riding out her efforts to free herself. "Kate, you did everything you could."

"I can save him! I've brought people back that were gone longer than he's been!"

Wrapping her with his arms, Shane held on to her. He knew he was leaving himself open to attack. She could knee him, punch him or bite him at any moment. The fact that she didn't meant that she knew she needed to accept what he was saying.

"Listen," he whispered. "You did everything you could do. He just didn't have much left to give. He's gone. You just can't call back someone that far gone."

Gradually, she stopped struggling and stopped crying. She turned rigid in his grasp.

"Let me go," she whispered hoarsely. "Let me go."

Shane did, unwrapping his arms and stepping back.

Without a word, Kate turned on him and slapped him so hard it turned his face. He tasted blood as his already split lips reopened. He throttled the savage instinct in him to respond in kind. Maybe he hadn't had that coming, but she'd needed to hit somebody. He could understand that. He'd been feeling like that himself the last couple days.

"Okay," he said. "Okay."

She walked away from him, causing Ernie to step back hurriedly.

Ernie took his ball cap off and held it. "I appreciate what you tried to do for Deke, Ms. Garrett. Truly I do. And I'm sorry about what happened last night. I mean, sometimes I just can't control myself."

"That's some friend you have there," Kate accused as she stopped in front of him. Then she looked back at Shane. "Both of them."

Red-faced, Ernie looked down at his feet.

Entering the bathroom, Kate slammed the door behind her. And locked it. He knew she was aware the flimsy door wouldn't hold, but he also knew she needed some kind of wall between her and her enemies.

Shane let out a long, low breath and looked at Deke dead on the bed. Ernie walked slowly over to his cousin's side, then dropped on to his knees by the bed, put his hands together before him like a child, and started praying for Deke.

Anger, dark and relentless, stirred inside Shane. He needed out of this assignment. He needed to get it finished. And he was prepared to do that. Mr. and Mrs. Martini would have to wait just a little longer to find their daughter's body. Sooner or later it would turn up. They nearly always did.

But he was going to put a stop to Raymond Jolly's hit parade. Right now.

Shane strode into the living room and found Jolly out smoking on the porch under the tin canopy. He appeared to be watching the rain, as though nothing had ever happened in that back room.

"Don't come at me riled up," Jolly said, removing the cigarette from his mouth. "That damn woman was lying about everything she said in there." He shifted, coming around, his hand a scant inch from the .357's butt.

Shane held up, knowing if he kept approaching Jolly in the mood he was in that the man would draw and fire before he could reach him.

"She was lying," Jolly repeated, "just the way she was lying the other night when she put on that act like you and her were planning on taking the ransom money." He breathed out smoke, then hit the cigarette again. "She's trying to split us up, Shane. Any fool can see that." His eyes narrowed. "I guess my question is, are you going to get bent out of shape about it? Or are you going to go with me today to get that ransom money?"

Today? The opportunity buzzed into Shane's head. Today. He took a deep breath and let it out. Just one more day.

"She wasn't lying about you killing Deke," Shane said. "I know you killed him."

Jolly's smile spread, but he didn't look relaxed. He rested his hand around the gun butt. "You think so, do you?"

"I *know* you did," Shane said. "Smothering someone can cause petechiae. It nearly always happens with ligature strangulation."

"What's petechiae?"

Shane kept himself calm, detached. He'd had a lifetime to learn how to do that. He pointed toward his eyes. "It's caused by small blood vessels rupturing in the eyes." He paused. "Deke had petechiae. You smothered him."

"How do you know about petechiae?"

"One of my mother's boyfriends strangled her," Shane said. For just a moment he was back in that small one-bedroom apartment in Mobile, Alabama, and his mother was on the couch, hours dead and already cold to the touch. That was the trick to doing good undercover work: cutting the lie with so much truth that the lie almost wasn't a lie at all but just one turn that hadn't been taken. Sometimes he wondered how he kept from becoming the person he so often portrayed. "I found her in the living room the next morning." Years of telling the story kept his voice from breaking. "I was eight years old. It's something that kind of sticks with you."

"Man, you are all out of family, aren't you? Dead father. Dead brother. Dead mother."

Shane kept all the old pain from balling up on him through a sheer effort of will. "Keeps the Christmas card list short."

Jolly looked a little uncomfortable but didn't say anything.

"I know," Shane heard himself say, as though he was someone else entirely, "that you did what you had to do with Deke. There's no way we could have taken him with us. And he would have died anyway."

"Yeah," Jolly said.

"If you look at it right," Shane made himself say, and added a slight smile, "what you did was put Deke out of his misery."

Jolly nodded. "Damn right I did."

"And out of *our* misery." Shane took a breath, knowing that Jolly was taking in the callous attitude with a newfound respect. It also better balanced out the shift in power since Kate Garrett had shown up. Both of them had weaknesses now, and they both knew what they were. "I don't think Ernie's going to be that understanding or generous about his cousin's death."

"You're probably right," Jolly said. "So it would be in our best interests not to tell him, wouldn't it?"

"It would."

Jolly took a deep breath. "What do you want, Shane?"

"We're down to three people," Shane said. "I want a full cut of the ransom. Three and a third million dollars."

"You're getting greedy."

"Some might say that. But when we escaped prison, you were in for twenty percent of a ten-million-dollar pie. That's two million bucks. With Phil, Deke and Monte out of the way, you're up over fifty percent."

"A fifty-fifty split between Ernie and me sounds better," Jolly said laconically. "Minus what you and I agreed on for a finder's fee on the boat."

"Sure," Shane said. "If Ernie could get you a boat out of Florida, you'd probably be better off doing that. But he can't." He paused. "I can. More than that, I can watch your back if Ernie starts thinking too hard about how *conveniently* Deke died before we left today."

Jolly flicked his cigarette butt into the water far below. "All right," he said. "Just don't get too greedy, Shane."

"Sure," Shane said. But he couldn't wait to find the ransom and Desiree Martini's corpse so he could take Jolly off the board. All he had to do was make sure he kept Kate and himself alive while he did it.

In the hallway, Kate stood frozen, replaying what Shane and Jolly had just said. She couldn't believe Shane could be so cold, so callous. Then she thought about the losses he'd suffered in his life. All of his family was dead.

If it's true. Still, she remembered his eyes when he'd told her about his granny and his father and brother. She'd believed him. She still did.

Not having family made a difference. She knew that from having seen it in people she knew and clients she'd met. Even

Tyler Jordan was better off having a father who was a functioning alcoholic than having no one.

But Shane had just sold away the truth of Deke's murder. *For a few million dollars.* Maybe it was easier, she decided, when the numbers were bigger. Big numbers had always attracted Bryce, and he had had a family he'd walked away from time and again.

For a moment, Kate was lost in thought, exhausted by everything she'd gone through, especially the guilt over Deke's death—*It was murder!*—and the realization that Shane Warren had reached an all-time low in her estimation even though he'd dived into the water with her to rescue Deke from the alligator.

All of the parts of the man, even in the short time she'd known him, were confusing. She still couldn't reconcile what Shane had done with what she knew about him.

"You all right?"

Startled, Kate looked up. Shane stood at the other end of the hallway. His blond hair hung wetly down to his shoulders.

"Yeah," she answered, lifting her chin and crossing her arms over her breasts. "I'm fine." She stared into his eyes until he finally looked past her to the bedroom.

"How's Ernie doing?" he asked.

"Don't know."

Shane nodded. "We're going to be pulling out in a few minutes. Get your stuff together or you're leaving without it." Cold and impersonal, he turned and walked away.

Kate hated him then, with everything in her. But she couldn't forget how soft his touch had been when he'd pulled her back off Deke's body, how soothing he'd sounded talking to her and telling her she'd done all she could, not realizing that Jolly had killed Deke with her watching to drive home his point to her.

She had the point now: she was going to live if she got along to get along. Till the exact minute Jolly decided she was going to die.

And Shane Warren wasn't going to stand in Jolly's way because he was receiving a bigger cut of the ransom money now. Her life wouldn't be hers again until she escaped.

Hurricane Genevieve had hooked back around after driving across Florida, according to the portable radio Ernie had found back in the mobile home. There were extra batteries as well. The storm was now headed back inland and would make the coast by evening. Kate knew from past experience that it would stick around for another couple of days till it blew itself out.

Kate sat in the johnboat's stern. The cuffs felt heavy on her wrists. She was conscious of Shane watching her from behind a pair of sunglasses he'd taken from the mobile home.

Jolly seemed more antsy than ever. "Ms. Garrett," he said politely.

Pointedly ignoring him, Kate looked out at the flooded swamp. A parade of five drowned ducklings floated past the johnboat, yellow puffs of feathers against the gray-green murk of the water. They'd passed five dead white-tailed deer, two of them fawns, a number of rats, nutria, dozens of wild turkeys and even a bear. The flooding had impacted the area in ways that would take years to recover from. In the wetlands, even an inch rise in the water table affected life cycles for miles and years. Some of them, Kate knew sadly, wouldn't recover at all.

Despite the large land masses involved, the Everglades were a fragile eco-system. Man had hurt it most of all, but the tropical storms were devastating.

"Ms. Garrett, don't ignore me," Jolly said. "If you do, I'll hurt you to get your attention."

Kate turned to him, squinting her eyes against the rain. "What?"

"Good." Jolly showed her a self-satisfied smirk. "Which way is Everglades City?"

Kate pointed. "Five or six miles. That way."

"You'll keep us on course then?"

"Yeah."

"See that you do."

Less than half an hour later, the outboard prop got caught in a trotline that had floated loose from some fisherman's private fishing area.

Shane leaned the motor forward but couldn't clear the prop quickly. His back and shoulders ached from the last few days in the water and from sitting hunched over in the stern, slowly guiding the johnboat through the morass and murk. There was no clear path, no true way to go that guaranteed safe passage.

"We need to put in somewhere," Shane said, pushing his sunglasses up because the evening gloom was deepening the constant gray of the stormy sky.

"Can't you clear it?" Jolly demanded.

Shane took a deep breath and let it out. "That's a trotline. It's old rope filled with fishhooks. If I don't watch what I'm doing, I'm going to end up with my hands cut to pieces. Then I'd have to worry about infections. Not only that, the rope is old and frayed. The prop, which wasn't in great shape to begin with, chewed the rope up pretty good. I'm going to have to break it down to get it cleaned out enough to trust."

Jolly frowned.

"Unless you want me to do a half-ass job and we can all cross our fingers that it won't break down somewhere between here and Everglades City. If it does, we can row in, but in a boat this size, we could be at that for a while." Shane nodded at the sky. "Plus, as dark as it's getting, we wouldn't make Everglades City before nightfall anyway. Trying to pilot this boat through that mess isn't a good idea."

"There's an island over there," Ernie said, pointing a halogen flashlight at a hilltop that jutted above the flood level.

"That's not an island," Kate said. "It's just a hill that didn't get submerged."

"Whatever," Ernie said. Now that they had left his cousin's body in the mobile home and out of sight, he seemed to have forgotten his newfound respect for the woman. "Looks like an island to me."

The knob of land was maybe a hundred yards across, filled with bald cypress and brush. Birds—gulls, songbirds, blue herons, owls and anhingas—lined the tree branches, all of them forced into closer proximity due to the submerged swamplands.

A scream tore through the night, sounding almost like a woman in pain.

"What the hell was that?" Ernie asked.

Kate spoke quietly. "There are some who say the swamp is haunted. People tell me all the time that they see ghosts out here." She looked at Ernie. "Do you believe in ghosts?"

Ernie gripped his shotgun a little more tightly but didn't answer.

"That was a bobcat," Shane said. "Nothing to worry about. They rarely attack humans." He nodded at the hilltop. "With all the flooding, there are probably a lot of animals holed up there. Play your cards right and, if we find a dry place to have a fire, you can be eating fresh roasted turkey."

Ernie grinned. "Sounds good to me."

Breaking out the oars, Shane inserted them into the locks.

He and Ernie rowed them to shore. They stopped at a shelf of limestone that jutted out of the ground, then Ernie waded ashore and moored the boat to a tree.

The rain picked up in tempo, answering the call of the storm. Under the thick canopy of tree branches, the rain and the wind was somewhat blunted. Dry firewood was impossible to find, but Ernie had brought a sack of charcoal briquettes from the last mobile house in the trees. He dug a fire pit, lined it with the driest brush he could find, then poured half of the big bag into the pit and set it ablaze. After only a few minutes, the charcoal started to gray and the makeshift semi-tent warmed considerably.

Shane removed the outboard engine from the johnboat and carried it into the shelter. Fatigue chewed into him, and he almost jumped out of his skin when he heard the shotgun bang. His head swiveled and he looked for Kate, making sure she was still there. She was, lying down at the back of the shelter and sleeping, her cuffed wrists resting lightly across her stomach below her breasts. He'd gotten so wrapped up in finishing the outboard motor up that he'd lost track of time.

"Easy," Jolly said. He sat in a folding camp chair at the shelter's edge and peered out at the night. Vivid veins of lightning chased through the dark sky. "It's just Ernie. He decided to try for one of those turkeys we keep hearing in the woods."

Shane nodded, then stood and stretched in an effort to alleviate the compression in his back.

A moment later Ernie came strutting back into the shelter carrying a dead turkey. "Got one," he declared proudly.

Shane figured it was a lot like when cavemen first started bringing food home to the cave.

Ernie walked over and kicked Kate's boots.

She glared up at him without saying a word.

"You know how to clean game, right?" Ernie demanded.

"Yeah," she answered.

"Let's grill that up."

Shane expected Kate to object, but she surprised him. Instead, she sat up and asked for a knife and to get the cuffs off. Then she expertly plucked the turkey's feathers while letting it finish bleeding out. Afterwards, she gutted the bird, then cut it up to put on the grill stand over the fire pit.

Within minutes, the smell of fresh meat roasting over charcoal filled the shelter. In spite of the situation, Shane listened to his stomach rumble.

Without a word, Kate tended to the meat while Jolly and Ernie made small talk. As he put the prop back together, Shane kept listening, hoping they would say something about the Desiree Martini kidnapping, but they never did. He ate pieces of turkey, missing salt and pepper and seasoning, but enjoying the almost home-cooked meal.

But he wondered why Kate had been so willing to prepare the turkey for them. He'd learned over the last couple of days that she never did anything without an ulterior motive. She was like him in that regard.

Kate waited till the time was right to make her move. As Jolly and Ernie sat and told stories, and Shane watched them both closely, though without showing too much interest, she'd listened to the animal noises outside the shelter. She'd known that the smell of the kill, the blood and the cooked meat, would bring the creatures from the brush to inspect the shelter.

They were curious, after all, like any wild thing. And after having been trapped on the limited land space, they were hungry, driven near to desperation and falling upon each other to survive.

Something already dead provided an easy meal for those that would eat carrion, and there were a number of them that hunted nocturnally. Shane remained quiet as the two other men talked. To look at him, no one would really notice how much attention he was paying to them. But Kate saw because she was used to watching predators. Especially feline predators.

Shane was hunting. Just like a big cat, he was biding his time.

He's probably planning on taking *all* the ransom money, Kate told herself sourly. He's already muscled his way into a third of it. He's only one more body away from half. Looking at things in that light, it was easier to understand why Shane had snapped Monte Carter's neck a few days ago. And she had to wonder more about Phil Lewis's death.

Maybe the bus mishap had happened *exactly* where he'd wanted it to, giving him the opportunity to whittle down the competition.

More snuffling sounded in the brush behind the tent. Kate knew she had to act fast, before the others figured out what she was up to.

She sat up and announced, "I need to go to the bathroom."

Jolly looked at her for a moment, then turned to Ernie. "Take her."

"Me?" Ernie was aghast. "I'm always taking her."

"And you'll take her now," Jolly said.

Kate relaxed a little, there was always the chance that Jolly would take her. She knew she'd have more trouble overcoming him. But she felt certain Ernie was afraid of the dark.

She got to her feet and held her hands out. Jolly stood long enough to take the cuffs off, then dropped back into the camp chair.

"If she tries to run," Jolly told Ernie, "shoot her."

"I will," Ernie replied.

Outside the shelter, cold rain hammered Kate. She turned and walked into the brush behind the shelter.

Ernie played his halogen light over her. "It's cold an' wet out here," he complained. "Ain't no reason to go far. Just far enough."

"Sure," she said, senses acute to the movements around her that Ernie hadn't quite caught. She turned toward the one she wanted. The scar on the back of her right leg tightened.

Only two steps farther on, a wild hog jumped into motion. It was a smaller one of the wild ones, no more than a couple hundred pounds. But he made a lot of noise tearing through the brush.

Ernie jumped, trying to bring the flashlight and the shotgun to bear at the same time. Taking advantage of his confusion, Kate stepped into him, grabbed the shotgun's barrel, and threw her elbow into his face, wishing she had the Asp baton because the contact wouldn't hurt so much and Ernie would already have been down.

As it was, he managed to hang on to the shotgun even while he was going down. It discharged, firing into the air. Pellets skidded along branches and brought down a deluge of rainwater and freshly shorn leaves.

Kate shoved a leg out and tripped Ernie, shoving into him with her hip and using the leverage for all it was worth.

"Damn bitch!" he snarled. "You ain't gettin' my gun!" He hung on to the weapon viciously.

Kate doubled up her right hand into a fist and slammed it into Ernie's face. In addition to the fear that filled her, knowing that neither Jolly nor Shane would keep the animal off her now, she stoked the anger from the way he'd attacked her the previous night. She hit him three times, as quickly as she could, listening to him yell for help the whole time, then kneed him in the crotch twice.

One of them kicked the flashlight and sent it skidding off into the brush.

Then something cut the wind in front of her face. She heard the harsh report of the .357 Magnum a moment later.

Releasing Ernie, Kate threw herself forward, stumbling over the man, aware of the animal eyes in the darkness watching her. They scattered as she stayed low and went through them. A bobcat, three wild hogs, mink and otters scrambled from in front of her, adding to the confusion Jolly was firing into.

Running to the nearest tree, Kate took cover and looked back. As she watched, Jolly and Shane were getting to their feet. Jolly seemed to be a little wobbly, but he was conscious and lifting the heavy Magnum to aim at Shane.

A burst of buckshot tore into the tree just above Kate's head, leaving jagged streaks of white bark in its wake. She turned and fled, charging through the forest, wondering if she'd ever understand what Shane's motivations were.

The Magnum emptied quickly. Kate kept running, hoping just to stay alive.

Chapter 12

The sound of the shotgun blast brought Shane up from the ground in a heartbeat, but fast as he was, he was a step behind Jolly when they left the shelter. Outside, the brush seemed alive with animals. He didn't know how that had happened, but he assumed Kate had had something to do with it. She hadn't needed to go to the bathroom; this had been part of an escape attempt.

Shane swore to himself as he paced Jolly. Instead of passing the man, Shane stayed a step behind him and to his right, so it would be easy for him to move against Jolly if he had to, and hard for Jolly to turn and point the pistol at him.

The wind had picked up strength again as the storm hit the coastal areas once more. Driving rain slashed through the trees. Lightning arcs blazed across the sky, igniting the heavens for brief periods and ruining Shane's night vision.

Then, ahead, between a copse of cypress trees, the lightning blazed again and lit up the struggling figures of Kate and Ernie Franks. She hit him in the face with her fist, obviously trying to separate the big man from the shotgun.

Jolly came up short and brought the .357 Magnum in a two-handed grip. Shane dived for the man, throwing his arms wide to take Jolly down. He hit Jolly across the back, driving him forward, hoping that the big pistol would get jarred free.

When Shane hit the ground, he hadn't counted on the mud. He tried to hold on to Jolly, but the man's shirt ripped in his grasp and the mud caused him to slide a few feet away.

Shane shoved himself to his feet, intending to throw himself back at Jolly, but he couldn't get any traction in the mud. His feet kept sliding out from under him. When Jolly raised the pistol, Shane dove into the bush. The bullet intended for his face smacked into the mud.

"I'm gonna kill you, Shane!" Jolly screamed.

Already a believer, Shane ran, staring through the shadows that filled the darkness as he tried to spot Kate. Jolly's bullets chased him, tearing through the brush and screaming into trees. Slightly ahead of Shane, the side of a tree suddenly erupted into a shower of bark splinters that he ran through.

The land mass was only a hundred yards across. Shane grew grimly aware that not too many good hiding places existed. He also knew that Jolly and Ernie didn't seem too keen on following them into the darkness at the moment. Then he realized they were staying there to protect the boat.

That made Shane feel a little better. Jolly wouldn't let them escape, but at least pursuit might not be immediate. All Jolly would have to realize was that he could take the spark plug out of the outboard motor and shove it into his pocket to ensure it would be there when he got back for it.

"Kate!" he yelled. He was in it now. There was no way he could rebuild what little trust Jolly had had in him. "Kate, I need to talk to you! Damn it!"

Realizing he'd lost her in the mad scramble and could no longer tell one shadow from another, Shane stopped. He locked his fingers behind his head and lifted his arms to open his lungs to their maximum potential, then he breathed.

He tried to listen, but the drumming rain took away all other sounds.

"Kate!"

A noise sounded to his left. He charged after it, thinking that if he could somehow just look her in the eye and talk to her, she would listen.

Instead of Kate, though, it was a wild hog that charged him. It had eight-inch long tusks that could slice a man to ribbons.

Shane leaped to one side and let the fear-maddened creature rush by him. But he stumbled and fell over a downed tree, falling back heavily on to his back and shoulders.

Lightning flared again as he lay dazed on the ground. He picked up movement from the corner of his right eye, and saw the snake rise up from the ground, jaws distended to strike.

The wedge-shaped head streaked at Shane's face. Reflexively, he raised his arm and tried to block the snake. He felt the snake's fangs bury deeply into his arm. There was pain at first, then a burning sensation and finally numbness.

The snake continued to hold on to him and Shane couldn't pull it loose. Panic slammed through him and his arm started to feel hot.

Poison! he thought.

The snake coiled its cold, muscular body around his other arm, hanging on to him as it pumped venom into his body.

* * *

Kate hid in the brush only a few feet from where Shane had come looking for her. Her heart thudded almost painfully in her chest. Glancing back at the shelter they'd made, she saw by the two flashlights walking a perimeter that Jolly and Ernie hadn't left the campsite.

That left just Shane.

A moment later, she saw him. Watched as the wild hog ran at him and caused him to stumble over a moss-covered log.

Kate went forward immediately. If he was going to come looking for her and he didn't have a pistol or shotgun, she intended to take him out. She noticed him struggling on the ground and froze for a moment until she figured out what had happened.

She saw the snake. From the size and shape of the head, she knew it was a cottonmouth. She ran forward and dropped to her knees beside Shane. He was panicked, which was understandable if it was the first time he'd been snake-bitten. But yanking on a snake only made the bite worse and spread the venom farther and faster.

She dropped to her knees beside Shane. "Shane!"

He looked up at her, still pulling at the snake.

"Stop pulling," Kate said. "Let me do this." Normally when she had to detach a snake the victim was too panicked to listen. Then again, normally when a snake bit someone, it didn't stay attached.

"Get it off me," Shane whispered hoarsely.

Moving quickly, Kate seized the viper's head by the jaws and squeezed them together. The snake's mouth popped open as the hinge buckled. The fangs slid free of Shane's arm. She broke the snake's neck and threw its writhing body into the brush.

Shane cursed, already shaking. Grabbing his elbow, he tried to look at the wound. "Tell me that was just a mean snake and not a venomous one."

"It was a cottonmouth." Kate took his arm and examined the wounds. There were two of them, both large holes.

"Are they poisonous?"

"Yeah."

Shane started to get up.

Kate put a hand in the middle of his chest and pushed him back. "Lie still."

"So the poison won't spread?" Shane lay on his back.

"So you don't hurt yourself running around in the dark," Kate replied. "Or maybe trip over another snake. You don't find cottonmouths by themselves very often. And they're water snakes, so getting wet or getting flooded doesn't bother them."

Shane lay back and swallowed hard. "Aren't you supposed to suck the venom out or something? I can't reach my arm or I'd do it."

Kate listened intently and looked back towards the make-shift shelter. A golden glow of light defined it in the distance. She didn't see or hear any signs of pursuit.

"You're supposed to suck out the poison," Shane insisted. "I've got a knife in my pocket."

"Do you?"

"Yeah."

"Let me see it." When he produced the clasp knife, Kate opened the blade and found it was razor-sharp. At less than five inches long, it was better than nothing. Barely. She closed the knife again and shoved it into her pocket.

"What are you doing?" Shane asked.

"Waiting."

"For what?" Anger knotted his face then. "For me to die?"

"You're not going to die. Do you have an ink pen?"

"An ink pen?" Despite the situation and how scared he was, Kate thought Shane was holding up remarkably well. Most people would have been screaming idiots by now, making the situation worse by getting jacked on adrenaline.

"So you can write your last will and testament," Kate said. Shane cursed.

"See? You sound better all ready. I really need that ink pen, though, if you have one." Since she was soaked through already, Kate sat cross-legged on the ground, grateful for the brush and that they were out of most of the mud.

Reaching into his pocket, Shane took one out and handed it to her.

"This is going to hurt a little." Kate pressed the retractable button and pushed the point out. Then she held his arm and encircled the wounds, marking the edema. Then she glanced at her watch and marked the time 11:27 p.m. She'd check again at 11:42.

Shane cursed and swore during the process, jerking his arm away. She didn't let go of the limb till she was finished.

Kate didn't blame him. Snakebite wounds were painful, and scary as hell.

"What did you do that for?" he demanded.

"To mark the envenomation. When you're bitten, you measure how far the venom spreads for the first few hours. Take readings every fifteen minutes to find out how big a problem you're dealing with is."

"That's why you suck the venom out, Kate. So it won't spread."

Kate sighed and tried to be patient, but it was hard. She knew he was scared and hurting, even a non-lethal snakebite hurt. The

problem was, she considered Shane Warren to be more dangerous than any cottonmouths that might be crawling around.

"What do you think I should do? Cut *X*'s over the snakebite and try to suck the venom out?"

Shane just looked at her, one part pissed and the other part
perplexed. "Yeah," he said finally.

"If this was a cowboy movie," Kate told him, "maybe I'd
do that. But the truth of the matter is that cutting into your
arm is only going to spread the poison faster and farther. If
you do have venom in your arm, which we've got to wait
to see, it already has necrotic properties—if you've never
heard the word before, it means that it kills living tissue, and
I said *tissue* not *people*—and spreading that necrosis over
your arm is going to leave a scar worse than your granny
did. Not to mention leaving your body open to all kinds of
infections."

He lay quiet for a moment, trying to get control of his rapid
breathing. His eyes searched her face. "You're not just lying
to me are you? So I'll just lie here, never knowing my heart
is about to stop?"

"Man," Kate said, smiling in spite of the situation, "you do
have an imagination."

"I mean, you could still be pissed about me helping with
your kidnapping—"

"That I'm not too happy about," she agreed. She kept talking although she didn't want to because she knew talking
would help keep Shane focused on something other than his
condition and because it would relax him.

Personally, she found talking to Shane confusing. Despite
the fact that she was running for her life and was presently
stuck on a hilltop with cottonmouths and potentially rabid

swamp creatures, she was all too aware that he was a handsome man.

But all she had to do was remember his talk earlier with Jolly, about how he was going to keep quiet about Deke's murder for a bigger cut of the Desiree Martini ransom. Handsome he might have been, and sexy, but he was also a rat.

"—and you could be telling me to lie here so I'll die instead of going back to the camp and getting help," Shane said.

"That would make me a real bitch, now wouldn't it?"

He blinked at her, not knowing how to handle that. "Yeah," he said finally, "yeah, it would."

"Well, for your information, I'm not. What I'm doing here, the way I'm treating you, is the best thing we can do."

"You're *treating* me?"

"Yeah." Kate did feel increasingly irritated at his attitude.

"Lying here, with my arm throbbing, with poison coursing through my body, that's treating me?"

"This is what you do for a snakebite just after it happens. You observe." Kate looked at him then and decided to unload somewhat. "You know about petechiae. I know about snakebites. We're both experts in our own fields." She cocked her head at him as he lay back. "I just haven't figured out what your field is."

That stopped him dead in his tracks. "You heard Jolly and me talking this morning. About the fact that he killed Deke."

"I *saw* Jolly suffocate Deke with a pillow," Kate said, her voice more strained than she would have thought. "I knew he killed him. What I didn't know was that you knew."

"It was too late to save Deke," Shane said defensively. "There was nothing I could do."

"Except leverage more of the Martini ransom money."

Shane sighed. He looked at his arm. "Has it been fifteen minutes?"

Glancing at her watch, Kate discovered that it had. She took his arm when he offered it, then waited for a lightning strike to see. When the sky lit up, she saw that the edema had spread beyond the encircled areas.

"Okay," she said, "it injected you with some venom."

Shane paled at the announcement. "So *now* I'm going to die?"

"No, you're not going to die. I've never known anyone to die from a cottonmouth bite."

His expression showed doubt and great concern.

"If you don't believe me," Kate said, "then hike back to your friends—"

"They're not my friends."

"—and maybe they'll suck the poison out of you. Maybe they grew up on the same John Wayne movies you did."

"Clint Eastwood was more my style."

"Whatever. But I'm betting Jolly will kill you the next time he lays eyes on you."

Shane shifted his injured arm and grimaced in pain.

"And I'm keeping your knife, just so you know."

"Somehow, I'm not surprised."

Kate sat and watched him lying there on the cold wet ground. She saw the fear in him.

"I just want to know if I'm going to die," he said finally.

"You're not going to die," Kate repeated.

"Everybody in my life died without knowing they were going to, Kate," Shane told her. "My father, my brother, my mother. Every one of them. His voice turned brittle. "And I didn't know until they were already gone."

"That's all true?"

"Yeah. It's all true."

For a while, Kate sat there in the rain, feeling it beat down on her as the wind whipped through the trees and branches clacked against each other. "I'm sorry."

"So am I," he said. "Not just for myself, but for you because you got caught up in this." He looked at her. "That wasn't supposed to happen."

"You've been poisoned," she told him, "but you're not going to die. You're lucky you were bitten by a full-grown cottonmouth. Adult pit vipers don't usually release all their venom at one time. They hold some back in case they have to strike again."

"Okay."

"Twenty-five percent of the time, you get what is known as a *dry* bite. That's one where there's no venom injected. It'll still hurt because you're talking about a certain amount of trauma anyway. And getting bitten is always scary. You get jacked on adrenaline, you're going to think you're having heart seizures. And you're going to get dizzy. That's all natural."

He lay quiet, listening to her.

"Cottonmouths are poisonous, but not as poisonous as a lot of snakes. Copperheads and rattlesnakes, which we have here in Florida, are much worse. But even then you rarely see a death associated with a bite. Generally you have people die from a subsequent heart attack brought on by anxiety or fear. Or, on rare occasions, you have people who are allergic to a snakebite and go into anaphylactic shock, then die."

"And if I was allergic?"

"You'd already be having problems. You're not allergic. But you may get sick since poison is present."

* * *

Shane did get sick. Less than twenty minutes after she told him he wasn't going to die, he thought she'd been lying. Nausea swept through him and turned his stomach to water. He rolled over to his hands and knees, head swimming, and threw up everything he'd eaten earlier.

He got really scared then, because he truly didn't know how much he could trust Kate Garrett to tell him the truth.

But she stayed there with him, helping him through it, dealing with the vomiting and the weakness. Every time he finished throwing up, his head pounding like it was going to burst, she scooped up a handful of rainwater and washed his face. Then she guided him to a different spot that kept them at least partially protected from the elements.

"I'm not dying?" he asked through chattering teeth after the last round of sickness. He sat huddled with his back to a tree, his arms wrapped around himself in an effort to stay warm.

"You're not dying," she repeated just as patiently as she had the first time.

He watched her as she sat with him. Maybe it was the pain, but at that moment he believed she was the most beautiful woman he'd ever seen. And the most resourceful. None of the women he'd dated before entering the army or the FBI knew the things that Kate Garrett knew. None of them could have done what she did. He was willing to bet none of the Bureau agents knew a woman who jumped into flood zones and cut the throats of alligators.

She was one of a kind.

And she thought he was the scum of the earth.

"Do you have any analgesics?" he croaked.

"No. And if I did, you couldn't take them. They thin the blood, and that would—"

"Spread the poison," Shane said. "Yeah. I got that." He shifted, trying to figure out how to do what he knew he needed to.

She leaned back against the tree on the other side of him. Her eyes watched the forest. He knew she was thinking and planning. She'd already cut a half dozen branches that were as big around as his forefingers and were three feet long. She'd also sharpened them on one end.

"Kate," he whispered, "I have to tell you something."

She looked at him.

"I'm not who you think I am," he said, thinking maybe that was the dumbest opening he'd ever tried to use.

"Well," she said, "you're definitely not who I thought you were. I was figuring on someone a little less callous and bloodthirsty."

Okay. I had that coming. I deserved that. Shane took a deep breath and wished that his head would stop spinning.

"I'm a special agent for the Federal Bureau of Investigation," he said.

She just looked at him, not impressed.

"You know," Shane said, "the FBI."

"I think I had the acronym figured out," she said sarcastically. "Even down here in the rural areas we've heard about the FBI." She paused. "This is the part where you flash your badge, isn't it?"

She was still being sarcastic, Shane realized. "I don't have my ID. I'm undercover."

"Oh," Kate said, rounding her eyes and her mouth as if she were in on the joke.

"It's the truth," Shane said, getting irritated.

"That whole not-having-identification thing gets in the way a little, don't you think?"

Shane forced himself to go on. This was turning out a lot differently than he'd believed it was going to.

"My assignment was to get close to Raymond Jolly," he said.

"You've managed that quite nicely, too," she observed. "Except for the part where he wants to kill you now."

"I did that to save your life."

"I can see it's really working out for you."

"He had you in his sights."

"It was dark," Kate argued. "People have a tendency to aim low in the darkness. I'm betting he might have missed, so I'm thinking maybe I saved my own life. Just like I saved yours."

"How?"

"From the snakebite."

"You said the snakebite wouldn't kill me."

"It won't, but running back to Jolly for medical assistance would have. I've seen his bedside manner for patients."

Shane sighed and willed himself not to throw up as nausea twisted his stomach again. During the last hour he seemed to be getting better. Or maybe there was just nothing left.

"My Director wanted me to find out where Jolly and his crew left Desiree Martini's body. I was supposed to get the location so she could be recovered and her parents could get some kind of closure on their grief. I know about grief, and about losing family. The Director didn't have to ask twice."

She regarded him curiously then. "To get close to Jolly, you had to go to prison."

He nodded and regretted it. "I've done that three times before. The longest time was for a year, to put together the cover I needed to bring down the Colombian cartel that killed my brother."

She looked surprised but said, "I can't imagine willingly going to prison."

"I couldn't imagine letting my brother's killers go free."

"So you were here to find Desiree Martini's body? Not the ransom money?"

"That's right."

"But you're thinking probably they're in the same place."

Shane knew then how neatly she'd laid the trap for him, making it look as if he could still be after the money. "I'm not here for the ransom, Kate. I give you my word on that."

"And how much is your word worth?" she asked.

He was quiet, wishing he knew what to say to make her trust him.

"You're here for Desiree Martini's parents," Kate said. "Is anyone here for the maid's parents?"

Shane leaned back against the tree. There's no winning with her. He sat still and tried very hard not to throw up.

Kate stood and gathered the sharp sticks she'd made. "I'll be back."

"Where are you going?"

She looked at him, her face mottled by the rain, and he saw there was no mercy in those jade-green eyes. "I was on my way back to Everglades City two days ago when Jolly and you popped out of the swamp into the path of my truck. My two kids are there. They were right in Genevieve's path. I need to make sure that they're all right." She nodded in the direction of the shelter. "Your two friends—or *suspects* or whatever you want to call them—have got the only boat that I know of. I'm going to get the boat."

"I'll go with you."

"You'll stay here," she said. "You'll only get both of us killed."

Stubbornness brought Shane to his feet, but sickness swirled inside his head and his stomach, bringing him back down again. After he'd retched up nothing a dozen times or more, the spasms finally went away.

When he looked for Kate, he discovered that she'd already gone.

Chapter 13

Kate crept up on the shelter in the darkness. Thoughts of what she was about to do almost made her sick. Taking out drunks like Mathis or would-be rapists who thought her presence out in the brush was an open invitation to rough sex were never premeditated. And those men had only ended up with bruises and bruised egos.

She took one of the sticks she'd sharpened and waited at the back of the shelter. Hours passed. At 4:08 a.m., Ernie emerged from the shelter and went to empty his bladder.

Moving stealthily, Kate crept up behind him and drew back the sharpened stick. She hesitated just a moment, hearing the sound of him relieving himself, and thought about Steven and Hannah and how she didn't know if her son and daughter were alive or dead.

Trying to knock Ernie out with a rock would have been one choice, but she knew that she couldn't guarantee unconsciousness. So she chose to incapacitate and scare instead, because she knew she could do those things.

Pushing aside all doubt, Kate struck, putting her weight into the stick and pushing the sharpened point in deeply. She felt the shock of the stick coming to a stop, not sharp enough to penetrate more than a couple of inches.

Ernie loosed a bloodcurdling scream and brought the shotgun around. Kate dove to the side, rolling and coming up at once, ducking behind a large bald cypress.

Jolly came out of the shelter with the pistol in both hands, moving constantly as he tried to find a target. Ernie was jerking around, groaning every time the makeshift spear jerked in his flesh.

"What is it?" Jolly demanded.

"Don't know," Ernie replied, grabbing for the stick in his back. "Somebody stabbed me." He finally caught hold of the stick and yanked it out. Blood streamed down his back, not enough to be threatening, but Kate knew the wound was painful.

Jolly lifted his voice. "Shane! Is that you?"

Kate stayed flat against the tree, breathing as quietly as she could. She had another stick in her hand. When Ernie turned his back to her again, she launched herself from the brush and stabbed him again, this time in the side as he turned toward the sound of her rushing at him.

"Damn!"

Still in motion, Kate ran through the woods. The shotgun boomed behind her. Pellets screamed through the trees overhead, missing Kate by inches, shredding leaves and splintering small branches.

"Over here! She's over here, Jolly!"

Kate dropped to one knee in the brush and held her position. She took up another sharpened stick and breathed out again. As she'd hoped, Ernie and Jolly gave pursuit, cursing her and calling out to each other so that she could have found them in the dark with her eyes closed.

"Did you see which way she went?" Jolly asked.

"No, dammit! An' she stabbed me with another one of those damn spears!"

"Kate!" Jolly yelled.

She tracked his voice, guessing that he was twenty yards away, moving almost tandem to Ernie.

"You're seriously beginning to irritate me, Kate," Jolly threatened. "I was going to let you live. Just leave you here in the morning and go our own way. I'm not willing to do that any more. The only way you're getting out of here now is as 'gator food."

Keep talking, Kate thought. That way I'll know exactly where you are.

Ernie and Jolly both tried to be quiet as they moved through the brush, but they had no woodcraft. They even stared directly ahead of them, trying to see in the dark instead of letting their peripheral vision do the work.

Letting Ernie creep past her again, Kate moved quietly after him again, coming up once more before he knew she was there. "Ernie," she whispered.

Frightened, already expecting to feel the bite of another spear, Ernie spun around. The shotgun went off, hurling a load of double-ought buckshot over Kate's head as she ducked and shoved her next spear into Ernie's stomach.

He looked down at the spear jutting out of his stomach in horror. "No!" he whimpered, and wet himself.

Kate reached for the shotgun and tore the weapon out of the man's grasp as he reached for the spear in his stomach. Like the others, the sharpened point had only gone in a couple inches, not enough to be life-threatening, but more than enough to be scary.

Ernie's knees buckled and he dropped to them, pulling the spear from his stomach and looking down at the damage. He whimpered and cried. Then his head evaporated into a mass of splintered bone and blood.

The sound of the .357 Magnum came almost at once.

Kate dived away as the corpse jerked to the side and sprawled to the ground. She moved through the forest, circling around behind Jolly as he stood his ground and peered into the darkness.

"Ernie!" Jolly called. *"Ernie!* I think I got her!" He took a couple of hesitant steps forward, letting the .357 lead him.

Kate came up out of the darkness behind him. She wanted to just squeeze the trigger and put an end to him. She'd never felt that way about a human being before. But after what she'd seen him do to Deke, and just now to Ernie, she wanted him dead.

My Director wanted me to find out where Jolly and his crew left Desiree Martini's body. I was supposed to get the location so she could be recovered and her parents could get some kind of closure on their grief.

Shane's words sounded again in her mind. Jolly was the only one left who knew where Desiree Martini lay buried. She tightened her grip on the shotgun and tried to tell herself that she didn't care.

But she did.

Even if Shane was lying about being an FBI agent, he hadn't been lying about the parents' inability to find their daughter. That had been in the news a lot.

She shifted the barrel slightly, then fired into the ground beside Jolly. The shotgun slammed against her shoulder with bruising force. As she expected, the man dove for cover at once. She moved forward quickly, putting a foot on his gun hand and aiming the shotgun at his eyes.

"If you so much as twitch, I'm going to blow your head off," Kate promised. "At this range, double-ought buckshot will get it done."

Jolly grimaced at her. "Sure, Kate." He released the pistol and took his hand away. She didn't let him up, making him crawl on his hands and knees back to the shelter so he couldn't try to escape.

By the time they got there, Jolly had some of his nerve back. He started threatening her. After she tied his hands behind his back with tent rope and secured his feet, she gagged him with a dry sock.

"Kate."

She had the shotgun across her thighs, fully loaded once more, and it came up in her hands naturally. Peering across the barrel, she watched Shane stumble into the light. He had a rock in one hand and a stick in the other.

"I came to help as fast as I could," he said.

Trust him or not trust him? she wondered. Then she realized how long that trip through the woods was in the shape he was in. She didn't believe what he claimed about being an FBI agent, but she didn't think that he'd try to hurt her either. At least, not while she had the shotgun and the .357 Magnum. And not while he was so weak.

"It's all right." Kate stood and left Jolly lying facedown on the ground.

Shane walked into the shelter and gazed around warily. "Where's Ernie?"

"Dead," she answered.

He frowned.

"I didn't kill him," Kate said. "Jolly did. He thought he was shooting me."

"Okay." Tiredly, Shane dropped to his haunches and sat by the fire. "I'm just going to sit here and try to get warm."

Later, Kate woke, surprised that she'd gone to sleep. She hadn't intended to because it was too dangerous. She didn't think Jolly could have gotten out of the handcuffs, but she didn't know.

She felt immediately better with the shotgun still resting across her lap. Jolly was still where she'd left him, asleep now.

But Shane was convulsing in the sleeping bag that they'd salvaged from the last mobile home. When she touched his forehead, she discovered he was burning up with fever. That was one of the side effects of being envenomed. Probably by morning he would be better and most of the sickness would have passed. But for now he was in misery.

He looked up at her as she knelt beside him. His eyes were glassy, feverish. "C-c-c-cold," he whispered hoarsely. "I'm j-j-just so c-c-cold, Kate."

He was scared, too. The fire pit had banked low and there wasn't any more charcoal. With the reemergence of Hurricane Genevieve, the temperatures had dropped again. Now that she was awake, she realized how cold she was too.

"Roll over on your side," she told him. "Facing Jolly." She didn't want to let Jolly out of her sight.

When Shane did as she asked, Kate lay on the ground behind him. Molding her body against his to share their mutual warmth, she held him as he quaked. She left the big pistol between them. Despite the sickness, he felt big and strong, and she could only imagine what it might feel like to be held by him. Right now, after everything she had been through, having someone hold her would have been good.

If he wasn't a convict, she told herself. But lying next to him, smelling the musk of him that somehow overrode the dirt and sweat, mixed with a hint of soap left over from that morning, she inexplicably felt comforted. She was asleep in minutes.

Someone was watching her.

Kate woke immediately with that sensation. She looked through the opening of the shelter and tried to find Jolly, but the man wasn't where she'd left him. Panic set in then and she reached for the pistol, only realizing then that she didn't feel it. More than that, somehow during the middle of the night Shane had turned over and taken her into his arms. He slept now with his head pillowed on her breasts. At least he didn't feel feverish any more.

But Jolly was missing and so was the pistol.

She rolled out of Shane's arms and looked up to find her ex-husband sitting in the camp chair drinking a cup of coffee.

"Hello, Kate," he said with that smarmy smile she'd learned to hate.

"Bryce," she said automatically.

"I remembered how I used to watch you while you slept and it would wake you. Like you were some kind of forest animal sensing a predator."

Looking back on things, Kate thought that comparison fit.

"It makes me happy to see that some things don't change." Her ex-husband waved the porcelain cup toward the downpour that was sluicing down the hillside toward the water's edge. "Particularly dreadful weather we're having, isn't it?"

"You didn't come here to talk about the weather." Kate looked around the shelter and discovered there were three other people in the shelter. It had gotten crowded and she'd slept right through it.

Two of the men looked like hired muscle outfitted in bush clothes. Jolly, now in handcuffs, stood between them. He didn't look happy to be there.

"How did you get here?" she asked.

"By boat. It's moored outside. A big, beautiful boat." Bryce beamed. Everything he owned was big and beautiful. "And through luck. We've been searching for you for over thirty hours. Even with an assist from some satellite experts I do business with, I was about to give up. If the storm hadn't cleared for those few hours, I'd never have found you at all in time."

"What are you doing here?" she asked.

Bryce frowned. Even here in the swamplands he looked immaculate and clean. He wore expensive clothes, khakis and a heavy black knit shooting sweater with a rifle pad on the right shoulder. He looked like he was on safari. Despite the inclement weather, his dark hair lay perfectly, his gray eyes were clear, and his teeth were immaculately white.

"A couple of days ago, the Coast Guard rescued a young man named Tyler Jordan who insisted you and he had been taken prisoner by the escaped convicts."

The knowledge that Tyler had pulled through thrilled Kate.

"The young man had quite a story to tell," Bryce continued. "Of course, with the storm going on—especially this second bout of it—not many people were listening. Hugh Rollins was. He sent for me because he thought I would have better luck finding you, and would be able to recognize and reason with you when I did."

"He doesn't know us very well, does he?" Kate asked acidly.

"My being here is a direct result of your insufficiency and

irresponsibility, Kate," Bryce accused. "I sent Steven and Hannah down here for you to keep out of harm's way. That didn't exactly happen now, did it?" He nodded toward the storm, which chose that moment to unleash a concert show of lightning and a cannonade of thunder that shook the shelter.

"Maybe if you had told me—"

Bryce held up an authoritative hand, silencing her. Kate knew trying to keep talking would only have been a waste of time. Even if he'd heard her and understood her, he would have acted like he hadn't.

Rain slapped at the tarp overhead and wind tried to suck it away.

"What I told you or didn't tell you is beside the point," Bryce said. "You have endangered my children by not staying with them as you should have."

"Where are they?" Kate stood and started toward him.

One of the bodyguards stepped between them.

"Please sit down," Bryce said. "You're alarming Mr. Fisk, and I promise you you won't like it when you do."

Kate took a deep breath and relaxed.

"As for Steven and Hannah, that's a bit of a quandary. For the moment, they're all right. Fortunately, Rollins got them out of your house before the storm surge flooded all of Everglades City's lagoons and low-lying areas. Saved them from drowning at the very least." Bryce shrugged. "The unfortunate part—and there's always an unfortunate part when you're dealing with someone of Rollins's ilk—is that he's going to kill them if I don't deliver the Desiree Martini ransom money your friend Jolly hid those months ago."

The declaration hit Kate like a physical blow. Her children were in danger. Her mind seemed to lock.

"He's not my friend," Kate whispered.

"Perhaps Jolly isn't your friend," Bryce said, looking pointedly at Shane, who was now starting to wake up, "but you've made at least one new friend, haven't you?"

"He's not an escaped prisoner," Kate said. "He's an undercover FBI agent."

"Enchanting," Bryce said, letting her know he both didn't believe her and didn't care.

"Who's our company?" Shane asked groggily. He'd missed out on the conversation.

"The ex-husband," Bryce explained. "And a few business associates."

"Well," Shane said, taking in the situation, "this is awkward."

Kate hated Shane more than ever in that moment. His presence was bad enough, but he had to antagonize her ex too?

"Bryce has a problem," Kate said.

"*We* have a problem," Bryce said.

"He was short of prisoners so he decided to take yours?" Shane asked.

"There's a man holding my son and daughter prisoner," Kate said, looking at Bryce. "A man named Hugh Rollins."

"A true criminal sociopath," Bryce interjected.

"Rollins says he's going to kill Steven and Hannah unless Bryce brings him the Martini ransom money."

Shane took that in and didn't say anything. Kate was grateful for that. She was also glad he seemed to be over most of the sickness from the snakebite.

"How did this guy Rollins know you would be able to find the ransom money?" Shane asked.

"The news stories revealed that Kate was with you. And she is my ex-wife. To Rollins, the math was simple," Bryce said calmly. He switched his attention to Kate. "Rollins means what he says. He'll kill the children, Kate."

And that, Kate knew, meant everything.

"What do you need me to do?" she asked.

"Your friend Jolly is going to tell us where the ransom is—" Bryce began.

"The hell I am!" Jolly snarled.

Hardly were the words out of Jolly's mouth before Fisk hit him and knocked him off his feet. Fisk grabbed Jolly by the jacket and yanked him upright again. Crimson threaded down his chin from his split lips.

"I can do this all day," Fisk said, smiling. "And if I get tired, my friend can take over for me. Understand?"

Reluctantly, blood dripping from his chin, Jolly nodded.

"What do you want me to do?" Kate asked, feeling hollow and empty.

"This man," Bryce jerked a thumb at Jolly, "is going to give us directions. I want to know that we're not being led on a wild goose chase. You know this area. I want you along to do what you do best: guide us to our destination."

Kate knew there was no choice to be made. Not with Steven and Hannah's lives at stake. "All right," she said.

The storm worsened as they headed north toward Tamiami Highway. Kate knew they wouldn't go that far. According to the news reports, the night of the Martini kidnapping Jolly and his crew—who were all dead now, she couldn't help thinking—had been picked up on Chololoskee, the island community southeast of the Everglades National Park coastal area.

At least, Kate amended, where the Everglades National Park used to be before Hurricane Genevieve came in to rearrange the geography.

It only made sense that Jolly and the others had buried the ransom and the bodies of the two women—Desiree Martini and the maid, Luisa Becerra—somewhere nearby. The swamps held a lot of secrets, though. Even jetliners had been known to disappear there. A suitcase of money and the bodies of two women were no problem.

She hadn't mentioned Jolly's use of the GPS unit to Bryce. Neither had Jolly or Shane. For the moment, that remained a secret the three of them shared.

"Do you know where we're headed?" Shane asked.

"Yeah," she answered.

He waited expectantly.

She didn't say anything further.

"That's all you're going to say?" he asked.

"Yeah." Kate remembered how good it had felt to rest in his arms. It was the best night's sleep she'd had in years. If only she trusted him.

"I'm sorry to hear about your kids," he said.

They stood in the stern and the storm drummed into them. Bryce stood back in the pilothouse of the big boat. The boat was either one of his toys she'd never seen or one that he'd recently acquired. Maybe he'd even bought it for the business they were about now.

"Me too," she said.

The sound of the boat's engine filled the darkness around them while the powerful lights lit up the murky chop of the floodwaters.

"So answer me one thing," Shane said.

"What?"

"Your ex is a jerk."

"What did I ever see in him? Is that what you're going to ask?"

"No." Shane waved that aside. "He has money. I get the money part. And he's good-looking, so I'll give you that too. I'll bet the jerk factor is usually well hidden."

"You'd be surprised how well most men can hide it when they want to," Kate said.

If Shane took any insult from the comment, he didn't show it.

"What I want to know," Shane said, "is why he allowed me to come. He could have stranded me back there."

"Oh. That." Kate took a deep breath. "He brought you along to embarrass me. To point out how far beneath him you are because you can't even take care of yourself."

"You know," Shane admitted ruefully, "I'm sorry I asked."

Less than an hour later, Bryce guided the boat into Butcher's Hog Lagoon by one of the two crumbling wooden piers. Back in the 1920s, when the oilmen had been in the area, they'd used the lagoon as a weekend party location. They'd gotten into the habit of trucking in booze and women, and killing wild hogs to dine on. After it had had its heyday, the name stuck, but only the locals knew about it.

"This is as far as we can go by water," Kate said. "It's too dry here. We'll have to go the rest of the way on foot."

"All right," Bryce said, "let's do it."

In minutes, they docked at the small wooden pier that thrust out into the dark water. Overhead, the storm clouds swirled and lightning flared again and again. The hard-driving rain turned the world to a constant wet gray and reduced visibility to only a few feet. Thunder crackled.

Kate was looking out at the coast, wondering how bad the trails were going to be and how Jolly—even with the GPS unit—was ever going to find the bodies and the ransom in an area that tended to look the same during good weather and now looked like nothing he could possibly have seen before.

That was when Kate saw the woman coming up alongside

the boat. She was tall and slender, dressed in a rain hat and an ankle-length duster that shimmied in the wind. In the storm and with the hood over her head, she couldn't see her features.

The men aboard the boat were looking to the other side and she knew all of them were thinking about the money that lay out there. In the noise of the storm, the woman's approach seemed virtually silent.

At first Kate thought the woman was one of Bryce's snuggle bunnies, brought along to keep him warm while he went on his treasure-hunting expedition. Then the woman's arm came up and a silver, snub-nosed revolver filled her hand.

"Look out!" Kate yelled, moving toward the stern where Shane stood. A surprised expression filled his face as he started to turn toward her, then she had both hands in the center of his chest and pushed him over the railing.

The woman fired like a seasoned pro, putting two rounds in each of the security guards and dropping them before they could draw weapons or take cover.

"Don't shoot him! Don't shoot him!" Jolly yelled to the woman, throwing his body in front of Bryce.

She halted and turned her weapon on Kate, locking eyes just for a moment. But Kate threw herself over the railing backward, not even bothering to try to turn around because there was no time.

Chapter 14

Arms stretched before her, Kate dove deeply, hoping she didn't bottom out and knock herself unconscious. Her hands touched mud and she changed the angle of her descent, twisting around to come up under the boat as it bobbed on the turbulent water. When she surfaced, she found Shane already there in the shadows, treading water next to the boat.

Thunder pealed as lightning turned the surface of the water silver.

"What the hell happened?" he demanded.

"A woman came up alongside the boat," Kate answered. "She's still out there."

"I never saw her."

"I don't think anyone did until it was too late."

"Who is she?" he asked.

Kate shook her head. "Jolly knew her. He told her not to shoot Bryce, and threw himself in front of him."

One of the dead men surfaced for just a moment only a few feet away. Then the body disappeared in the water again.

"Well, she didn't have any problems shooting the other guys," Shane observed.

"Really?" Kate asked sarcastically. "You think?"

Frowning, Shane said, "Maybe we could maximize the team-work potential a little here and save the backbiting for later."

Kate knew she was taking her anger and frustration out on him. And she didn't like that she was all too aware of him, aware of his body, in the cold water next to her.

He reached out and gently stroked her face. "You shoved me off the boat so fast I didn't even see her." His voice softened. "When I heard the shot, I thought she'd killed you."

She liked the warmth of his flesh against her skin. In seconds, that warmth spread to other areas too, which made her mad all over again. Teach you to sleep with someone who's been snake-bit.

"She missed," Kate said.

"I'm glad." Then Shane turned and looked out, watching as Kate pushed away from the boat. "If you get out there, she'll have a shot at you."

Water jumped to the right of Kate's head, then the sound of a pistol thundered over the roar of the storm. Kate drew back behind the boat at once.

Looking back at the shoreline, Kate saw Jolly kneeling with some kind of rifle in his arms. The woman stood behind Bryce, holding a pistol to his head.

"They don't want to hurt the boat," Shane said. "In case they have to use it to get out of here."

"Depends on how flooded the land north of us is," Kate said. "If it's not too bad, they could walk out of here. And if they do, Steven and Hannah—" She didn't—*couldn't*—finish the thought. *Damn you, Bryce Colbert!*

* * *

After a few more minutes passed, during which the wind picked up to gale force again, and Jolly, Bryce and the woman disappeared inland, Shane figured it was safe enough to attempt climbing up on the boat. There was a ladder on the stern.

While Kate went forward to the pilot cabin, Shane knelt beside the dead men and went through their pockets. Both of them were missing their weapons, though the holsters had been left behind. They also both had ID that identified them as private security guards for a New York City agency Shane had heard of.

"No keys," Kate said when she returned.

"Maybe I can hotwire it," Shane told her.

"They teach you to do that in the FBI?"

He looked at her then, watching her hair blow around and those deep-green eyes studying every move he made. *And here you are, going through the pockets of dead men like it's something you do every day.* He sighed, knowing that he looked entirely too used to such an activity.

"Their weapons are gone," he said.

"But they still have their cash and credit cards, right?"

"They do," Shane agreed. He showed her the IDs he'd found.

"So?"

"Just checking." Shane also turned up an unexpected bonus: a phone.

"That won't work out here. Even if you could hit a cell tower, all of those frequencies are being used by emergency services."

"This is a satellite phone," Shane said. "Not a cell phone. It can hit a satellite all by itself." He punched in numbers from memory, hoping he got through.

"Who are you calling?"

"Dennis Carlyle. He's my contact for this assignment. He's not just my contact, he's a friend."

"I don't want the FBI involved," Kate said.

"Kate," Shane said, "the FBI can—"

"The FBI can get my kids killed," Kate told him. "Just like they got Desiree Martini killed seven months ago."

"This is different." Shane looked into her eyes and willed her to believe him. He also wished the throbbing in his wounded arm would calm down.

"It's not different," she insisted. "It's another kidnapping, another demand for payment."

"The Martini kidnapping was an inside job, Kate. The Bureau knew that as soon as they stepped into the picture. But there wasn't anything they could do about it. Everyone suspected the maid, Becerra, was in on it. Jolly and his guys took Desiree Martini while she was out shopping. They knew exactly where to find her."

"Carlyle," a firm male voice answered at the other end of the satellite phone connection.

"Denny, it's Shane." The connection actually sounded pretty good.

"Where the hell have you been? You've been off the grid for almost three days. You were supposed to check in."

"There's a storm going on down here, Denny."

"I know there's a storm going on down there. Genevieve. That's all anybody's been watching on the Weather Channel for the last three days. And now it's picking up again. There's another storm surge building out in the Gulf. This one's supposed to be even higher than the last."

That wasn't good news.

"Look, a new wrinkle has come up," Shane said, watching as Kate grabbed gear from the boat. He lifted his voice to address her. "Are there any guns on the boat?"

"Guns?" Carlyle echoed.

"I didn't find any," Kate replied. "But I found this." She held up a compound bow and quiver of arrows.

"I've never shot a bow," Shane said.

"I have. I've hunted wild hogs and white-tailed deer with them."

"A bow?" Carlyle repeated. "Shane, we need to talk."

"Can you get a fix on this phone's GPS?" Shane asked.

"Already done it," Carlyle said.

"I need a strike team assembled and sent to this twenty," Shane said.

Kate clambered off the boat and crossed the pier. She wore the bow across her shoulder, and somehow the weapon looked natural there. The arrow quiver hung at her hip.

Shane hurried to catch up. God, he'd never met a woman like her in his life.

"Shane," Carlyle said patiently, "there's a tropical storm going on down there. Millions of dollars in damage. Sixteen people are confirmed dead in the area. I can't just send a—"

"I've got innocents down here, Dennis. A woman and her two kids. I need whatever you can do for me." Shane broke the connection and pocketed the phone.

He hurried to catch up to Kate as she came to the treeline around the lagoon. He reached for her elbow, but she slapped his hand away. Pain from the snakebite hurt so bad it rattled his teeth and his brain.

"Kate, talk to me," he said, matching her long-legged stride.

"There's nothing to talk about."

"What are you going to do?"

She looked at him then, her deep-green eyes dark and cold. "I'm going to get that ransom money, and I'm going to make the deal with this Rollins guy. I'm getting my kids back, Shane."

"I think you should wait for backup."

Just then, another boat arrived out in the lagoon. This one wasn't big or expensive, but it moved fast through the water. Searchlights flicked across Bryce's boat. Then the second boat glided in next to the first and a small group got off.

At the distance, even through the driving rain, Shane saw that two of the figures were a lot smaller than the rest.

Kate's heart nearly stopped when she saw the two small figures sandwiched between the six armed men as they walked along a narrow, twisting trail. She rummaged in the knapsack she'd filled aboard the boat and took out a pair of sport binoculars with light amplification abilities. Bryce never stinted when it came to his toys.

She focused the binoculars with intermittent success across the rain. But she saw enough of the two small figures to recognize them.

"Are those your kids?" Shane asked.

Unable to speak, Kate only nodded.

"Looks like they're coming inland," Shane said. "This guy Rollins, he must have had your ex's boat bugged. He was covering his bases all the way around."

Kate silently agreed. More than anything, she wanted to touch her children, to hold them and keep them safe. Instead, they were marching through one of the deadliest storms Florida had ever known in the middle of an armed group of criminals.

"What did you say Rollins was into?" Shane asked.

"Bryce said money laundering."

"For who?"

"I don't know." Kate packed all her fear up and put it away. She had to be at her best if she was going to get Steven and Hannah back safely.

Beside her, Shane took the satellite phone out again and

punched in a number. Then he said, "Hugh Rollins. OrgCrime. Money laundering. Who is he?"

Silently, hidden in the trees and the brush, Kate watched as the six armed men walked into the forest. She worried about Steven and Hannah, thinking about everything that might happen to them. And that fear only made her heart grow harder.

Shane closed the phone. "My guy says that Rollins is one scary son of a bitch, Kate. Evidently your ex accidentally exposed some kind of money-laundering empire that's still causing repercussions. Everybody who's mobbed up and moves cash through that computer company of his is getting the microscope treatment from the IRS and RICO." He was silent for a moment. "Sounds like your ex burned himself on the deal too. Evidently whatever he did uncovered some of the insider trading he pulled off to put the whammy on Rollins' little empire. He may be looking at some time away."

Bryce? In jail? That didn't seem possible. "Bryce has a fortune in off-shore accounts. Switzerland. Maybe leaving behind what he has here will bother him on a pride level, but he keeps his finances protected."

"Yeah, well he's not going to be able to live in the United States any more," Shane said. "There's an indictment against him coming down the pipe."

And that caused a whole new fear to strike Kate as suddenly as one of the lightning bolts around her. If Bryce left the country, he'd take Steven and Hannah with him before she could fight him again for custody.

Out in the lagoon, the second boat rolled back and went back to the east.

"See the way that boat's moving?" Shane asked. "Going around to the other side of the lagoon? They're doing that so they can take two readings on the bug that's on your ex."

"Triangulation," Kate said, understanding.

"Right. They do that, they're going to find him damn quick."

Kate knew that.

"The thing is, Kate," Shane said, "according to what Dennis said, Rollins isn't a man to forgive past sins. He's not just going to make a trade for the money. This is a pride thing for him. He'll take the money, but he'll also kill your ex. And your kids."

"I know," Kate said quietly, her helplessness making way for a calm rage. They had her kids, but they had walked in on her turf. She'd hunted and fished and trekked across this swamp for years. They'd made a mistake coming here.

And now she was going to make sure they paid for it.

Remaining hunkered over, she fisted the bow and faded back into the woods, moving slightly ahead of and parallel to the armed men. It was time to hunt.

Once the men found a game trail and decided to stay with it rather than fight the bush, Kate and Shane sped ahead of them and set up what Shane called a trip line using some of the nylon cord she'd taken from Bryce's boat. She'd intended to use the cord to tie Jolly and the woman if it came down to that. But Shane had had the better idea.

Kate left Shane in the brush and climbed a nearby tree. Because of the rain and the dark, the lead man didn't see the cord until he fell over it. Then he got up, cursing and pointing his rifle in all directions. A moment later, he did what Kate had hoped he would do; he sent scouts out into the brush.

Hunting the men reminded her of hunting wild hogs that ran in groups. If the hunters were in stands a fair distance away where they were safe, they could simply take their shots and remain safe from the hogs' razor-sharp tusks. When the prey was armed with hunting rifles that shot farther than her bow, tactics had to change.

Ten feet up in a bald cypress, balanced on a wide branch and buried in shadows, Kate drew back the bowstring and peered down the arrow shaft at the lead guard. She squinted and shook a little as she thought about what she was about to do.

Killing Monte Carter, even though Shane had finished the job, had been easier because Carter had been about to kill her. This was more cold-blooded. Still, her dad had taught her how to hunt. One should never kill unless there was a need. To make meat, as the old-time hunters called it. Or to cull a predator that was attacking livestock.

They're going to kill your kids, Kate, she told herself. Be the hunter. She shut off the part of her that thought too much, closing down everything inside her mind but the hunter.

The bow was a good one. It felt right and balanced, a marksman's weapon. Kate had been surprised to find it aboard Bryce's boat, but Jolly and the woman had taken the rest of the weapons.

From a distance of forty yards, holding her breath when it was halfway out, Kate released the string. The arrow leapt from the bow.

Kate was already reaching for a second arrow when the first struck its mark.

The man screamed, dropping to the ground and gripping the few inches of the arrow that hadn't penetrated his chest. "Trent, dammit! Help! I've been shot!"

The other man went slower, staying close to the ground. Kate shifted and took aim again, sighting along the arrow. Neither of the men had any idea where she'd fired from. With a bow, there was no telltale muzzleflash.

She released again and reached for a third arrow.

The second arrow caught the other man in the back, piercing him and the ground he lay on. He shuddered and went still. From the position of the shaft, Kate felt certain she'd put the arrow through the man's heart.

"Help!" the first man yelled, looking in all directions. "Indians! We're being attacked by Indians!"

Kate sighted on the man again, but then saw Shane coming out of the darkness of the nearby trees at a dead run. Rollins' man saw him coming and tried to bring his assault rifle to bear.

Shane grabbed the rifle barrel and pushed it away, then swung into an incredible natural and athletic roundhouse kick that caught the man full in the face and stretched him out unconscious. Without hesitation, Shane picked up the rifle, sorted through the unconscious man's pockets and gear for extra magazines, and disappeared back into the woods.

"Antonio!" someone yelled. *"Antonio!"*

The four men dropped back, getting closer together. They shoved Steven and Hannah on to the ground. Kate's control almost slipped when she saw her son and daughter huddled together crying. Steven had his arms around Hannah and her head pulled into his shoulder.

Kate breathed out. Steady, she told herself. First rule of survival is being able to save yourself. If you can't save yourself, you can't save anyone. But it was hard to remember that when it was her kids on the line. And taking hostages from armed gunmen was nothing she'd ever had to do as a wilderness guide.

"Antonio!" the man yelled again.

Kate dropped to the ground. At this distance, through the trees, she'd never get a shot without an arrow deflecting and potentially hitting Steven or Hannah. There were four of them to go and it might as well have been an army.

She made her way to Shane as he was pulling on the unconscious man's field jacket. "What are you doing?" she asked.

"The only thing I know to do," Shane answered.

"You think you can pass yourself off as one of them? That's stupid!"

Shane glared at her. "You got any other bright ideas right now?" he challenged. "Because this is the best I can come up with on short notice."

"Antonio! Bobby!"

"I'm not exactly crazy about this either," Shane said, "and I'm going to be depending on you. When I walk over there, I'm going to be buying a few seconds' distraction at the most. After that, everything's going to go to hell." He picked up the man's rifle. "But I'm not going to leave those kids in that mess with those men. Even if they weren't your kids, I couldn't do that."

Looking into his hazel cat's eyes, Kate saw the old hurt in him and thought about all the family he'd lost. She'd lost her mother and that had been devastating. She couldn't imagine losing everyone.

But that was what she was facing now.

"Bryce!" the man called. "Bryce Colbert, is that you? Because if that's you, you need to know I've got your kids here!"

"It's your call," Shane whispered. "They're your kids."

"They're not going to be fooled," Kate whispered. "They're going to see you're not one of them."

"Negativity is not a good thing right now," Shane said. "This is the part where you tell me how clever I am and I get to go in and be the hero. Heroes fool everybody. Kind of like a natural Jedi mind trick." He took a breath. "Hell, at least I'm not jumping into the swamp and taking on an alligator with a straight razor. If you ask me, that was pretty—"

Kate was leaning in before she knew she was going to act

on the impulse. Or even knew what the impulse was. She slid
her hand behind his head and through that long blond hair,
pulled his head down to hers and kissed him.

Chapter 15

Electricity ran through Shane, making him feel as if he was going to explode right out of his skin. He felt Kate's heat against him, tasted her lips, and felt her firm breasts pressing into his chest. Instinctively, he put his arms around her and maximized their proximity.

Over the years, Shane had known a lot of women. The ones that were hell in bed and the ones so cold they could put a bullet between a man's eyes before post-coitus had time to truly kick in.

But he'd never known a woman like Kate Garrett. He felt a hunger for her like nothing he'd ever felt before. He was aware of the rain sluicing down on them, felt the vibrations of the thunder booming and saw the silvery sheen the lightning left on her skin as it lit up the dark skies.

He found something of himself in that instant that he'd never known existed. All the need in him to keep distant from other people suddenly eluded his grasp. He realized then the price he'd paid for that solitude, for the safety from losing anyone else he cared about.

Then she pulled back and looked at him. She tried a smile, but it didn't fit and he knew she was worried. "For luck," she whispered. Then she was gone, fading into the swamp brush around them like a ghost.

"Bryce Colbert!" the man yelled. "I'm going to kill one of your kids if you don't come out of there!"

Shane gathered the rifle into his arms. It was an army-issue M-4 assault rifle. In the army, he'd carried one for three years, and he'd trained with a variation of them for the FBI for urban strike teams.

He eased through the forest, not daring to look over his shoulder because he wouldn't see Kate. She's there, he told himself. Just accept that she's there.

"Bryce—"

Shane stepped out on to the trail so the other four men could see him. He hoped the darkness held and the lightning didn't rip it away—at least for a moment or two longer.

All four men swiveled their rifles toward him.

That's not a good sign, Shane thought. He held up a calming hand. Took a step. Then put his finger to his lips and pointed to the woods.

"How many, Bobby?" one of the men whispered.

Shane whispered back, "Five."

"Is it Colbert?" the man asked.

Shane grunted and kept moving forward. He looked past the man, seeing Kate's kids huddled on the ground. They looked small and vulnerable.

"Hey," one of the men said, "that's not Bobby."

In that instant, an arrow zipped into the man's neck, coming out on the other side. The man stumbled back and grabbed the arrow on both ends. His lips parted and he gave a gurgling yell.

A second arrow arrived almost immediately, striking a second man in the back, but it didn't put him down. He yelled in pain and dove into the trees.

Shane brought his rifle up as he broke into a run straight at the man ahead of him. He yelled and fired into the center mass of the man, putting three rounds into him and pushing him over with the rifle barrel.

Then Shane was on top of the boy and girl, scooping them up and running for the trees, running back in the direction he thought Kate might be. He lost the rifle in the confusion and cursed his luck. He was unarmed again. He ran as far as he was able, slipping, sliding and falling down a hillside and ending up in a slough. He skirted the edge of it, not daring to try to run across because they would be exposed.

Then he couldn't run any farther and he fell, taking the kids down with him in a loose spill of arms and legs. They cried out and Shane didn't blame them because he was scared as hell too. He heard footsteps behind him and knew they'd been pursued.

The boy—Steven, Shane remembered—grabbed the little girl's hand and tried to drag her away.

"No," Shane gasped. "I'm an FBI agent. I'm here to help you."

Steven kept trying to drag Hannah away. Fear twisted the boy's features and he was crying.

Damn, Shane thought. Even her kids don't believe you. He moved closer again and they shrank back. "I'm—" He struggled with what to tell them, listening to the footsteps grow closer. "I'm—I'm here with your mom."

"Mom?" Hannah said, wiping her face.

"That's right, Hannah," Shane said. "She came to rescue you."

"How did she get here?" Steven asked.

"She tracked you."

Doubt knitted the boy's brows. He was no one's fool. "Across the swamp?"

"Your mom's a tracker, Steven. One of the best I've seen. I don't think a bloodhound could keep up with her when she gets started." Shane was trying to give them something to believe in. Kids, especially small kids, always believed their parents were capable of superhuman things. Shane had remembered thinking that about his own mom. Until he'd found her strangled that morning. "She's here. I swear she's here."

"Where?" Steven asked.

Hannah pointed over Shane's shoulder and screamed. He turned, throwing his arms wide and putting himself between the kids and the gunman. The guy had them cold. There was no room to maneuver.

"Hey man," Shane said. "Don't hurt the kids. You don't have to hurt the kids."

"Should have thought of that before you broke up the party," the guy rasped. He centered the rifle on Shane's face.

Something whizzed by Shane's ear, like a really fat, really fast mosquito. Then an arrow sank into the gunman's chest beneath the shouldered rifle. In disbelief, the gunman looked down, touched the arrow fletchings with the fingers of his left hand, then dropped to his knees and fell forward.

Shane turned around, watching as Kate stepped out of the shadows, another arrow already nocked. She looked like a goddess draped in darkness. Like Artemis, he finally remembered, the goddess of the hunt in one of the mythology books his granny had read to him when he was a kid.

Then she was on her knees, taking her kids into her arms. They were all crying, and even Shane found tears in his eyes.

But he was an outsider. He'd always been an outsider when

it came to family life. Turning away, he went back to the gun-man and picked up the dropped rifle.

Kate came up behind him. He felt her standing there even though she didn't touch him. Slowly, he turned to face her.

"I don't know who you are," she told him in a voice tight with emotion. "I don't know if you're an FBI agent or a con-man. But what you did for Steven and Hannah—" Words or her voice failed her.

"It's okay, Kate," he said. "I know."

"It's not okay," she whispered. "The number of men I've met that would do something like that? I could count them on one hand and have fingers left over. Thank you."

"You're welcome," he said, but he wanted her to hold him again, and to give him the chance to hold her.

The dead man's radio crackled. "Davey," the radio called. "What's going on over there?"

"We got hit!" an excited voice called back. "Somebody in the forest came in and took the kids! Took out the rest of the team! I think I'm the only one left!"

"Hold your position. We'll get another team over there."

Shane grimaced and looked at Kate. "Unfinished business," he said. "Looks like we're not out of the woods yet."

"We'll take Bryce's boat," Kate said. Her tears dried up as he watched. He was amazed again at how together she was. Her kids clung to her waist, obviously more at ease now but still frightened. "We need the key."

"Maybe I can hotwire it," Shane suggested.

Kate shook her head as she knelt and stripped a long-handled flashlight from the dead man's backpack. "We can't take that chance. We need the key."

"Bryce has it," Shane said. "And the other guys have got re-inforcements on the way. Smart money says to go to the boat."

"We could get trapped there," Kate argued.

Shane sighed. "I know."

"If we're on the boat and we have no key, we can't get away."

Shane thought quickly. "Do you think you can find Bryce?"

"Yeah."

"Then do it." Shane hoisted the rifle. "I'll see if I can delay the reinforcements."

She took her children by the hands. Looking over her shoulder, Kate said, "Stay safe. And if you don't get to the boat before me—" She hesitated and he knew it was hard for her to say.

"Leave without me," Shane said. "Get the kids out of here as soon as you can."

She gave him a tight nod, then hurried away.

Shane got his bearings, remembering the direction the other boat had gone. He set out at a distance-eating jog, wondering if any of them were going to get out of this alive. The forest seemed alive with enemies. And the storm was gathering intensity.

Kate found what she was looking for in a matter of minutes. The hollow between the copse of hardwood trees was mostly dry.

"I'm going to have to leave you here for a minute," she said, slipping the bag she'd packed aboard the boat from her shoulder.

Both of them protested at once. Their pleas were so scared and plaintive it was hard to leave. *If you don't, they're going to die out here.*

"I have to go," Kate repeated as she spread out the contents of the bag, bringing out blankets, bottles of water and trail bars. She didn't know when Steven and Hannah might have last eaten. "I'll be right back. I promise."

"But you'll lose us in the dark, Mommy," Hannah wailed.

Kate took her daughter into her arms. "I won't, baby girl. I promise." Reluctantly, she pulled Hannah off her shoulder and looked at Steven for help. For all these years, he'd always looked down his nose at her, always faulted her for what she couldn't give him that his father could.

"You killed that man back there," Steven said.

Tears filled Kate's eyes. She would have given anything for her children not to see that. How are they going to be all right after this?

"Yeah," she whispered, meeting it head-on. "I did."

Steven nodded. "He was going to kill us."

"Yeah."

"Because of something Dad did."

Kate didn't answer. She just couldn't be that cruel.

"When you leave us," Steven asked, "can you find us again?"

"I can," Kate whispered, feeling the lump in her throat.

He smiled at her a little then. "I knew you could." Turning to Hannah, he took his little sister into his arms and guided her back to the hollow.

It hurt Kate to see how grown-up he acted, but she took pride in it too. He looked back at her as she got to her feet.

"Mom?"

"Yeah," she replied.

"Be safe," he told her.

"I will," she said. "And if anyone comes this way, anyone but Shane or me, hide. Hide really good. Understand?"

Back on the game trail, Kate ran, heading in the direction her ex-husband, Jolly and the woman had gone. She used the flashlight to cut their trail, spotting the deep impressions they'd left in the soft loam with ease.

Then she was hunting again.

* * *

Shane found the reinforcements with no problem. He climbed into one of the cypress trees and took up a sniper position. The second team carried flashlights against the storm's darkness, looking like a glowing caterpillar snaking through the woods.

The satellite phone vibrated against his leg. Looking to his left, he thought he saw where Kate was. She intermittently used the flashlight she'd taken from the dead man. Less than a hundred yards ahead of her position, two other flashlights glowed in the darkness.

Evidently Jolly and the woman had found the site he was looking for. The GPS unit had guided them straight to it. Bryce had to be with them.

Shane felt scared for Kate, but knew she would probably see Jolly and the woman before she walked up on them. He slipped the phone from his pocket and answered.

"Shane," Dennis said.

"Tell me you've got a team coming," Shane said.

"I would if I could. They've upgraded Hurricane Genevieve again. She's at Force Five again. Not only that, but it gets worse. I've pinpointed your position by GPS. Hurricane Genevieve has whipped up a wall of water. The weather guys say it's going to hit the area where you are within minutes." Dennis was quiet for a moment. "The meteorologists think this one is going to be even worse than the last one. The storm surge is bringing in another thirty feet of water. If you've got a boat where you are, buddy, climb in. Because you're at ground zero to become a new, temporary sea floor."

Kate! Shane looked north and saw her flashlight blaze again, then die out as she closed on her target. He shouldered the rifle, using open sights, and started firing, two rounds per target, aiming for the center mass. He had four rounds off, two men down before they knew they were getting fired at. Another two shots narrowly missed a third target, but by then they had his location tracked back to the muzzle flashes of the rifle.

As bullets tore through the branches around him, Shane leaped to the ground and started running for his life, leading the men southwest, away from Kate and the kids.

And the boat that he'd need if they were going to survive the latest storm surge.

Kate kept an arrow nocked to the bow as she crept up to the clearing where she'd seen the flashlights. When she'd heard the rifle shots back in the direction where she'd left Shane, she'd gone to ground automatically. She hoped that he was all right, and that the sudden silence didn't mean that the new arrivals had killed him.

Don't think like that. She forced herself to breathe. Kneeling, she stayed low as she surveyed the ground.

The flashlights had disappeared, either turned off or down and around a section of the swampland and trees.

After a moment, Kate got up and kept moving. Her mind raced. Evidently, the night of the kidnapping Jolly had had a GPS unit then too. With the police and FBI hot on his trail, he'd had no choice but to bury the money in case they were caught and memorize the coordinates.

Even in the storm, the GPS must have worked.

Only a few minutes later, with the rain hammering her like a determined prizefighter, Kate reached the target area. She glanced around the clearing and spotted the hole at once.

It looked like an open grave, mud piled up around it.

They hadn't had to dig very deep. The wet ground had been easy to work through.

They never found the kidnapped woman's body. The thought shot through Kate's mind. She crept forward, and as she did, a shape materialized out of the darkness.

A body lay on the ground next to a mound of dirt. Two shovels thrust up from the dirt.

Bryce! Kate hoped the prone figure wasn't her ex. Maybe Bryce wasn't really close to Steven and Hannah, but they loved him.

More gunfire sounded out in the swamp. Evidently the reinforcements were still in pursuit of Shane. She just hoped he lived through the experience.

Pushing those fears out of her mind, Kate crept closer. Aside from the body on the ground, no one else appeared to be around.

Lightning flickered and she recognized the prone figure: *Bryce!*

Circling the clearing, checking from several angles, Kate figured Jolly and the mystery woman were gone. Whatever they'd come for—presumably the ransom money—they'd evidently gotten it and departed.

Kate eased out into the clearing, using her ears and her peripheral vision, knowing she was now more the hunted than the hunter. Step by step, she made her way to Bryce. Blood caked his head, looking black in the lightning. When she put her fingertips to the side of his throat, she found a pulse.

She let out a breath of relief. Then, remembering the satellite phone Shane had found on the bodyguards, she searched her husband's clothes and found a similar one.

She opened it and dialed her father's phone number. It made a strange sound and she at first thought the phone had dropped the signal. Then she heard it ring.

"Hello," her dad answered.

"Dad," Kate choked out, biting her lip to keep from crying.

"Baby girl," he said. "Are you all right?"

Kate took a shallow breath. "I'm getting there. Things have been confusing."

"I know. Sheriff Brannock an' me been lookin' for you an' the kids since Tyler Jordan got back. Somebody done took your kids—"

"I know, Dad. I've got them. But we may need some help getting out of here."

"I'm with the sheriff now. Using this satellite phone of his. Had my home an' business numbers forwarded to this one in case you called. I was hopin'."

"Good. I'm glad you're all right."

"I am. But what about you?"

"We're okay," Kate said. "So far. There's a man looking for us. His name is Rollins. Hugh Rollins." She had to lift her voice to be heard over the wind. "He kidnapped Steven and Hannah because Bryce stole money from him and left him exposed to the police. It's a long story. But they're here now, looking for us."

"Where are you?"

"Butcher's Hog Lagoon. I can take the kids and go to ground for a few hours. Maybe even a day. They won't find us."

"Baby girl," her dad said. "You can't stay there. Not in Butcher's Hog Lagoon. There's another storm surge. That whole area's right in the path of it. It's all going to be underwater in just a few minutes."

Kate couldn't believe it. She looked up at the dark sky swirling overhead, the jagged veins of lightning flashing through it, and felt the cannonade of thunder pounding through her.

"There's a boat here, Dad. We can get to the boat. It's

Bryce's. Marine authorities somewhere ought to have a record of it. If we go back to the boat, we could be caught. But we don't have a choice."

"We'll get there soon as we can, Kate. I swear to you."

"I know. I love you." Kate punched the phone off and stood up. Then, when lightning flashed overhead, she saw the bottom of the freshly dug hole. There was something there, something that sent primeval fear jarring along her nerves.

It was the body of a woman.

Chapter 16

Frozen with horror, numb from everything she'd faced tonight, Kate stared at the body in the bottom of the shallow grave. It held the mortal remains of Desiree Martini.

If Kate hadn't already been drained by her recent experiences, if Steven and Hannah weren't dependent on her to get them to safety, she might have felt more sorry for the dead woman. As it was now, she could only think of her children, and Genevieve. The hurricane was building again, summoning up another storm surge that would engulf the area where she and her children now were.

Rainwater pooled in the grave, filling the hole with surprising speed. By the time the storm abated, the grave might well have been swallowed up.

Seven months in the grave had left a barely recognizable corpse. If it hadn't been for the dress, the one that Desiree Martini had been wearing in all the news footage of the nightclub she'd been at prior to the kidnapping, Kate wouldn't have known the young woman at all. The twisted, ravaged features looked like something out of a horror movie.

C'mon, Kate told herself. Shake it off. You don't have time to fall apart. Not now. Steven and Hannah are depending on you. Genevieve isn't going to wait until you're ready for her.

Through sheer force of will, Kate looked past the body, shifting the flashlight to the left where a waterproof ammunition case sat open, collecting rain. A handful of papers lay soaking on the ground.

Kate played the flashlight beam over the paper and saw presidential faces and national buildings. Hypnotized, she reached down and plucked one of them from the mud. Andrew Jackson stared back at her from the twenty-dollar bill.

We want ten million dollars, the disguised voice had announced on the recorded phone call. *In small, non-sequential bills. Nothing smaller than twenty-dollar bills, nothing larger than one hundred dollars. Pay the ransom. You'll get your daughter back in one piece.*

But they didn't get her back, did they, you bastards?

A moan sounded to the right.

Kate flicked the light back to Bryce. His clothes and hands were covered in fresh, thick mud.

Gunfire sounded out on the swamp, rolling in hard and loud, warring with the thunder.

Then she thought about Rollins's men somewhere in the brush behind her. Bryce might have been a selfish cheat and a greedy thief, but he wasn't a killer. Rollins's men were.

And you left Shane out there with them. Kate pushed past the guilt. She had her kids to think of. Playing the light over her ex-husband again, she saw him turn away from the bright beam this time.

Bryce was coming around. She flashed the beam over his scalp again. The tear was already starting to clot. The rain only made it look like there was more blood. A few stitches and he was going to be fine, other than a headache and a possible concussion or fracture.

You're not responsible for him, either. Kate stood and shone the flashlight into his face. And you can't trust him. He'll put his own welfare ahead of Steven and Hannah's. He's already done that by exposing them to all the danger.

But she couldn't just walk away either.

She leaned down and slapped his face, blocking the driving rain from him for just a moment.

He moaned.

"Bryce," she said in a steady voice.

He moaned and put a hand to his head, turning away from the light.

"Wake up," she said. She slapped his face again, knowing it had to hurt a little. She forgave herself the perverse pleasure she got in the act. Bryce deserved even worse than the lump on the head and the cut he'd received from whoever had cold-cocked him while he was rooting around in Desiree Martini's grave for the ransom money.

"Leave me alone, you bitch!" Bryce snarled. He wrapped his arms over his head. "Don't you dare hit me again!" He didn't sound exactly lucid, but he was getting there.

"Get up." Kate pulled at him, shaking him awake. "Get up or you're going to die."

He cursed her.

She wanted to slap him again just for that, and the control almost slipped beyond her. "Rollins is somewhere out there. So is Jolly. You're going to have to get up."

A shot cracked through the air back in the direction of the

boat, away from the area where Shane had engaged Rollins's reinforcements.

Steven! Hannah! Kate was in motion before she knew it, running toward the boat. If Jolly took the boat, her kids were going to be left at the mercy of the storm's newest flooding.

Her boots splashed through the water and mud, packing deep and feeling like they were filled with lead. Her legs and back ached now from the constant physical demands she'd faced. Her breath rasped and burned the back of her throat.

She drove herself on when she felt as though she didn't have anything left to give, following the game trail through the woods, chasing the light. Reaching the hollow where she'd left Steven and Kate, she knelt and shone the beam into the dry area where she'd left them.

They were gone. The beam tracked the empty space, playing over the blankets, the first-aid kit and the trail-bar wrappers and water bottles.

Steven and Hannah were gone.

In that moment, Kate's heart emptied in a rush. Someone had taken her kids! The realization slammed into her like a blow. She staggered and fell to her knees on the muddy ground, sinking deeply. Black spots swirled in her vision as a ragged cry tore from her.

For just a moment she gave into the helplessness. Then she stood and forced herself to stop crying, playing the flashlight beam around the ground, sorting through all the tracks there, knowing there were more than just hers and her kids'. Someone else had been there. From the size of the feet, she guessed it had been a man.

Taking a deep breath, she made herself be calm. Panic wasn't going to do anyone any good. The flashlight beam picked up a set of tracks that were washing out even as she found them. Her kids were lost in the wilderness, but she could find them. That was one of the things she did best. She started to follow the tracks.

"Mom!"

Steven's voice came from behind her. Kate whirled, already moving to the side herself in case Rollins or Jolly or Shane had them.

Steven stepped out from behind a tree, leading Hannah by the hand.

They're all right! Kate rushed to them and dropped to her knees, hugging them tightly. Then all of them were crying, holding on to each other fiercely.

"We had to leave the shelter!" Steven said, looking at her, his small face pinched with hurt and fear. "I know you said not to. But I saw a flashlight coming. I knew it wasn't you, so I took Hannah and we hid."

Kate forced herself to laugh and give him a smile. "It's all right. You did good."

Steven calmed but still looked scared. "The guy found the shelter. He went inside and looked."

"But he didn't find you, did he?"

"No."

"Momma," Hannah said, "we hided good. Like you told us to."

"Yes, you did, honey." Kate stood and took Steven's hand. "We've got to get out of here. The storm's getting worse again."

"Where can we go?" Steven asked.

"To your dad's boat." Even if they couldn't start the boat, Kate knew it would be safer there when the land flooded. "Stay close to me. Do what I tell you. No one talks until I say it's all right. Okay?"

They both nodded. Hannah mimed a key locking her lips and threw it away, then took a tighter grip on her doll.

"Are you going to get us out of here now, Mom?" Steven asked.

"I am," she told him with the complete conviction she knew he wanted to hear, even though she didn't know how she was going to accomplish that feat yet.

She led them into the darkness, switching off the flashlight because she didn't want Rollins or Jolly to spot them in the darkness. Steven and Hannah slowed her, but they weren't far from the boat. Kate kept thinking about the single gunshot she'd heard, wondering what it meant.

Another lightning flash caused Hannah to scream.

Kate turned to her daughter immediately, sliding a hand across Hannah's mouth. "Shhhh, baby," Kate whispered into her daughter's ear. "We've got to be quiet. There are bad people out here. We don't want them to find us."

Hannah nodded.

Kneeling, Kate looked into her daughter's eyes. They were big and filled with fear. Kate kept her hand in place. "What's wrong?" she asked.

Hannah pointed.

Slowly, heart thudding in her chest, Kate turned to look at the side of the trail.

Jolly lay crumpled against a cypress tree, mostly covered by brush but Kate recognized his clothes. Then lightning flashed again, revealing the torn and bloody flesh that covered the side of Jolly's face.

Hannah quivered and screamed again. A little of the noise made it past Kate's hand. She turned her daughter away from the sight.

"It's all right," Kate said. "He can't hurt us."

Hannah nodded, but she was still trembling and Kate felt the rush of hot tears across her fingers and the back of her hand. She felt bad because she knew Hannah wasn't afraid that Jolly was going to hurt them. Hannah was afraid because she'd never seen a man wearing a gunshot wound where a large section of his face had been.

"Steven." Kate looked at her son and saw that he had his own hand over his mouth. He looked at her with big eyes. "I need you to take care of Hannah. Can you do that?"

He nodded and slipped his hand in place of Kate's. Hannah held her brother's hand to her mouth.

"He may have the keys to your dad's boat," Kate said, hoping she sounded calm and not panicked. Sounding panicked wouldn't keep her kids from getting more panicked. *Please let him have the keys!* "I've got to get them. We're going to take your dad's boat out of here. Okay?"

They nodded.

Turning, Kate gripped the flashlight near its end so she could use it like a club if Jolly wasn't as dead as he looked. She went down the small incline, walking through several inches of water that told her how bad the flooding conditions had already gotten.

Keeping control of herself, Kate rapped Jolly's foot with the flashlight, ready to bail at the first sign of movement on his part.

He remained inert.

She tried to see his face in the darkness and couldn't. From the best she was able to remember, the bullet had hit Jolly somewhere under the left eye. Evidently he'd had his head turned to the side because the bullet had plowed through the soft tissue of his cheek and torn through his left eye socket. It might even have ricocheted into his brain.

Taking a deep breath, she made herself go forward till she

was beside him. She thought about checking for a pulse, but after seeing the ruin of his face, she knew there wasn't one. And if there was, she couldn't do anything that would help.

Quickly, breathing shallowly to control her fear, she went through his jacket pockets. She found a key ring almost immediately and felt a surge of hope and happiness so strong that she laughed a little, surprising herself.

A quick flash of the flashlight revealed that the key ring was Bryce's. Shoving the keys into her jeans pocket, she stood and returned to Steven and Hannah.

"Is he...dead?" Steven asked.

For just a moment, Kate thought about lying to her son. Just to protect him. But there was so much more between them now that hadn't been there before. She couldn't risk it.

"Yes," she said.

"And he was one of the bad guys that I saw on television? The one that kidnapped and killed that woman for all that money?"

"Yes."

"Okay." Steven took a deep breath. "At least he can't hurt us now."

Pain touched Kate's heart. Kill or be killed. It was one of the most instinctive and savage edicts of animals and people, but she didn't know how jarring that feeling could be coming out of the mouth of an eight-year-old boy.

"That's right," she made herself say. "He can't." Then she took Steven by the hand and they went on. She couldn't help wondering who had killed Jolly. Rollins might have done it. But Shane was still out there too, and she felt he was definitely capable.

After eluding the reinforcements Rollins had sent, Shane ran through the forest, slipping and sliding, falling twice but pushing himself back up immediately. Carlyle's warning kept echoing through his head, adding urgency to the fear and anger that was already fueling him.

Hurricane Genevieve has whipped up a wall of water. The weather guys say it's going to hit the area where you are within minutes.

And Kate didn't know.

Topping the hill leading to the low area where Bryce Colbert's boat was docked, Shane told himself that the course of action he'd decided on was the best he could do. Kate and her kids were somewhere in the middle of this part of the Everglades and he couldn't immediately find them.

Helplessness battered him as relentlessly as the rain that soaked him to the bone. He didn't like feeling helpless. Not helpless. Hell no. You're way past that. Ineffectual is what you've been. Shane Warren was supposed to be the Answer Guy at the FBI for getting tough cases solved. Always-Thinks-Outside-the-Box Warren. That was him. But he'd been like a fish on a bicycle ever since he'd helped Jolly and his crew escape prison.

If it hadn't been for Kate Garrett, he'd have already failed his assignment. He pushed his breath out angrily as he ran. Get off it, Warren. Without that woman, you'd have been dead a couple times in there, too.

And if she hadn't been trying to look out for him, Kate would have already gotten her kids and herself out of harm's way. He was responsible for them being here. Right where a wall of water was already rushing inland to take out everything in its path.

Some hero, he told himself. Some big-shot FBI agent. You're just a hotdogger.

Lost in his thoughts, overrunning existing conditions and

way too fast for the trail, Shane felt his feet slide out from under him. He fell. Gracelessly and flat on his ass. The incline was sharp and slick enough with mud that he careened down the hillside. He wrapped his arms around his head as best as he could and took the beating delivered by the branches and trees, crashing at last into a tree so hard that it knocked the wind out of him.

For a moment, he was stunned, drifting toward a lazy blackness. The rain pounded him, locking him into the here and now, and at that moment he was grateful for it. It hurt to move but he did it, knowing Bryce Colbert's boat was the only chance he had at saving Kate and her kids.

As soon as he was up, he started running again. At the bottom of the hill, he glanced at his compass and got his bearings. He headed to the right, knowing he had to be close.

Light bloomed against the trees ahead of him. A short distance farther on, he made out the elegant lines of the powerboat. Lightning flashed and brought the boat out of the darkness, making it look as out of place there in the swamp as a unicorn at a construction site.

Tied up at the pilings, the powerboat pulled restlessly at her tethers. Water slopped over the top of the pier now, several inches higher than it had been, letting him know the level was rapidly rising.

Shane ran down the pier and clambered aboard the powerboat. On the deck, he felt her sway and thud against the pilings as she fought the restraints. He searched the shore, hoping for some sign of Kate, Steven and Hannah. Only the darkness greeted his efforts.

Raymond Jolly and Bryce Colbert were out there, too. He hoped Kate and the kids didn't run into either of them. Jolly would kill them, but Bryce would be more useless than helpful.

About the way you are now, Shane chided himself. He turned his attention to the powerboat's ignition. He knelt and tried to remove the access panel. Unfortunately, it was locked as well. Probably with the same damn missing key. Rocking back on his butt, he kicked the panel.

On the third kick, the access panel caved. He had to admit that tearing up one of Bryce's expensive toys felt pretty good.

Back on his knees again, Shane grabbed the panel and yanked it out to reveal the circuitry. He took his cigarette lighter out and flicked the roller. Holding the lighter inside the circuitry panel, he started chasing the ignition wires. He knew how to hotwire cars and motorcycles. Boats couldn't be that different. Looking at the bundles of plastic spaghetti, he frowned. There were a hell of a lot of wires, though.

The boat shifted a little, working against the current. That tipped Shane off that he wasn't alone on the boat. He turned around, starting up into a crouch, intending to position himself to one side.

"Don't move," a woman said.

Shane's heart beat more frantically as he looked at the slender woman draped in shadows in front of him. "Kate?" he asked softly.

"Don't move," she repeated more forcefully. "I'll shoot you if I have to."

Lightning blazed, revealing the cold blue metal finish of the snub-nosed .357 Magnum she held pointed dead center at his chest. It also revealed her features. He didn't know if he was more surprised by her presence and the gun, or that he knew her and she was supposed to be dead.

Chapter 17

"Mom," Hannah whispered. "I can't walk any more."

Kate stopped and looked back at her daughter. "It's only a little farther."

"I just can't," Hannah whined. "I've tried to be brave. Really I have. My legs hurt. They hurt really bad."

That was something Kate understood. Despite her conditioning, she was hurting too. "I know." She picked her daughter up and shifted Hannah to her hip, leaning just a little to balance out the load. Hannah was almost too big to carry comfortably. Kate's heart nearly broke as she thought about all the opportunities she'd missed to carry her daughter when she was smaller. Six weeks of visitation a year hadn't been enough.

"Hold on to me," Kate said. She tucked the long-handled flashlight into her waistband.

Hannah threw her arms around Kate's neck. "Thank you, Mom."

"She can't carry you, Hannah," Steven growled. "She's too tired."

"It's okay," Kate said. "I can do it."

"It's not fair," Steven said. "You shouldn't have to carry her when you're so tired."

Life isn't fair, Kate thought, remembering how many people had told her that over the years when they'd found out she wasn't getting to see the kids very much. People had meant it as a positive saying, something that acknowledged that bad things happened to good people, that she didn't deserve how she was being treated. But she hadn't realized how negative it would become when she heard it over and over. She stopped herself from telling Steven that now.

"This is what we have to do," she told him instead. "I can do it."

"Dad should have helped you," Steven said. "He should have. He just didn't want to."

A pang of guilt about leaving Bryce by the grave passed through Kate. There was nothing she could do about that. Both of them had made their choices. She held out her hand. Steven took it, holding it tightly, and she felt how cold his fingers were. It was a good thing Raymond Jolly was dead. After putting her kids through this, she knew she would have been tempted to kill him herself when she laid eyes on him.

Carrying her daughter and holding on to her son's hand, Kate started down the incline. She hoped she was right about the boat's location. She didn't have the stars or a compass to guide her, only her instincts and a memory of the land before it had been storm-tossed.

At the bottom of the incline, she saw the edge of the swamp. The waterline had crept up, flooding more of the bottomland, turning the mud into soup. She slogged on, feeling Hannah's extra weight push her right down into the ground. If she stopped moving, she was afraid she'd sink till she and her daughter were buried.

"Mom," Hannah whispered, leaning down over Kate's head, "I see a light." She pointed.

"I see it too," Steven agreed quietly. "Is that Dad's boat?"

"Yeah," Kate said, hope dawning in her. "Yeah, I think it is."

"Yay," Hannah said quietly, as if she'd just found out they were going to McDonald's. "We've got a boat!"

"We do," Kate agreed. The fatigue dropped away from her a little then. Her steps lengthened. Just before she hit the edge of the trees lining the boat dock, a shadow ran down the incline, lithe and fleet as a deer. The figure carried a suitcase-sized box in one hand.

Just about the size of a ransom drop.

Kate stopped, holding Steven back and pulling him into the deeper shadows among the tree.

"What's wrong?" Steven asked.

"Shhh," Kate told him.

The figure trotted down to the pier, then froze when someone started banging something aboard the powerboat. Lightning flared and shone on the pistol in the figure's hand.

"Oh no," Hannah wailed softly. "She has a gun!"

She? Kate wondered. None of the men Kate had seen were that small. She had to be a woman. Then, thinking about the gun in the woman's hand, Kate had to wonder if she was the one who'd shot Jolly. And why.

The figure started moving again, creeping stealthily aboard the powerboat.

For a moment, Kate sat in the darkness with her children, hoping that nothing happened to them. Unfortunately, she needed the powerboat if they were going to get away. To the southeast, she saw the sky roiling, clouds bumping and ripping as the storm increased her fury.

Can't wait much longer, she told herself.

"Don't move!" the woman yelled aboard the powerboat. *"Don't move!* I'll shoot you if I have to!"

Knowing that if the woman was friendly with Jolly—even if she'd killed him later—then she wasn't going to be supportive of her and her kids, Kate knew she had to take action. Evidently whoever was aboard the boat wasn't someone the woman trusted.

"Steven," Kate whispered.

"Yeah."

"I need you to stay here with your sister." Kate shrugged out of the bow and quiver, leaving them hanging in the tree off the ground.

"Don't leave, Mommy! Please don't leave!" Hannah pleaded softly.

Kate held her daughter's face in one hand, watching Hannah's tears mix with the rain. "I need you to be a big girl, Hannah."

"I don't want to!"

"I need you to, Hannah. Please. I need to make sure it's safe for us. Just stay here with Steven and be quiet." Kate looked her daughter in the eye. "Understand?"

Hannah nodded, but her lower lip trembled.

"I love you," Kate said, kissing Hannah. "Both of you." She kissed Steven as well. "Stay here. Till I come get you."

Solemnly, fear in their eyes, they both nodded.

Steeling herself, telling herself that they would be fine and that she was the one that she needed to be worried about, Kate turned and ran toward the boat.

* * *

Shane looked at the woman and took away the brunette hair, substituting it with blond. He said her name without knowing he was going to. "Desiree Martini." As soon as he recognized her, nothing seemed to make sense.

Her gun didn't waver, but the woman looked at him harder. "I don't know you." She motioned with the pistol. "Get your hands up."

Reluctantly, still stunned by who he was seeing before him, Shane raised his hands. "I thought you were dead," he said. "Even your parents thought you were dead."

"Who are you?" she asked. "I saw you with Raymond Jolly on the news. You were part of the prison bus break."

"I was with Jolly," Shane said. "But only to find you."

She frowned. "What are you talking about?"

"My name is Shane Warren. I'm a special agent with the FBI." Shane studied her brown hair and decided it was a wig. "Your parents have friends in Washington. They pulled enough pressure to get the FBI looking for you again." He paused. "*Everyone* thought you were dead."

Desiree shook her head. "Do you have any ID?"

"Not when I'm this far undercover." Shane knew she shouldn't trust him. He didn't think he would trust him in these circumstances.

She looked him over from head to toe. Indecision tightened her eyes and pinched her features.

"Look," he said gently, "I don't know what you've been through, but I came out here with Jolly and his buddies hoping just to find your body and get it—you—home so they could bury you." He smiled. "I know they'd prefer you get home safe."

Desiree shook her head. "You don't know what I've been

through." Tears ran down her cheeks. She wiped them away with the back of her free hand.

"Tell me," Shane invited.

Thunder rumbled ominously.

She hesitated.

"We don't have a lot of time," Shane said. "I've got a contact in the FBI that I managed to get through to a few minutes ago. He said there's a flood headed this way. Genevieve has started a series of storm surges that are going to cover this entire area. This place is about to be overrun by the ocean." He lowered his hands to his sides. "You're going to have to trust me." And I've got to find Kate and her kids. "There are people out there who are depending on me."

"Jolly kidnapped me," Desiree said. "For the last seven months, some of his men have held me captive. They were supposed to meet him in Everglades City if he ever escaped. But after they heard the news they decided to come here. At a camp in the woods. They were going to reclaim the money from wherever it was buried. Jolly wouldn't tell them where it was when they visited him in prison, but he told them to hang on to me, that he'd be ransoming me back to my father again. I just got away from them during all the confusion. There are a lot of guys with guns in the woods now. I knew about this boat because we came by here earlier, and I decided to see if I could find someone who could help me."

Damn! Shane thought, knowing the kind of rough treatment she would have had at the hands of Jolly's men. It was a wonder that she'd still had enough courage to save herself when she had the opportunity.

"Is anyone following you?" That would be good to know. Shane scanned the banks and the forest but didn't see anything.

"No. I don't think so. I shot the guy I escaped from."

That didn't make Shane feel entirely comfortable. If Desiree could drop the hammer on one of Jolly's men and she still believed he was one of them, she might not have a problem shooting him either. "Okay," he said. "That's good."

"Can you start the boat?"

"I think so." Shane held out his hand. "Can I have the gun?"

Desiree took a step back and shook her head. "No."

Okay, we're not exactly working with complete trust here. Shane let out a breath. "Could you at least point it somewhere else?"

Reluctantly, Desiree lowered the pistol to her side.

Feeling a little better, Shane knelt and flicked his lighter to life again. He studied the wiring once more, searching out the hot wire to the ignition. He wanted to keep her talking, and he also wanted to know more of her story. "Why did they keep you alive?"

"Jolly was going to ransom me again. He figured if my dad paid the ransom once, especially since it was something he could pay so easily, then he'd do it again."

"He didn't count on your dad going to the FBI."

"No. Neither did I. My dad could have gotten me killed." Desiree's voice turned hard.

Shane didn't blame her. She had a right to be scared and pissed.

"Your dad thought you were already dead. Someone reported that they'd seen Jolly shoot you."

"That was Luisa."

"The maid?" Shane found a promising wire and held on to it with his forefinger while he dug his utility knife from his jeans pocket.

"Yes. Jolly wanted me to know how easy it was for him to kill somebody."

Sick bastard, Shane thought. When this was over, he intended to run Raymond Jolly to the ground. "When Luisa disappeared, investigators thought she was in on it."

"No. Jolly took us both. He was going to leave her body after he got away with the ransom, just to show my father that he meant business the second time around."

Thunder rumbled again, sounding closer and more forceful. The powerboat shuddered and rocked on the water as the flooding increased. Shane tried to work faster, but it was difficult with only the lighter to work with. Another set of hands would have been useful too, but he didn't think he'd talk Desiree into getting that close. He concentrated on his task, knowing the storm was sweeping in.

Kate stayed low as she approached the powerboat. She kept her hands trailing the ground in front of her, adding her sense of touch to her vision to warn her of anything she might trip over while she watched the powerboat.

Dim, wavering light filled the boat's pilot area. Lighter, she thought. She felt the long-handled flashlight she'd confiscated in her waistband at her back. When she ran out of brush, still sixty yards distant from the pier, she decided to go into the turbulent water in an effort not to be seen. Whoever had shot Jolly had been close. The woman she'd seen earlier could easily have been that person.

Wading into the water, she felt the cold seep into her until she was numb. Teeth chattering, she swam against the current to reach the boat. Coming up behind it, she found the ladder in place.

Kate pulled herself up and listened as Shane talked to the woman. When she learned that the woman was Desiree Martini, and that the heiress wasn't dead after all, Kate was shocked.

She clung to the ladder for a moment, thinking about the situation. If Desiree was there because she'd managed to escape Jolly's men, then there was no reason not to call Steven and Hannah out of the trees. The water was rising by fast inches around Kate's hips, swirling higher and higher and growing stronger as it tried to pluck her from the stern.

"Jolly wanted me to know how easy it was for him to kill somebody," Desiree said.

But Kate's mind whirled and latched on to the image of the dead woman in the shallow grave. She'd been dressed in Desiree Martini's clothes. Why would Jolly do that? It didn't make any sense.

She's lying, Kate thought, peering through the gray sheeting rain into the pilot area. Jolly had been shot at close range. He wouldn't have allowed Rollins or his people to get close enough to do that. Besides, Kate and Shane had kept Rollins and his men busy during that time. And Jolly hadn't been dead long. His body had still been warm.

The powerboat's engine tried to turn over with a basso rumbling that momentarily rivaled the thunder. In the pilot area, Desiree lifted her pistol and aimed at the back of Shane's head as sparks briefly outlined him. Kate recognized the woman as the one who had been aboard the boat earlier and had freed Jolly.

Desiree Martini had been in on her own kidnapping. It had been an inside job.

She's going to shoot him! Kate almost hauled herself up over the stern, but she got control; she would be too exposed.

The boat's engines died.

"Dammit!" Shane said.

Desiree lowered her weapon as he turned back to look at her.

"Almost had it," he said, sucking on a finger. "Shocked me."

"That's okay," Desiree said, as if she was depending on him to rescue her. "I know you'll get it."

Kate damned Shane for falling for the soft-voice routine. Get men into the role of the rescuer and they could be so pathetically stupid. Desiree Martini was punching all the right buttons in Shane Warren. She had his number.

But she only needs him to start the boat, Kate thought. Then she'll kill him.

As the sound of the powerboat engine faded away, a shadow lumbered down the pier, walking slowly. Lightning blazed and revealed Raymond Jolly's bloody features.

Jolly walked slowly, but he walked. He worked his mouth, dripping blood and saliva, and his left eye was a gleaming mass of crimson. He carried a pistol at the end of his right arm and walked with determination toward the boat.

Neither Shane nor Desiree saw or heard him, both of them intent on the engine.

"I'll get it this time," Shane promised. He flicked the lighter to life once more and leaned into the control panel.

Jolly paused on the pier just for a moment, then he grabbed hold of the boat and leaped over the side. The sudden shift of weight, something Kate had intentionally avoided by easing out of the water, caught Shane and Desiree's attention.

"Damn bitch!" Jolly snarled as he turned toward Desiree and lifted the big pistol. "You shot my face off!"

Desiree started to raise the gun in her hand.

"Do it, you backstabbing bitch!" Jolly swore. "I'll put a bullet right through your black heart!"

"Jolly," Desiree said, fear showing on her face. "You don't want to kill me."

"The hell I don't!" Jolly roared.

"You can ransom me back to my father," Desiree said.

"No!" Jolly shook his head. "You were the one who wanted to get cute with the plan in the first place! If it hadn't been for you changing things, none of us would have gotten caught!"

"That wasn't my fault," Desiree pleaded. "I thought my father loved me. I didn't think he'd do something to jeopardize my life."

"I should have had you killed then," Jolly said. He spat blood and twisted his head on his neck as if he were in great pain.

Beside Desiree, Shane tensed and Kate knew he was going to try something stupid.

Kate almost hauled herself up then. Instead, she reached down and caught a dead rat by the tail, lifting it from the water. It was heavy and solid, a limp weight at the end of her arm. The hairless tail felt like rope.

"Hey," a voice called from the pier. "That's my boat!" Bryce stumbled along the pier, one hand to his head.

Jolly's attention wavered, and he was further handicapped because Bryce was coming up on his blind side. He shifted his pistol toward Bryce.

"Oh hell no!" Bryce yelped, diving to the pier.

Chapter 18

Jolly's first bullet split the air over Bryce's head. By then Shane was in motion, throwing himself forward. Quick as a snake, Jolly swung the pistol back around and fired at Shane from point-blank range. Shane's leap turned into a sprawl as he went down. Desiree fired three times, hitting Jolly in the chest each time.

Staggered by the rounds, Jolly stepped back, holding his free hand to one of the bullet holes that pumped crimson. "Damn you!" he said hoarsely. He tried to pull his pistol up but didn't have the strength.

Desiree Martini fired at him one last time. The bullet smashed into Jolly's already-ruined face and knocked him backward. Kate hugged the ladder as the big man spilled over the side and disappeared into the swirling water. She made herself not cry out and turned her attention back to Desiree and Shane. Bryce cowered on the pier.

Blood covered Shane's right thigh. He stripped his belt off, obviously intending to use it as a tourniquet to stop the bleeding.

"Don't bother," Desiree said, holding the pistol on him. "You're not going anywhere."

Shane tried to get up, but the wounded leg wouldn't hold his weight. "So it's true?" He scooted to the side and threw an arm over the gunwale.

"About me helping stage my own kidnapping?" Desiree smiled and arched an eyebrow. "Yeah. And it would have worked, too. If dear old Daddy hadn't cared more about his money than he did about me." She sighed theatrically. "And if Jolly had told me where he *really* hid the money that night. He lied to me about that. When he didn't come to Everglades City for me, I came out here and waited. I've got a camp up in the woods. I knew the money was out here somewhere, but I could never find it. I was just about to run out of savings when you guys escaped the bus. If Jolly had trusted me, I could have already been gone. Ten million dollars richer."

"Maybe he suspected that you'd called in the anonymous tip that got him arrested," Shane accused. "You don't come across as exactly trustworthy."

"Really?" Desiree smiled and shook her head. "Say what you want, Mr. FBI-Guy, but I think you were buying into it before Jolly arrived." She waved the pistol. "It wasn't Jolly's money anyway. It was mine. I didn't need him. You're just lucky I need you to start the engine."

"You don't need him," Bryce called from the pier. "There's a spare key." Slowly, he stood. "You need me. I know where the key is, and I can pilot the boat."

Desiree turned slightly and pointed the pistol at Bryce.

"Can you pilot the boat?" Bryce demanded in that holier-than-thou tone that Kate had learned to hate.

Desiree didn't say anything.

"If you can," Bryce went on, "do you really want to bet that you can handle everything that storm is throwing our way?"

Shane finished getting to his feet. The stain spreading down his wounded leg grew bigger and bigger. He was finding his balance, timing the rhythm of the boat, and Kate knew he wasn't going to lie down and die.

"I can pilot the boat," Bryce said. "I can get us out of here. More than that, I can back your story up and tell everyone that you were being held captive all this time. You don't really want to continue hiding, do you?"

Thunder pealed while Desiree considered her options. A fresh wave of water spilled into the lagoon, causing the powerboat to violently rock and smash against the pier.

"Why would you do that?" Desiree asked.

Bryce nodded toward the suitcase on the boat's deck. "That's the ransom money, right?"

Desiree didn't reply.

"I'm not greedy," Bryce went on. "I want half."

"All right," Desiree said with a smile. She turned back to Shane. "You've met my new partner. I don't need you anymore."

Shane tried to throw himself at her, but his wounded leg gave out beneath him. He went down and tried at once to push himself back up. He was never going to make it.

Curling her fingers tightly around the dead rat's tail, Kate whipped her arm forward and over the boat's stern section, throwing as hard as she ever had when pitching for the beer-league overhand softball games.

The rat crossed the distance in a hairy blur and smacked into the center of Desiree's chest. The tail slapped her across the face. Staggered by the impact, she stumbled back. She looked down and saw the dead rat rolling across the heaving deck, then screamed.

By that time, Kate had hauled herself over the boat's stern and rolled on to the deck. She reached behind her and slipped the flashlight from her waistband, sliding it through her hand till she gripped it by the end as she threw herself forward.

"Kate!" Bryce called.

"Don't!" Shane yelled, trying to get to his feet again.

Kate threw herself forward, desperate. No matter what else she did, Desiree wouldn't allow Kate to bring Steven and Hannah aboard. The woman would leave them to drown when the storm surge rolled across the swamp.

"Get away from me!" Desiree yelled as she leveled the Magnum.

Mercilessly, Kate swung the flashlight as hard as she could. The blow connected with the pistol and Desiree's hand. Metal rang and bone snapped, followed immediately by Desiree's scream.

"You bitch!" Desiree dodged Kate's next blow, then set up in a martial arts stance. She ducked under Kate's next swing and stood toe-to-toe with her. Then she powered a palm-heel strike to Kate's face.

Kate turned her head just enough to keep the blow from breaking her nose as Desiree had intended, but not from avoiding the explosion of pain that filled her head. She swung and missed as Desiree crouched and shot a foot into her stomach.

Air left Kate's lungs and she crashed back against the pilot cabin. Her head struck the metal frame and stars swirled in her vision. She barely saw Desiree set herself and lash out with another kick till she felt it crash against her forehead.

Kate's knees went weak and she dropped. She caught Desiree kicking out at her again. This time she rolled beneath it, coming over swinging the flashlight into the back of her opponent's knee. Desiree's leg buckled and she came down.

Desiree cursed in pain but she scrambled and tried to get up. Kate didn't let her, going after her at once. She swept Desiree's ankles in her arm and pulled her feet out from under her. Desiree scratched and bit, screaming in fury. Kate rode her, trying to stay on top. In her peripheral vision, she could see Bryce at the side of the boat, frozen in fear or surprise.

Grabbing Kate's hair in her fist, Desiree yanked, still cursing and kicking. Somehow they came up together in the pilot cabin, reaching their feet while pushing and pulling each other. They banged against the interior of the confined space and skidded over the battered control-panel cover.

Then Desiree's good hand closed on the hunting knife at Kate's hip. The other woman ripped the blade free and slashed at her face. Kate blocked the blow with the flashlight. Somehow she'd maintained a hold on it. The sharp blade stopped less than an inch from Kate's eye. Both of them were breathing hard, shaking from the strain of the fight. Kate felt Desiree's body trembling against hers.

"I'm going to kill you!" Desiree screamed.

Thinking of Steven and Hannah waiting for her out in the dark forest, Kate shook her head. "Not today." She forced Desiree's hand back with the flashlight, banging it against the metal bulkhead. Once, twice, three times, all of them as hard as she could.

The knife fell limply from Desiree's grip. Then, unexpectedly, she headbutted Kate in the face. Kate's nose broke and she immediately tasted blood. Unable to move for a moment, she watched as Desiree bent down for the hunting knife. The blade sparked, catching the lightning that strobed the whirling storm clouds.

Desiree drove the knife forward. Kate ducked inside the blow, then whipped the flashlight back across her body, catching the woman in the face and knocking her back through the doorway out on to the deck.

Shane was on his feet now, but still bleeding badly. He started toward them.

Kate didn't wait, didn't hesitate. Desiree Martini's kidnapping, aided and abetted, had turned Kate's life inside out. She struck, putting her body behind the blow as she swung the flashlight into Desiree's jaw. The lens cover broke and batteries shot across the deck as the flashlight emptied.

Desiree dropped in a loose sprawl of limbs.

Standing above her, chest heaving, pain shooting through her nose and face, Kate hated the woman at the same time she hoped she hadn't killed her.

Shane knelt beside her. His fingertips pressed against her throat. Then he looked at Kate. "She's alive."

"Thank God," Kate said. She threw the broken flashlight away then grabbed Shane's belt from the deck. "Sit down."

Shane hesitated a moment.

"Your leg," Kate said. "If you don't take care of it, you're going to bleed out."

Shane sat.

Without a word, Kate dropped to her knees and expertly wrapped the belt around his thigh. She pulled it as tight as she could, then used the clasp knife to cut a new hole so she could buckle it.

"Where are your kids?" Worry sounded in his voice.

"I found them," Kate told him. "They're nearby."

Bryce jumped aboard and ran to the pilot cabin. After a frantic search, he announced, "They found the spare key too."

"Maybe I can hotwire it," Shane said. "I almost had it before Jolly arrived."

Kate reached in her pocket and took out the key. "I've got that, too."

"I'll be damned," Shane said, shaking his head and smiling in amazement.

"I'll take that." Bryce crossed to her and tried to snatch the key from her hand.

Kate closed her fingers over it and made a fist. "No."

"No?" Bryce glared murderously at her.

"No," Kate repeated, and she knew the word sounded strange due to the swelling caused by the broken nose. She stood straight and tall, looking up at him.

"It's my damn boat."

"Not tonight." Kate started for the pilot cabin.

"Hey, just a damn minute." Bryce grabbed her by the arm and spun her around. "This is my boat and we're going to do things my way."

"I know the swamp," Kate said, trying to reason with him. Surely now, with the storm unfolding all around them again, he could see that she was the best gamble they had.

"I don't care," Bryce said. "This is *my* boat."

The wind suddenly rose again, howling now and tearing branches and limbs from the trees surrounding the lagoon. The powerboat slammed harder against the pier.

"Bryce," Kate said, trying to think of some way to negotiate with her ex-husband.

"Mr. Colbert," Shane said in a tone that suddenly sounded totally official.

"I told you," Bryce yelled, putting his hands out to shove Shane, "this is my—"

Shane hit him, putting all of his weight behind the blow

and snapping the punch as he connected with Bryce's chin. Bryce's eyes rolled up into his head and he sank like a stone to lie beside Desiree Martini.

"Damn!" Shane swore, shaking his hand. Then he turned to Kate. "What *did* you see in that guy?"

"He was a jerk," Kate told him evenly, walling off the confusion of emotions that swirled around inside her head and her heart when she thought of Shane. "I've never been able to pick a guy who wasn't a jerk."

He started to say something, but closed his mouth, shook his head and growled. "The storm's getting worse. One of the agents I talked to said a whole new front is moving in. This area is about to be sea bottom for a while."

"Cast off," Kate said, turning to the pilot cabin. "We've got to go get Steven and Hannah."

She started the engine and watched as Shane climbed from the boat, then threw the lines on to the deck. Kate fought to keep the boat close enough to the pier for him to jump, and he barely made it. He fell heavily to the deck, then pushed himself back up.

"You need to stay off that leg," she said as she reversed the engines and backed out into the lagoon.

"Got it on my list of things to do," Shane replied. He dragged Desiree and Bryce to the stern and rolled them into the small cargo hold.

"If the boat goes down, they'll drown," Kate said.

"So don't let the boat go down." Shane stood at the railing. "Where are the kids?"

"In the treeline. I told them to wait for me." Kate guided the powerboat toward the trees, then switched on the spotlight. She yelled over the noise of the approaching storm front. "Steven! Hannah!"

They didn't answer.

She called again, worried that something had happened to them.

"Mom! Mom!" Steven yelled. He came running toward the boat, charging through the shallow water with Hannah in tow.

"Hold up, Steven," Shane called. "Let me come to you." He'd taken two child-sized float vests from under the seats and had them under an arm as he jumped over the side.

So much for staying off that leg, Kate thought. But it took everything she could do to hold the boat in place.

Shane swam a short distance, then waded through the shallows. He tied the float vests on her son and daughter, then looped the rope through both of them. At his direction, they began swimming through the water to the boat.

Monstrous roaring and grinding from the port side drew Kate's attention. As she stared in disbelief, she saw the huge wave approaching them, rushing across the land with inexorable force and speed.

"Oh my God," Kate whispered, and it was as though she was trapped in a bad dream. The wave was twenty feet high. It ripped up trees and shoved them before it, a roiling mass of destruction.

In all the years she'd lived in the Everglades, through all the storms she'd weathered, she'd never seen anything like the horror that swept toward her now. The dull roaring of the churning water filled her ears. White curlers appeared and disappeared at once.

The sea had raised a mountain of water. And it was all about to slam into the boat.

Kate turned back to Steven, Hannah and Shane, seeing that they were nearly to the boat. *"Hurry!"* Her voice came out more as a scream than a yell.

The roaring sound increased, growing closer in a rush. Above them, the eye of the storm whirled, dark and mysterious and ravenous. The eye looked like a hole that had been poked into the cloud cover. It was calm, serene, but the clouds around it whirled, spinning faster and faster.

Oh God! Kate thought. *It's right on top of us!*

Steven reached the boat first and hauled himself aboard. He didn't even notice the coming wave. It was everything Kate could do not to leave the controls and go to them. But if she did the boat might come around and hit them or catch them in the twin props. Her heart hammered in her chest.

Steven leaned over the railing and caught Hannah's hands. By then the boat was bucking, getting harder to control as the rising water pushed in front of the main body of the surge slammed into the vessel. He pulled her up while Shane pushed her from below. She spilled over the side and fell on to the deck.

"Get over here!" Kate called. She struggled with the engines, trying to find the best power to use that would allow her to hold the position, knowing in her heart that she was doomed to futility.

In fact, it was already too late. The water raced toward them and hit the boat just as Shane came over the side. He had time for one startled glance, then he flung himself at Steven and Hannah, dragging them down.

Kate lost sight of them when the monster wave slammed into the boat. Spray and water filled the air, sluicing over the vessel in a deluge that covered everything.

For one minute she was terrified that they'd been shoved to the bottom of the sea in a watery coffin. She hung on to the wheel and the throttles, knowing she didn't have a choice. She could only hope that her kids were still on the boat.

She slapped the throttles forward, giving the engines full

power. The sea was a surging monster that the boat had to find the will and power to ride. The boat was submerged beneath the roil of water for a minute, then it powered through, ripping apart the curtain of the sea.

A trailer house came up out of the water and hit them. That close in to the coast, Kate knew the surge had ripped the home from the trees, offering further proof of how deep it was.

A grinding noise ripped through the storm's fury as the trailer house battered the boat. Kate was certain the fiberglass hull would cave in.

Kate reversed the throttles, hoping to pull away from the trailer house before it caught hold of them and pulled them under. Then the home disappeared once more beneath the water, gliding like a shark. The tops of trees raked at the boat's hull, clawing like a skeleton's fingers. Kate shoved the throttles forward again, cutting the wheel hard to bring the boat around so it would be caught broadsides.

For a moment, she didn't dare look back. She watched the sea crashing all around her, steering the boat as much as she was able to for the open water. She turned toward the retreating wave, hoping to climb it fast enough that she could stay on top of it instead of getting swamped by the next one. The roaring sound of the plunging, wild sea filled her ears.

Finally, she was able to glance back, heartsick and thinking that she would find only an empty deck where Steven and Hannah, and even Shane, used to be.

Instead, she saw Shane, his arms wrapped tightly around her children, hanging on for all he was worth, his uninjured leg hooked under one of the benches to help brace them. They were crying and scared, holding on to Shane just as tightly. Then she noticed that Shane was crying too, looking from one to the other to make sure they were all right.

He looked up at Kate. "They're okay," he said, his voice thick with emotion.

"I know," she said. She felt the hot tears running down her face. "I know."

Shane got Steven and Hannah up and herded them into the pilot cabin so they could be out of the rain. He searched through the compartments and found dry blankets, wrapping each of them up to stave off the cold. They huddled on the floor, teeth chattering. But they were alive.

Unable to stand any longer, his pant-leg nearly completely stained with blood, Shane's leg went out from under him and he sat heavily on the deck. He started shaking uncontrollably.

"What's wrong with him, Mom?" Steven asked worriedly.

"He's in shock," Kate said. "He was hurt really bad."

"Did that man shoot him?" Hannah asked.

Kate nodded, checking the sea, then looking back. "Steven, could you look for another blanket to—" She stopped when she saw Steven sitting beside Shane on the deck, extending his blanket to cover him.

Hannah slid over and joined them, holding out her blanket so she could share it with Shane as well. "You can have some of mine, too."

"Thanks," Shane said.

"Were you crying?" Hannah asked in innocent curiosity.

Shane hesitated just for a second. "Yeah. Maybe a little."

"'Cause you were scared?"

"Yeah," Shane answered. "'Cause I was scared."

"You don't have to be scared," Steven told him solemnly. "My mom's the greatest wilderness guide in the world. She'll get us home."

"Maybe you should think about doing commercial spots for your mom." Shane looked up at Kate. "You've got great kids."

"I know. But thank you anyway." Kate checked the sea and it was mostly smooth, flat and dark ahead of them. She thought about everything Shane had done, all the things he'd said. Taken as a whole, it was confusing. Thinking about his ultimate goal of finding Desiree Martini's body for her parents kind of put things in perspective.

But in the end, she chose to remember how he'd saved her kids. And maybe she remembered a little too fondly the way he'd punched Bryce.

She looked back at him. "Are you really an FBI agent?"

"Yeah," Shane said. "I really am." He frowned. "I may be an unemployed FBI agent after this fiasco. Things did *not* go as planned." He sighed. "Got any openings for a wilderness guide-in-training? I may need to explore my options."

Kate looked at him huddled there with her son and daughter. Her first instinct was not to trust him. She hadn't been attracted to a man yet that she could trust. And she was definitely attracted to Shane.

Finally she said, "You're not much of a guide, Special Agent Warren. You're too much of a hunter. You see the game trails in the world, not the whole world."

He looked a little sad, and maybe hurt.

Kate's heart went out to him but she steeled herself against those old familiar and untrustworthy feelings. She made mistakes with men. Now was not the time to start making them again when Steven and Hannah were going to need her so much.

"Yeah," he said finally. "You're probably right about that." Then he leaned his head back and closed his eyes.

By the time Kate thought of something more—something better—to say, Shane had passed out.

"Mom," Steven said.

"Yeah," she replied.

"Is he going to be okay?"

"I think so," Kate said. "He seems like a guy who comes through things that would stop a lot of other people. There aren't many guys like that." But they're not guys you can always depend on, or ones you should get attached to.

She pushed that thought out of her mind and concentrated on getting her bearings. All she had to do was ride out the rest of the storm and find the closest harbor that was still operational. Reaching up to the navigation center, she switched on the radio.

"—are advised to continue staying inside," a calm-voiced newscaster was saying. "Most of Hurricane Genevieve has passed over southern Florida. Emergency squads continue to rescue people caught in the storm, but meteorologists confirm that we've come through the worst of it."

Yeah, we have, Kate thought, looking back at her kids. Hannah was already asleep on Shane's shoulder. Steven, though still a little uncertain, smiled up at her. We've come through the worst of it.

Epilogue

Two Months Later

Dressed in jeans, a T-shirt, and an unbuttoned, sleeveless green-and-white-plaid flannel shirt, her hair pulled back under a Marlins baseball cap, Kate swung the framing hammer and soaked up the warm afternoon sun. She finished driving in the last nail, then stepped back and took a look at the bones of her new house.

Dozens of people had shown up to help her. Tyler and his father, fishermen and guides who were temporarily shut down till the storm waters finished receding. Even people like Jolie Meacham—who was the biggest flirt in Everglades City and who worked at The Stone Crab Pot restaurant—volunteered time. Several vehicles had gathered, and labor and tools and raw materials all came together.

Kate had been surprised by the number of people who had shown up at her house. She and her dad had interacted with most of them on a regular basis. But she hadn't expected them to help her. She thought part of it might have been because she'd become something of a minor celebrity in the community.

Still, even with them helping her, the house was coming along *so* slowly. Kate felt like screaming, but she knew it wouldn't do any good. There were just so many things up in the air at the moment.

Bryce was working out some kind of plea bargain for turning evidence against Hugh Rollins, but from what Kate was hearing through Mitch Tomlinson, the local attorney she'd hired to protect her interest in Steven and Hannah, Bryce was still going to spend some time inside a penitentiary for insider trading. Permanent custody was one of the balls she had up in the air, but Tomlinson was giving her hope. But she was going through her savings putting the house back together.

The insurance money hadn't kicked in, and there was some question as to if, when and how much. She tried not to think about that.

"Take a break, kiddo."

Turning, Kate saw her father walking over to her with an ice-cold can of tea in each hand. A red bandanna held Conrad Garrett's hair back and the carpentry belt looked at home around his hips. The sleeveless gray sweatshirt was darker gray with sweat.

"Thanks." Kate pulled the tab and took a deep swallow. The tea cut through the fatigue, tasted clean and pure.

Her dad sat on a keg of nails. "You know, baby girl, you might be pushin' yourself a little too hard."

Kate sat on the ground in front of him the way she had

when she'd been a little girl. "There's a lot to do, Dad, and not much time to do it in."

"You took longer to remodel it the first time than to build it this time."

"I didn't have the kids with me then." That year she'd finally gotten it together, she'd worked at the house steadily, doing most of it herself, designing, framing and finishing. What she hadn't known, what her dad couldn't teach her, she'd learned from friends and from the Internet. Now she'd already been through the process once and this time through she had improvements she wanted to make. They cost money. She would have loved to hire extra help, but that would have cut too deeply into her budget.

"You and the kids are welcome to live with me as long as you like," her dad said. "You know that."

Kate sighed. "I feel like we're taking advantage of you too much now as it is."

He shrugged. "When I'm out salvagin', I'm not home. An' when I'm home, I'm helpin' you build your house."

"You do have a social life."

Her dad smiled. "I do. An' she has her own place all to herself, an' we like it there just fine."

"Yeah," Kate said, grinning and feeling just the least bit envious, "well, maybe I should let you fend for yourself when Steven and Hannah want to know where Grandpa Conrad goes when he goes out late and doesn't get home till the next day. Or later."

Her father had the decency to blush. He wiped at his face with a big hand. "You're a hard woman, Kate."

"It's a hard life." Kate looked back at the house. "We'll be done with the framing in a few more days." She sipped her tea. "The house is important, Dad. My attorney says that when we go to custody court, it's important that I'm able to show that I have a house for Steven and Hannah."

"Well, you can stay with—"

"I know," Kate said. "But the judge is going to be more impressed with me if I have my own house." She corrected herself. "*Our* own house." She really liked the sound of that.

"Well, we're not going to get it done sittin' here." Reluctantly, her dad got up, finished his tea, crunched the can and fired it toward the big yellow trash can nearby.

A dust storm rose out on the single-lane dirt road leading to Kate's house. She squinted her eyes and looked at the car. A knot of apprehension formed in her stomach.

"Isn't that your attorney's car?" her dad asked.

"Yeah."

"Was he supposed to meet with you today?"

"No." Kate walked toward the road, tossing her own can into the trash can. She had to make herself breathe slowly. Mitch Tomlinson showing up unannounced and unscheduled couldn't be good news.

Tomlinson pulled the car up and got out. A blond guy with wraparound sunglasses got out on the other side. He wore a dark suit that was nicer than Tomlinson's white seersucker.

At first Kate feared the young guy in the suit might be Bryce's attorney. Her stomach had spasmed over that. Bryce wouldn't have his attorney come down here alone to get Steven and Hannah. He'd want to come too, just to turn the knife himself.

"Afternoon, Kate," Tomlinson called. He was in his fifties, a slightly heavy man with good hair and a friendly smile.

"Afternoon, Mitch," Kate said.

"Well, I apologize for not callin'," Tomlinson said. "I know you're busy out here an' what you're doin' is important, but

I wanted to tell you the news myself. Actually, I wanted to be here when you were told the news." He shoved a hand in the blond man's direction.

Then Kate recognized him. She'd been so intent on trying to read Tomlinson that she hadn't paid much attention to the other man.

Shane Warren took his sunglasses off and revealed those hazel cat's eyes. He smiled, smooth-shaven for the first time since she'd known him. "Hello, Ms. Garrett."

Kate didn't know what to say. The morning they'd made it back to Everglades City, Shane had been out of it. She'd turned him over to the hospital, then gone to check on her dad. By the time she woke the next day, she'd found out Shane really had been an FBI agent, and that his director had ordered him medevaced out to Washington where his office was.

She hadn't expected to see him again.

"Special Agent Warren," Kate said cautiously. He'd made a few phone calls when he'd come to, and a few off and on after that. He'd been polite, asking her how she was and how Steven and Hannah were. Kate had talked to him, but had always managed to keep the conversations short and to the point, and he'd been busy himself. The bullet had broken his thighbone. He'd had to endure a couple of operations and some intensive rehab, as well as answer lots of questions about his undercover assignment and how it had gotten off track.

At least, that was what she'd last heard a few weeks ago. That had been on her dad's answering machine. She'd had her personal phone number changed to avoid the media people wanting to know more about the Desiree Martini kidnapping. Desiree was looking at some serious hard time for the death of the maid in addition to the faked kidnapping and the wounding of a federal officer.

"I'm the reason Mr. Tomlinson didn't call." Shane walked around the car. He had the trace of a limp, but he was probably still undergoing rehab. If he'd come that far after everything he'd been through, Kate felt confident he'd make a full recovery.

"I suppose you had a reason."

"I do." Shane smiled.

"It appears that Bryce has decided to relinquish rights to Steven and Hannah," Shane said.

Emotion whirled inside Kate. She felt her knees weaken a little. She put a hand to her mouth to keep herself from asking the question that she was so afraid to hear the answer to.

"They're yours, Kate," Shane said softly. "For now and forever. Bryce will never have any more rights to them than you care to give him."

Kate looked at Tomlinson.

The attorney laughed. "It's true," he said. "I was prepared to run this thing before every judge I had to, here and in New York City. But Agent Warren showed up on my doorstep today with these papers." He took a thick envelope from his back pocket. "They grant you custody—permanent custody— the minute you sign 'em."

Tears filled Kate's eyes and she fought against them. She hated to cry in front of anybody. "How?" she asked hoarsely.

"It appears Agent Warren has a few friends in the law-enforcement business," Tomlinson said. "Evidently some of the organized crime bureau people offered Mr. Bryce Colbert a little forgiveness in a few gray areas, enough to save him a few years in prison, during which you'd have custody of the kids anyway, if he'd sign these papers I hold in my hand. Apparently, he jumped on it like a rat on cheese."

Overcome, Kate didn't know what to say. She looked at Shane. "Thank you."

"My pleasure," he said. "It's the least I could do after everything I put you through."

"Actually," Tomlinson said, "I don't agree that it was the least Agent Warren could do. But however you want to measure it, he's delivered on another kicker to sweeten the pot." The attorney took out another envelope. "In this envelope, I hold a certified check for seven hundred and forty-eight thousand dollars. Made out to you."

"Me?"

"It's the finder's fee on the ransom money you found out there," Tomlinson said. "The insurance company had to pay off on the demand, which was one of the reasons Mr. Martini went through law-enforcement channels to get his daughter back. They were the ones who ultimately paid the ransom, not Mr. Martini. Agent Warren convinced them they should pay you the finder's fee." He smiled again. "I hear their agreement facilitated the FBI cutting loose the ransom money from their evidence locker a lot sooner than they could have."

Shane nodded toward the house. "After the flooding here, I knew you needed a new house. And I knew the insurance money was going to be slow. With that money, you'll be able to rebuild."

"I can," Kate said, dazed, not believing what she was hearing, "and I can make it the way I want to. I can put the rest into a college fund."

Shane grinned at that. "You might want to do that, because from what I'm seeing from the IRS and other agencies, your ex is going to be lucky to keep a roof over his head."

"You ask me, that couldn't happen to a more deservin' fella," her dad said.

"Amen," Tomlinson added. "Nothin' like helpin' bein' on the delivery end of a swift kick in the ass to somebody who sorely has it comin'."

Shane nodded toward the house. "Looks like you could use some help."

Some of Kate's old warning system flared to life. With his haircut and smooth-shaven in a suit that probably cost more than she made in a month, FBI Special Agent Shane Warren looked like trouble she didn't need. He was big city and she was small town. She wouldn't make that mistake again, not after she'd just gotten custody of her kids.

"We're doing all right," Kate said.

Shane retreated a little. "I've got some time on medical leave, and some vacation time I've piled up. When I was a teenager and going through college, I helped build office buildings." His voice softened. "I'd really like to help out."

Her dad nodded at Tomlinson.

The attorney dropped an arm across Shane's shoulders. "Special Agent Warren—"

"Shane," Shane said, dropping his gaze then looking at the attorney. "Just call me Shane."

"Well, Shane," Tomlinson said, "that's a mighty neighborly offer you've made. Considerin' that Ms. Garrett *does*, in fact, need a lot of help, I'd like to accept on her behalf."

Kate opened her mouth to object.

"Don't you dare," her dad told her.

Angrily, she closed her mouth and didn't say anything.

"Furthermore, while you're here, I'd like to offer you the spare room at my house," Tomlinson went on as he guided Shane toward the house. "You'll get breakfast in the morning if you've a mind, but after that you're on your own. I don't think you'll find a better deal in town. Let me show you what Ms. Garrett is plannin' on doin' out here." He looked back over his shoulder and winked at Conrad Garrett.

Kate wheeled on her father.

He held up his hands. "Now you know I don't interfere much—"

"The hell you don't," Kate said.

"Just an opinion or an observation ever' now an' again," her father conceded. "An' I do have a stake in how them grandchildren of mine are gonna be raised."

Kate folded her arms and seethed.

"That man there," her dad said in a quiet, authoritative voice, "is a hell of a man. I don't know what went on between the two of you while you was out there with Jolly and that bunch, an' I ain't gonna ask. But I'd be a damn fool to let you be a damn fool right now. No sir, that ain't gonna happen today."

A lump formed in the back of Kate's throat. "You don't know that I can trust him any more than I do," she accused.

"No, no I don't, Kate. An' that's the plain truth of it. But I'll tell you one thing: that man cares about you or he wouldn't have done the things he done. An' I'm not talkin' about the custody deal he worked out for you or that money he got for you. I'm talkin' about the way he saved your kids that night." He was quiet for a moment. "He's been a hero FBI agent in all the papers. Solved the Martini kidnappin'. All that. Why should he care about what goes on here—*unless*—he really cares?"

At that moment, the school bus pulled down the dirt road and let Steven and Hannah off. After a few weeks of no school while everything got back to normal, Kate had enrolled both of them into public school. The environment was different than both of them were used to, but they were handling the changes pretty well.

She expected them to come to her but they saw Shane and knew him in spite of the haircut and shave. Crying out, they ran to him. Both of them had been worried when he'd disappeared from the hospital. A couple of times, she'd let them talk to Shane because it had allowed her to get off the phone and not appear rude. Then she'd noticed how much they'd enjoyed talking to Shane, and how willing Shane had been to talk to them. Kate hadn't wanted Steven and Hannah to get hurt, so she'd quietly nipped that in the bud as well.

They ran across the yard, screaming out his name. "Shane! Shane!"

Turning, a big smile curving his lips, Shane caught them both around the waists and pulled them into his arms. They started asking questions at the same time.

Kate saw Jolie Meacham fluff up her blond hair, grab a can of tea from the ice chest and saunter over to where Shane sat holding Steven and Hannah.

"Of course," her dad said, scratching his chin, "you could just sit back an' let Jolie Meacham have him. She'll put another notch on her bedpost because she's still workin' her catch-an'-release program."

Shane took the tea and thanked Jolie. Jolie smiled at him, that hundred-watt flash of ivory that generally made men take leave of their senses, and added a hand-on-the-waist hipshot in her tight jeans that made someone up in the roof trusses bang his thumb with his hammer and curse like blue blazes.

Kate had never really felt jealous over Bryce when he'd turned his attentions to other women. She'd spent her time being more hurt and confused than anything else. What she felt now was totally alien to her, but she didn't like it.

She took her hat off and set her hair free. Then she handed her cap to her dad. "Hold my hat," she said. And before she knew it, she was striding across the yard to where Jolie stood smiling and talking to Shane.

Without a word, scared to death inside, Kate stepped in

front of Shane and crossed her arms over her breasts. Jolie shut up and took a step away, confused over what was going on.

Steven and Hannah and Shane all sat quietly, waiting for her to speak.

Kate was uncomfortably aware that every eye there was fixed on her. "I'm not much for beating around the bush," she said, "and I'm not about to start now. I've been hurt and used, and I'm not going to let that happen again. Not to me and not to my kids. So before you show up around here and start getting invited into people's houses, I want to know what you're really doing here."

Shane shooed Steven and Hannah out of his lap. They hung on to his hands as if they were afraid for him.

Shane's eyes were soft as he looked down at her. "I'm sorry we met the way we did, Kate. I can't change that now. But I'm glad we met, even though it's turned my world upside down and inside out." He shook his head. "I don't know what my intentions are. I came down here to find out. All I know is that I can't quit thinking about you. And Steven and Hannah. I don't know what that means because I've never felt like this in my life. Truth to tell, I haven't wanted to be around anybody or share myself with anybody in—well, a *long* time." He pulled his hands free of Steven and Hannah. "I came down here to be with you. To find out how you felt. Because sitting up there in that apartment in Georgetown, I wasn't going to find out." He breathed out, like he couldn't quite catch his breath. "I came down here to find out, and that's all I know to tell you."

She saw the fear in him then. It made her feel sorry for him. Almost. It also drove her crazy and made her want him in spite of her own fears. Both of them were taking a chance, and that meant something to her.

Without a word, she stepped in close to him, took his face in her hands, and kissed him deeply, bruising his lips and tasting his mouth. And then she was in his arms and he was holding her more tightly than she'd ever before been held.

Finally, unable to kiss him any longer without wanting to rip his clothes from him, Kate stepped back and looked him in the eyes. "Break my heart, mister, and I'll put you in the hospital."

He laughed at her then. "I can live with that," he said.

Then Kate took over showing him the house, telling him her dreams of what it would be like when she finished. He walked with her, holding Steven and Hannah's hands, and it felt like the most natural thing in the world.

She was out of the dark storm that had followed her around for the last few years. She was walking in the sun now, no longer feeling the heat, only the promise of the brightness.

* * * * *

Design Tip of the Day

Ambience is everything. Imagine eating a foie gras at a luncheonette counter or a side of coleslaw at Le Cirque. It's not a matter of food but one of atmosphere. Remember that when planning your dining room design.
—Tips from *Teddi.com*

"Now that's the kind of man you should be looking for," my mother, the self-appointed keeper of my shelf-life stamp, says. She points with her fork at a man in the corner of the Steak-Out Restaurant, a dive I've just been hired to redecorate. Making this restaurant look four-star will be hard, but not half as hard as getting through lunch without strangling the woman across the table from me. "*He* would make a good husband."

"Oh, you can tell that from across the room?" I ask, wondering how it is she can forget that when we had trouble getting rid of my last husband, she shot him. "Besides being ten minutes away from death if he actually eats all that steak, he's twenty years too old for me and—shallow woman that I am—twenty pounds too heavy. Besides, I am *so* not looking for another husband here. I'm looking to design a new image for this place, looking for some sense of ambience, some feeling, something I can build a proposal on for them."

My mother studies the man in the corner, tilting her head, the better to gauge his age, I suppose. I think she's grimacing, but with all the Botox and Restylane injected into that face, it's hard to tell. She takes another bite of her steak salad, chews slowly so that I don't miss the fact that the steak is a poor cut and tougher than it should be. "You're concentrating on the wrong kind of proposal," she says finally. "Just look at this place, Teddi. It's a dive. There are hardly any other diners. What does *that* tell you about the food?"

"That they cater to a dinner crowd and it's lunchtime," I tell her.

I don't know what I was thinking bringing her here with me. I suppose I thought it would be better than eating alone. There really are days when my common sense goes on vacation. Clearly, this is one of them. I mean, really, did I not resolve less than three weeks ago that I would not let my mother get to me anymore?

What good are New Year's resolutions, anyway?

Mario approaches the man's table and my mother studies him while they converse. Eventually Mario leaves the table with a huff, after which the diner glances up and meets my mother's gaze. I think she's smiling at him. That or she's got indigestion. They size each other up.

I concentrate on making sketches in my notebook and try to ignore the fact that my mother is flirting. At nearly seventy, she's developed an unhealthy interest in members of the opposite sex to whom she isn't married.

According to my father, who has broken the TMI rule and given me Too Much Information, she has no interest in sex with him. Better, I suppose, to be clued in on what they aren't doing in the bedroom than have to hear what they might be doing.

"He's not so old," my mother says, noticing that I have barely touched the Chinese chicken salad she warned me not to get. "He's got about as many years on you as you have on your little cop friend."

She does this to make me crazy. I know it, but it works all the same. "Drew Scoones is not my little 'friend.' He's a detective with whom I—"

"Screwed around," my mother says. I must look shocked, because my mother laughs at me and asks if I think she doesn't know the "lingo."

What I thought she didn't know was that Drew and I actually tangled in the sheets. And, since it's possible she's just fishing, I sidestep the issue and tell her that Drew is just a couple of years younger than me and that I don't need reminding. I dig into my salad with renewed vigor, determined to show my mother that Chinese chicken salad in a steak place was not the stupid choice it's proving to be.

After a few more minutes of my picking at the wilted leaves on my plate, the man my mother has me nearly engaged to pays his bill and heads past us toward the back of the restaurant. I watch my mother take in his shoes, his suit and the diamond pinkie ring that seems to be cutting off the circulation in his little finger.

"Such nice hands," she says after the man is out of sight.

"Manicured." She and I both stare at my hands. I have two popped acrylics that are being held on at weird angles by bandages. My cuticles are ragged and there's marker decorating my right hand from measuring carelessly when I did a drawing for a customer.

Twenty minutes later she's disappointed that he managed to leave the restaurant without our noticing. He will join the list of the ones I let get away. I will hear about him twenty years from now when—according to my mother—my children will be grown and I will still be single, living pathetically alone with several dogs and cats.

After my ex, that sounds good to me.

The waitress tells us that our meal has been taken care of by the management and, after thanking Mario, the owner, complimenting him on the wonderful meal and assuring him that once I have redecorated his place people will be flocking here in droves (I actually use those words and ignore my mother when she rolls her eyes), my mother and I head for the restroom.

My father—unfortunately not with us today—has the patience of a saint. He got it over the years of living with my mother. She, perhaps as a result, figures he has the patience for both of them, and feels justified having none. For her, no rules apply, and a little thing like a picture of a man on the door to a public restroom is certainly no barrier to using the john. In all fairness, it does seem silly to stand and wait for the ladies' room if no one is using the men's room.

Still, it's the idea that rules don't apply to her, signs don't apply to her, conventions don't apply to her. She knocks on the door to the men's room. When no one answers she gestures to me to go in ahead. I tell her that I can certainly wait for the ladies' room to be free and she shrugs and goes in herself.

Not a minute later there is a bloodcurdling scream from behind the men's room door.

"Mom!" I yell. "Are you all right?"

Mario comes running over, the waitress on his heels. Two customers head our way while my mother continues to scream.

I try the door, but it is locked. I yell for her to open it and she fumbles with the knob. When she finally manages to unlock and open it, she is white behind her two streaks of blush, but she is on her feet and appears shaken but not stirred.

"What happened?" I ask her. So do Mario and the waitress and the few customers who have migrated to the back of the place.

She points toward the bathroom and I go in, thinking it serves her right for using the men's room. But I see nothing amiss.

She gestures toward the stall, and, like any self-respecting and suspicious woman, I poke the door open with one finger, expecting the worst.

What I find is worse than the worst.

The husband my mother picked out for me is sitting on the toilet. His pants are puddled around his ankles, his hands are hanging at his sides. Pinned to his chest is some sort of Health Department certificate.

Oh, and there is a large, round, bloodless bullet hole between his eyes.

Four Nassau County police officers are securing the area, waiting for the detectives and crime scene personnel to show up. They are trying, though not very hard, to comfort my mother, who in another era would be considered to be suffering from the vapors. Less tactful in the twenty-first century, I'd say she was losing it. That is, if I didn't know her better, know she was milking it for everything it was worth.

My mother loves attention. As it begins to flag, she swoons and claims to feel faint. Despite four No Smoking signs, my mother insists it's all right for her to light up because, after all, she's in shock. Not to mention that signs, as we know, don't apply to her.

When asked not to smoke, she collapses mournfully in a chair and lets her head loll to the side, all without mussing her hair.

Eventually, the detectives show up to find the four patrolmen all circled around her, debating whether to administer CPR, smelling salts or simply call the paramedics. I, however, know just what will snap her to attention.

"Detective Scoones," I say loudly. My mother parts the sea of cops.

"We have to stop meeting like this," he says lightly to me, but I can feel him checking me over with his eyes, making sure I'm all right while pretending not to care.

"What have you got in those pants?" my mother asks him, coming to her feet and staring at his crotch accusingly. "*Baydar?* Everywhere we Bayers are, you turn up. You don't expect me to buy that this is a coincidence, I hope."

Drew tells my mother that it's nice to see her, too, and asks if it's his fault that her daughter seems to attract disasters.

Charming to be made to feel like the bearer of a plague.

He asks how I am.

"Just peachy," I tell him. "I seem to be making a habit of finding dead bodies, my mother is driving me crazy and the catering hall I booked two freakin' years ago for Dana's bat mitzvah has just been shut down by the Board of Health!"

"Glad to see your luck's finally changing," he says, giving me a quick squeeze around the shoulders before turning his attention to the patrolmen, asking what they've got, whether they've taken any statements, moved anything, all the sort of stuff you see on TV, without any of the drama. That is, if you don't count my mother's threats to faint every few minutes when she senses no one's paying attention to her.

Mario tells his waitstaff to bring everyone espresso, which I decline because I'm wired enough. Drew pulls him aside and a minute later I'm handed a cup of coffee that smells divinely of Kahlúa.

The man knows me well. Too well.

His partner, whom I've met once or twice, says he'll interview the kitchen staff. Drew asks Mario if he minds if he takes statements from the patrons first and gets to him and the waitstaff afterward.

"No, no," Mario tells him. "Do the patrons first." Drew raises his eyebrow at me like he wants to know if I get the double entendre. I try to look bored.

"What is it with you and murder victims?" he asks me when we sit down at a table in the corner.

I search them out so that I can see you again, I almost say, but I'm afraid it will sound desperate instead of sarcastic.

My mother, lighting up and daring him with a look to tell her not to, reminds him that *she* was the one to find the body.

Drew asks what happened *this time*. My mother tells him how the man in the john was "taken" with me, couldn't take his eyes off me and blatantly flirted with both of us. To his credit, Drew doesn't laugh, but his smirk is undeniable to the trained eye. And I've had my eye trained on him for nearly a year now.

"While he was noticing you," he asks me, "did *you* notice anything about him? Was he waiting for anyone? Watching for anything?"

I tell him that he didn't appear to be waiting or watching. That he made no phone calls, was fairly intent on eating and did, indeed, flirt with my mother. This last bit Drew takes with a grain of salt, which was the way it was intended.

"And he had a short conversation with Mario," I tell him. "I think he might have been unhappy with the food, though he didn't send it back."

Drew asks what makes me think he was dissatisfied, and I tell him that the discussion seemed acrimonious and that Mario looked distressed when he left the table. Drew makes a note and says he'll look into it and asks about anyone else in the restaurant. Did I see anyone who didn't seem to belong, anyone who was watching the victim, anyone looking suspicious?

"Besides my mother?" I ask him, and Mom huffs and blows her cigarette smoke in my direction.

I tell him that there were several deliveries, the kitchen staff going in and out the back door to grab a smoke. He stops me and asks what I was doing checking out the back door of the restaurant.

Proudly—because, while he was off forgetting me, dropping by only once in a while to say hi to Jesse, my son, or drop something by for one of my daughters that he thought they might like, I was getting on with my life—I tell him that I'm decorating the place.

He looks genuinely impressed. "Commercial customers? That's great," he says. Okay, that's what he *ought* to say. What he actually says is "Whatever pays the bills."

"Howard Rosen, the famous restaurant critic, got her the job," my mother says. "You met him—the good-looking, distinguished gentleman with the *real* job, something to be proud of. I guess you've never read his reviews in *Newsday*."

Drew, without missing a beat, tells her that Howard's reviews are on the top of his list, as soon as he learns how to read.

"I only meant—" my mother starts, but both of us assure her that we know just what she meant.

"So," Drew says. "Deliveries?"

I tell him that Mario would know better than I, but that I saw vegetables come in, maybe fish and linens.

"This is the second restaurant job Howard's got her," my mother tells Drew.

"At least she's getting *something* out of the relationship," he says.

"If he were here," my mother says, ignoring the insinuation, "he'd be comforting her instead of interrogating her. He'd be making sure we're both all right after such an ordeal."

"I'm sure he would," Drew agrees, then looks me in the eyes as if he's measuring my tolerance for shock. Quietly he adds, "But then maybe he doesn't know just what strong stuff your daughter's made of."

It's the closest thing to a tender moment I can expect from Drew Scoones. My mother breaks the spell. "She gets that from me," she says.

Both Drew and I take a minute, probably to pray that's all I inherited from her.

"I'm just trying to save you some time and effort," my mother tells him. "My money's on Howard."

Drew withers her with a look and mutters something that sounds suspiciously like "fool's gold." Then he excuses himself to go back to work.

I catch his sleeve and ask if it's all right for us to leave. He says sure, he knows where we live. I say goodbye to Mario. I assure him that I will have some sketches for him in a few days, all the while hoping that this murder doesn't cancel his redecorating plans. I need the money desperately, the alternative being borrowing from my parents and being strangled by the strings.

My mother is strangely quiet all the way to her house. She doesn't tell me what a loser Drew Scoones is—despite his good looks—and how I was obviously drooling over him. She doesn't ask me where Howard is taking me tonight or warn me not to tell my father about what happened because he will worry about us both and no doubt insist we see our respective psychiatrists.

She fidgets nervously, opening and closing her purse over and over again.

"You okay?" I ask her. After all, she's just found a dead man on the toilet, and tough as she is that's got to be upsetting.

When she doesn't answer me I pull over to the side of the road.

"Mom?" She refuses to meet my eyes. "You want me to take you to see Dr. Cohen?"

She looks out the window as if she's just realized we're on Broadway in Woodmere. "Aren't we near Marvin's Jewelers?" she asks, pulling something out of her purse.

"What have you got, Mother?" I ask, prying open her fingers to find the murdered man's ring.

"It was on the sink," she says in answer to my dropped jaw. "I was going to get his name and address and have you return it to him so that he could ask you out. I thought it was a sign that the two of you were meant to be together."

"He's dead, Mom. You understand that, right?" I ask. You never can tell when my mother is fine and when she's in la-la land.

"Well, I didn't know that," she shouts at me. "Not at the time."

I ask why she didn't give it to Drew, realize that she wouldn't give Drew the time in a clock shop and add, "...or one of the other policemen?"

"For heaven's sake," she tells me. "The man is dead, Teddi, and I took his ring. How would that look?"

Before I can tell her it looks just the way it is, she pulls out a cigarette and threatens to light it.

"I mean, really," she says, shaking her head like it's my brains that are loose. "What does he need with it now?"

AleX Archer
THE CHOSEN

Archaeologist Annja Creed believes there's more to
the apparitions of Santo Niño—the Holy Child—luring
thousands of pilgrims to Santa Fe. But she is not alone in
her quest to separate reliquaries from unholy minds who
dare to harness sinister power. A dangerous yet enigmatic
Jesuit, a brilliant young artist and a famed monster
hunter are the keys to the
secrets that lie in the heart
of Los Alamos—and
unlocking the door to the
very fabric of time itself....

**Available January 2007
wherever books are sold.**

nocturne™

WAS HE HER SAVIOR
OR HER NIGHTMARE?

HAUNTED
LISA CHILDS

Years ago, Ariel and her sisters were separated for
their own protection. Now the man who vowed
revenge on her family has resumed the hunt, and
Ariel must warn her sisters before it's too late.
The closer she comes to finding them, the more
secretive her fiancé becomes. Can she trust the man
she plans to spend eternity with? Or has he been
waiting for the perfect moment to destroy her?

On sale December 2006.

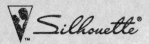

Romantic SUSPENSE

In February, expect MORE from

HARLEQUIN® *Romance*®

as it increases to six titles per month.

What's to come...

Rancher and Protector

Part of the

Western Weddings

miniseries

BY JUDY CHRISTENBERRY

The Boss's Pregnancy Proposal

BY RAYE MORGAN

Don't miss February's
incredible line up of authors!

HARLEQUIN®
INTRIGUE®

BREATHTAKING ROMANTIC SUSPENSE

Shared dangers and passions lead to electrifying
romance and heart-stopping suspense!

Every month, you'll meet six new heroes
who are guaranteed to make your spine tingle
and your pulse pound. With them you'll enter
into the exciting world of Harlequin Intrigue—
where your life is on the line
and so is your heart!

THAT'S INTRIGUE— ROMANTIC SUSPENSE AT ITS BEST!

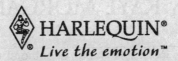

HARLEQUIN®
Live the emotion™

Don't miss

DAKOTA FORTUNES,

**a six-book continuing series following
the Fortune family of South Dakota—
oil is in their blood and privilege
is their birthright.**

This series kicks off with
USA TODAY bestselling author

PEGGY MORELAND'S
Merger of Fortunes
(SD #1771)

this January.

Other books in the series:

BACK IN FORTUNE'S BED by Bronwyn James (Feb)
FORTUNE'S VENGEFUL GROOM by Charlene Sands (March)
MISTRESS OF FORTUNE by Kathie DeNosky (April)
EXPECTING A FORTUNE by Jan Colley (May)
FORTUNE'S FORBIDDEN WOMAN by Heidi Betts (June)

COMING NEXT MONTH

#121 SEVENTH KEY—Evelyn Vaughn
The Madonna Key

In her heyday, Professor Maggi Sanger had harnessed the powers of her female ancestors to fight evil; now she had her hands full raising a daughter. But when her archenemies kidnapped members of the Marian sisterhood and their children and imprisoned them in Naples, Maggi had no choice but to fight for their legacy…and the future of the world. Did she hold the key to salvation—or would she unlock the door to apocalypse instead?

#122 THE MEDUSA PROPHECY—Cindy Dees
The Medusa Project

When Captain Karen Tucker and her all-female Special Forces group, the Medusas, uncovered a drug lab during an arctic training mission, the situation got hot enough to melt a polar ice cap. Exposed to a deadly mind-altering drug, Karen now had to help her team put the pushers out of business while she struggled to stay alive. And stay sane enough not to kill handsome allied soldier Anders Larson *and* her fellow Medusas…

#123 DEAD IS THE NEW BLACK—Harper Allen
Darkheart & Crosse

For Tashya Crosse, being a vampire wasn't a difficult cross to bear—she got to stay young forever, the male vamps were *hot* and she could still go out in the sun, provided she wore SPF 60 lotion. But the other two Crosse triplets—a slayer and a healer—were hardly amused by her new identity. And when a deadly enemy arrived in town, Tashya had to choose between vamping it up and saving her sisters from certain destruction.

#124 STAYING ALIVE—Debra Webb

All Claire Grant wanted was peace and quiet when she settled down as an elementary school teacher in Seattle. But the day terrorists took her classroom hostage—and she successfully fought back—she became a prime target for one of the most wanted, deadly men on earth. Soon the FBI's legendary and ultrasexy antiterror agent Luke Krueger stepped in with a new plan to take out the terrorists—using Claire as bait.

SBCNM1206